The Round Barn

Hardscrabble Books—Fiction of New England

Laurie Alberts, *Lost Daughters*
Laurie Alberts, *The Price of Land in Shelby*
Thomas Bailey Aldrich, *The Story of a Bad Boy*
Robert J. Begiebing, *The Adventures of Allegra Fullerton; Or, A Memoir of Startling and Amusing Episodes from Itinerant Life*
Anne Bernays, *Professor Romeo*
Chris Bohjalian, *Water Witches*
Dona Brown, ed., *A Tourist's New England: Travel Viction, 1820–1920*
Joseph Bruchac, *The Waters Between: A Novel of the Dawn Land*
Joseph A. Citro, *The Gore*
Joseph A. Citro, *Lake Monsters*
Joseph A. Citro, *Shadow Child*
Sean Connolly, *A Great Place to Die*
J.E. Fender, *The Private Revolution of Geoffrey Frost: Being an Account of the Life and Times of Geoffrey Frost, Mariner, of Portsmouth, in New Hampshire, as Faithfully Translated from the Ming Tsun Chronicles, and Diligently Compared with Other Contemporary Histories*
Dorothy Canfield Fisher (Mark J. Madigan, ed.), *Seasoned Timber*
Dorothy Canfield Fisher, *Understood Betsy*
Joseph Freda, *Suburban Guerrillas*
Castle Freeman, Jr., *Judgment Hill*
Frank Gaspar, *Leaving Pico*
Robert Harnum, *Exile in the Kingdom*
Ernest Hebert, *The Dogs of March*
Ernest Hebert, *Live Free or Die*
Ernest Hebert, *The Old American*
Sarah Orne Jewett (Sarah Way Sherman, ed.), *The Country of the Pointed Firs and Other Stories*
Lisa MacFarlane, ed., *This World Is Not Conclusion: Faith in Nineteenth-Century New England Fiction*
G. F. Michelsen, *Hard Bottom*
Anne Whitney Pierce, *Rain Line*
Kit Reed, *J. Eden*

Rowland E. Robinson (David Budbill, ed.), *Danvis Tales: Selected Stories*
Roxana Robinson, *Summer Light*
Rebecca Rule, *The Best Revenge: Short Stories*
Catharine Maria Sedgwick (Maria Karafilis, ed.), *The Linwoods; or, "Sixty Years Since" in America*
R. D. Skillings, *How Many Die*
R. D. Skillings, *Where the Time Goes*
Lynn Stegner, *Pipers at the Gates of Dawn: A Triptych*
Theodore Weesner, *Novemberfest*
W. D. Wetherell, *The Wisest Man in America*
Edith Wharton (Barbara A. White, ed.), *Wharton's New England: Seven Stories and* Ethan Frome
Thomas Williams, *The Hair of Harold Roux*
Suzi Wizowaty, *The Round Barn*

THE ROUND BARN

Suzi Wizowaty

University Press of New England HANOVER AND LONDON

Published by University Press of New England, One Court Street,
Lebanon, NH 03766

Printed in the United States of America

5 4 3 2 1

LIBRARY OF CONGRESS CATALOGING-IN-PUBLICATION DATA

Wizowaty, Suzi.
The round barn / Suzi Wizowaty.
p. cm. — (Hardscrabble books)
ISBN 1-58465-282-9 (alk. paper)
1. Moving of buildings, bridges, etc.—Fiction. 2. Round barns—Fiction. 3. Vermont—Fiction. I. Title. II. Series.
PS3623.I97 R68 2002
813'.6—dc21 2002005306

Though this novel takes its inspiration from an actual round barn in an actual museum, it is a work of fiction. All characters are imaginary. Any similarity to people living or dead is entirely coincidental.

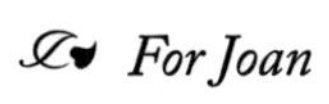
For Joan

Acknowledgments

I want to thank Peter Marsh of the Shelburne Museum and Craig Wooster of the Shelburne Fire Department for their patience in explaining such things as helicopters, security systems, and fires. Thanks, too, to Carol Thayer, M.D.; Lynda Goldsmith; and MariAnne Skodney for help in understanding ovarian cancer. Any failures here are of course mine alone.

Thanks to Deborah Lubar for permission to use my memory of her wonderful play, *Eve's Version.*

I am fortunate to have been able to attend several Vermont Artist Weeks at Vermont Studio Center and began this work there. I know of no place more conducive to writing.

Thanks to the Vermont Arts Council for a grant that helped me get to Bread Loaf. It was here that Susan Richards Shreve helped me think about this story differently, so I could rewrite it yet again, while Rob Cohen encouraged me to take time off in order to do so. They are both exceptional, generous teachers.

Thanks for their enthusiasm and patience to Ginger Knowlton and her colleagues at Curtis Brown, and to John Landrigan and his colleagues at University Press of New England, without whom this manuscript would not have become a book.

So many friends have encouraged me over the years that I cannot name them all. I deeply appreciated the support, during the writing of this novel in particular, of Rick Archbold, Cathy Wood Brooks, Judy Fitch, Paul Matthews, and Julian Thompson. Along with my beloved sister, Gigi, and my parents whose confidence in me hasn't wavered over nearly half a century, they have helped keep me going.

Finally, and most importantly, I thank Joan Robinson. For everything.

part one

I

At the top of East Hill in a small town in northern Vermont, there is a place where the earth flattens out and the surrounding woods give way to sloping meadows, upon which have grazed cows and sometimes sheep for at least a century. In one of these meadows there stood for nearly ninety years a round barn, one of about two dozen built in Vermont between 1899 and 1915. The Fletcher barn, as it became known, was completed in 1901, the largest of three built by Hoke Smith, a local carpenter who came to an untimely end soon afterward, amid much speculation as to the reason, if not the cause. His death followed not long after that of the barn's young owner, Thomas Fletcher.

The first round barn had been built in 1824 by Shakers in Massachusetts, but was viewed with suspicion, as a matter of religious experimentation rather than sound farming practice. Only when Wisconsin farmers began building round barns in 1896 did the idea catch on. In fact, round barns were cheaper to build and operate and represented the height of technology. They would likely still be in use were it not for the invention of the tractor which revolutionized agriculture. But that is another story.

The Fletcher barn consisted of three levels, and sixteen pie-shaped sections, arranged around the center silo, which provided the building's structural strength much as the hub of a wheel supports its spokes. From the basement to the top of its lightning rod, it stood sixty-seven feet high. The top floor, with its high, cathedral-like ceiling, served as a haymow. The earthen high-drive ramp led to this level. Below, at ground level, the dairy floor had ties for sixty cows facing inward toward a circular feed trough. Separate pens for bulls and calves took up two of the sixteen sections. At the rear of each pen was a trapdoor through which manure could be shoveled to the basement below. The mere half-hour it took a conscientious farmer to feed the herd arranged this way left additional time for milking and attending to the animals' health.

The bottom level, or basement, was built into the side of the hill—with a semicircular stone foundation on the hill side and a semicircular wall of stone and wood on the other, and wide doors that opened at ground level because of the slope. Had Thomas Fletcher lived, he would have driven his horse team and spreader through these doors, collecting manure from the floor above as he released trapdoors overhead. This lower third of the barn was built with long ceiling timbers, without support posts to interfere with movement, and thus he could have maneuvered his team in a way that would have been impossible in a traditional square or long barn.

The center silo was designed to store corn but was used mostly for hay silage and during its last ten years for ventilation. Atop the cedar-shingled roof sat a round, louvered cupola, which was both decorative and useful, allowing ventilation into the silo. Specialists praised its compactness and its efficiency.

For over eighty years, the barn was in use. But in the middle of the 1980s, its owners, like so many Vermont farmers, found themselves impossibly squeezed between the low price of milk and the high costs of small-farm dairying, and they sold their herd, and shortly thereafter the farm. The barn sat empty for ten years until new owners wanted to restore it. For them, too, the costs proved too high, and they gave up.

Mary Bailey Daly, co-owner of Daly's General Store, heard from a neighbor who dropped by the store that East Hill Farm was for sale again. She told the women in her church group. One of the women told her husband, who worked with Tuesday Bailey at the museum an hour away. Tuesday Bailey knew what a hundred-year-old round barn would mean to the museum. What the barn meant to Tuesday, what it meant to move the barn from here to the museum, was more complicated.

The land became available in June. By August, the museum had worked out a deal with the owners. By November, Tuesday Bailey had begun working with a crew of carpenters and the museum's curatorial staff to dismantle the barn. They labeled and numbered every beam, every post, every plank of siding. Carefully and methodically, they carted it all off by the truckload. Over the winter, on the grounds of the museum, they reassembled the barn just as meticulously, reconstructing the stone foundation, building the barn anew. They used as much of the original material as possible, replacing only those timbers they couldn't certify would hold the load. It took nearly six months. In May, the barn was ready. Once the silo arrived, the roof could be completed—just in time for the annual spring opening of the museum.

The section of the silo that still needed to be moved, the upper half that rose from the top-level floor to the peak of the roof, was seventeen feet across and twenty-nine feet high. It had been lifted from its base by crane last fall and deposited twenty feet away, so that the bottom two sections, relatively compact by comparison, could be disassembled and moved by truck.

The silo's walls were built of two-by-eight-foot vertical studs arranged in a circle, and covered both inside and out with thin, bent strips of pine. It would be tricky to move, but not impossible. Tuesday had hired the best outfit in the country at moving historic buildings. There was nothing to worry about, surely everything would go all right. Nonetheless, he was worried. Like everything else—love, for example, or life—a silo is a sturdy or a fragile thing, depending.

Tuesday Bailey met his crew at the top of East Hill at a quarter to seven, on the morning of May 3, 1999, a chilly day that would warm up soon. They had two hours; the helicopter was coming at nine. He didn't need to rush them; they were excited and moved quickly, his own two men and the air crane company's ground man. One by one they gulped the last of their coffee and left their thermoses in their trucks, parked just off the road, at the edge of the field.

The formerly smooth, grassy track that led to where the barn used to be, where now only the silo remained, had become deeply rutted last fall. The land immediately surrounding the barn had been scarred and flattened, worked over by trucks and machines. The circular site of the round barn itself, revealed to the world after a hundred years as a barren patch of earth immobilized and smothered by stone, had lain barren, snow-covered, all winter. But finally spring had come to northern Vermont, and the site of the round barn sprouted tiny clumps of new weeds—coltsfoot and dandelion, as lovely as they were opportunistic—and the field around it was green with clover. Even the earthen high-drive ramp, so heavily trampled last fall, had turned green again.

The men attached twenty-four metal plates to the inside and outside of the silo's walls with eyebolts. They secured twelve cables to the metal plates. They cut a fourteen-foot spruce from the nearby woods to serve as an anchor to keep the silo from spinning, thus unwinding the cables.

By eight-thirty, they were ready, with nothing to do but wait. A small group of locals had assembled at the edge of the field to watch the liftoff, which had been discussed for weeks. Tuesday Bailey lumbered over to his cousin Mary. Of course she would be there. It was because of her the museum had acquired the barn in the first place.

Jimmy would be at the store.

Tuesday might have heard about the barn's availability directly from Mary, but he didn't see her much. He stopped by the store now and then, to pick up something and say hello—the same way he had for the last ten years—but, well, since he worked in town, he got most of what he needed at one of the big stores there. Or so he said. The truth was, he had found he was happiest if he limited himself to one visit every month or two, a regime he had stuck to these many years as if his life depended on it. Anything extra, like running into her here, was a gift. A gift that both pleased and bit, like an encounter with a happy, unruly dog, who unintentionally left you bruised.

"So far, so good," he said to her now. They stood facing the silo, elbow to elbow, the short, round woman and the big, burly man. The woman seeking and cheery, with wild hair and sparkly eyes; the man quiet, prone to brood, with a coiled energy but an easy smile, tiny wrinkles around his eyes and a deep crease between the eyebrows.

"It looks like a dead bug stuck in the ground," said Mary, teasing, "with its skinny little legs all gone limp." She held her arms out from her body.

The wind clinked the cables against the side of the silo. It would be a windy couple of months, followed by an unnaturally still week in late July and a windstorm, a near-hurricane, that would knock out power at the museum for several days.

"Something's wrong," Mary said, tilting her head as if she were listening—her dowsing expression. He knew it well, not because he had seen her dowse more than a handful of times since she took it up, but because she had not changed in the forty-plus years he had known her.

"What?"

"Don't you feel it?"

He glanced at her sideways. "You look a little funny." Was she sick? Thinner, maybe. Her skin was a little gray, but her cheeks were flushed from the wind and her eyes were bright. Maybe she was just cold. "Are you all right?"

"Of course." A flicker of annoyance passed over her face. "I'm fine. But something here isn't."

Tuesday smiled, though he didn't understand her. Then he heard the helicopter. Whacka whacka whacka. Everyone looked up—Tuesday, Mary, the other visitors, the three men standing silently in a proprietary clump by their trucks. The ground man stubbed out a cigarette on the sole of his boot and strode back to the silo. Tuesday and his men followed. Within seconds, the sky crane appeared over the trees, bang-bang-bang-bang, as if it were beating the air.

Finally it maneuvered itself into place a hundred feet above the silo, lurching a bit in the gusting wind. It lowered to the ground its own rigging, which the men attached to the already existing cables. They checked the eyebolt attachments one last time, tugged on the cables, and backed away from the silo. The ground man signaled to the helicopter overhead with a wave. The radio wasn't necessary. The helicopter, so violently loud, rose imperceptibly, even gently. Slowly, unevenly, the cables tightened. The silo gradually tilted, swayed on its edge, testing the strength of the cables as if it might fall. It did not fall but lifted into the air, the felled spruce dangling like a sinker beneath it. Slowly, deliberately and without grace, whacking away at the air, the helicopter and its nearly ten-thousand-pound silo, trailing the small inverted spruce, rose and flew off over the trees.

Tuesday gave Mary a small wave as he jogged to his truck. He had less than an hour to make an hour-long drive on back roads—an hour on a good day, without snow, or heavy rain or fog, or school buses. In a straight race, he could easily beat the helicopter, which flew at twenty-five miles an hour at best, but it wasn't a straight race. Nothing ever was.

"So far, so good," Mary called after him cheerfully, with only a hint of distress.

Tuesday Bailey careened down East Hill Road in his pick-up, spraying gravel and dust, glad for the dry spell the past week that had left the roads hard-packed. He rolled down the window to feel the wind. He loved this, the moving of the silo by helicopter, the power of large machines capable of grand action, action beyond the scope of a mere man. What a sight, the silo rising and flying off over the trees, like a piece of a castle, or a squat bullet, or a toy. Tuesday had been working on this project—getting the round barn and now the silo to the museum—for nearly a year.

The museum. His museum, as he called it secretly. The museum that, through his devotion over the years, had become his. How else did something come to belong to you except through your care? Moving the barn had had its headaches, naturally, but never mind. Now the silo was on its way and with any luck, all would go well.

Tuesday Bailey lived for the museum. Ordinarily he was not overly concerned about harm coming its way; it was his job to keep the museum safe, to oversee its security and to supervise the care of its buildings, to maintain them in good condition. He did his job well. Therefore, why would any harm come to the museum—unless . . . He didn't dwell on the possibilities. He was not afraid of the silo not making it, he told himself. He was sweating under his jacket because he was excited, because he cared deeply that all go well. He took the curves in the road as fast as he dared.

Mary hadn't looked well. She didn't have the lively, bursting-out-of-her-skin feeling she usually had. Better to think of the silo swaying over the trees, making its way steadily over hills and woods to the congested western part of the state, to its future home at the museum.

Over his lifetime Tuesday had worked successfully at not thinking of his cousin when he drove to and from work, or any other time. This had been harder during the last year, because of moving the barn. Until then, even though he worked with one of his oldest childhood friends, Tuesday had still managed to keep his two lives separate. He'd grown up in Eustis and had lived here always, except for the years in Maine. It was odd to combine them—his working world, where he ran a large department, where he was in charge, and this, his home, where he was . . . nobody special. Just Tuesday Bailey, son of Alma and Madrid, pronounced MADrid, grandson of Old Bailey, also known as Olf'ck Bailey, short for Old Fuck. The intersection of his two worlds was unsettling, even dangerous.

Mary didn't look well. Her eyes.

As he drove, the two images flipped back and forth like photographs—the silo swinging below the helicopter, rising up slowly and flying off over the trees, and Mary, her skin pale, face flushed in the wind, looking annoyed when he asked whether anything was wrong. The silo, on its way to the museum; Mary, with her head cocked, listening, trying to figure something out, as always. Waiting for something.

And then he saw the dead dog by the side of the road, and though he hadn't thought of it in years, he remembered burying Harrietty.

He'd had her since he was eight. He and Mary, two years younger, had named her together, for Harry Houdini. Mary had been entranced by Harry Houdini since she'd heard about him in school a few weeks before and wanted to marry him, never mind that he was long dead. It was like Mary not to care about this detail.

Mary ran around Tuesday's barn clattering a stick on the siding, shouting, "Harry Houdini, Harry Houdini!" Tuesday ran after her, laughing, happy to be outside, running and yelling, happy especially to be playing with his cousin, whom he had adored with a childlike devotion since the time two years earlier when he rescued her from an apple tree. They made up a song together, a chant. Round and round the barn they ran, laughing and yelling at the top of their lungs.

"Harry Houdini, marry Houdini, marry Harry Houdini!"

In Tuesday's memory, they didn't stop. They were happy children, best friends, running and yelling and laughing forever.

His father won the scruffy little brown and white mutt in a football pool and gave it to Tuesday, the youngest of the Baileys' four children and the most likely to take care of it. ("Won?" his mother complained. "You must have lost!") Tuesday immediately took it down the road to Mary's—that is, the little dog trotted after him stopping every few feet like a puppy to poke its nose into the brush or run in and out of the scrub along the road. It was fall, and the dog buried itself in the leaves and disappeared more than once.

Mary and he named the dog Harry at first (before they knew it was a "she"—his father had called it an "it"), then Harriet, then Harrietty. Tuesday's older brothers called her Hairy Eddy, and referred to her as a "he."

Tuesday was sixteen when he came home from school to find Harrietty dead in the driveway. His brothers had moved to other towns, other states. He carried Harrietty gently to a spot beside the barn, out of the sun, though it was a cool fall day, and set out for Mary's.

He didn't call her his best friend anymore, or his favorite cousin. He thought of her simply as Mary, and somehow his. He found her waiting on her front steps. She always seemed to know when he was coming; she had a sixth sense for such things with everyone.

"What happened?" She sat hugging her knees, her hair wavy and loose, unruly around her like her clothes. It was 1968, and Mary's fourteen-year-old sense of fashion, idiosyncratic rather than rebellious, dictated overalls, faded and loose, and an old jacket of her father's. "Who died?"

"Harrietty."

"Oh Tuesday." She shook her head. "What of?"

He told her about finding the dog with no marks on her. She might have been hit by a car; she was the same brown as the last of the oak leaves, hard to distinguish at this time of year. They sat on Mary's porch step, shoulders touching, though he was nearly a foot taller, leaning on each other lightly like in the old days when they were young and closer to the same size.

"Maybe her breath just stopped," Tuesday said.

"Her ass or her heart?" It was an old joke; she was trying to cheer him up. Years ago, Mary had come into the kitchen one afternoon to find a friend of her mother's standing on her head, demonstrating yoga. As Mary came in, the woman farted. "My ass is breathing," she said. Mary ran outside laughing. She had been in second grade, and nothing was funnier.

Now she poked Tuesday gently with her elbow and said it a second time. He tried to laugh, for her sake. Instead, he began to cry. He sobbed as if he were a child.

Mary put her arm around him; he felt as though he were little and she big, rather than the other way around. He had to wipe his nose on his jacket sleeve, but Mary didn't let go.

When he stopped, she disappeared briefly and returned with a handkerchief. She sat down at the other end of the front steps, away from him.

"You need to bury her after the moon comes up," she said matter of factly. "That way, her spirit will find its way home. I'll help you. I'll come over."

But she never did. Tuesday buried Harrietty under the moon by himself, hoping Mary would come, knowing she wouldn't. He dug a hole close to the foundation of the barn so that she would never get churned up accidentally by a plough or someone laying a pipe. He laid her inside it and told her she was a good dog.

Afterward he sat outside on the single step to the mudroom. It was cold and still, the temperature dropping. He could see the outline of the barn against the starry night but not the place he'd buried Harrietty. Still he stood watch, waiting for he knew not what, standing guard over Harrietty in his way, folded into the doorway of the mudroom, his parents long asleep, the night silent around him but for an occasional skittering of a mouse or a chipmunk in the dry leaves. He watched and waited, and grew more and more angry.

He should have tied her up when he left for school. His father should have let her sleep inside during the day and he wouldn't have had to tie her up. The asshole who hit her should have been driving more carefully. Harrietty shouldn't have run out in front of the car. Mary should have come. *Mary should have come.*

Mary.

It wasn't the first time she'd let him down. But it was the first time that mattered.

Tuesday Bailey made it to the museum with a few minutes to spare. He parked in the visitors' lot and strode quickly to the barn, noting that the wind was stronger here, closer to the lake, than in the mountains. It was to be expected, but it was unfortunate. It would make lowering the silo in place that much harder.

The round barn itself had been painstakingly reconstructed at the entrance to the museum grounds. Newly painted a deep red, it sat sturdily upon its original stone base, also neatly reconstructed, stone by stone. The new high-drive ramp led properly to the upper floor, which with its dramatically high ceiling would serve as the new visitors' center. Recently seeded grass grew neatly all around the barn, and the newly planted shrubs that bordered the walkways, though bare of leaves, looked permanent, if not quite settled. The upper level had been sided like the rest of the barn with double planking, and the roof had been partially framed in but not completed—falsework held it up temporarily—as final construction depended upon the presence of the central silo for support.

A large crowd had assembled on the museum grounds to watch the silo arrive—museum staff, local dignitaries and merchants invited in a gesture of goodwill, a few major donors escorted by board members, a new board member whom Tuesday had met on the grounds yesterday in the company of the director, who seemed to be engaged in what he called "cultivation." Dean Allen was not among the staff, fortunately. Perhaps Didi Jamison had found a way to keep him out of sight; poor woman, to have the burden of monitoring how things looked.

In front of the barn, at the base of the earthen ramp, stood several of Tuesday's own crew, and two more men from the sky crane company, in radio contact with the helicopter. Before he could join them, Didi intercepted him.

"How'd it go?" she asked anxiously. "Are they late? The media's here."

"No, no, everything's fine. They'll get some great pictures. You'll see best from over there." He indicated the rise where the crowd stood. He spoke kindly; they were buddies of a sort, the serious, lesbian public relations director who made him feel lighthearted by comparison, and the confirmed bachelor. She was as devoted to the museum as he was. Didi touched his arm briefly and took the hint.

"A bit of trouble," said one of the sky-crane men as Tuesday approached, nodding deferentially toward the other, a short, stocky man with a headset.

Tuesday took off his jacket, though it was still cool, and tossed it on the grass.

"Come on in, let's try it. Over." The senior man spoke firmly into the mouthpiece.

This time Tuesday saw the helicopter before he heard it. It was flying in from the south, rather than from the east, from Eustis.

The junior man explained. "They're trying to avoid houses and highways. Three or four eyebolts popped loose, so it's not hanging straight. It puts a lot of strain on just a few plates, you know. They're nervous as shit up there."

"Why not set it down and reattach the cables, and *then* drop it in?" Tuesday asked, trying to keep the strain from his voice. *Not now! Don't let it fall now!* He wiped his palms on his sides.

The senior man held up his hand, listening. "Right," he said to the radio. "Affirmative. Bring her in. Clear." He told Tuesday that the greatest strain was placed on the silo at the point of lifting off; the less starting and stopping the better. The three men entered the barn. Tuesday stayed close to the senior ground man with the radio, who was in charge of the move, to give any countermanding orders in case of emergency.

When the helicopter had first come into view, the crowd behind him had murmured appreciatively. Now they *oohed* and *ahed* at every motion of the machine, as if watching fireworks on the fourth of July. They had no idea that the tilted silo meant a more dangerous operation. They seemed to assume it was supposed to be that way, as though it could slide into place more easily at an angle.

The sky crane rumbled into place above the barn, smacking the air, and began lowering the silo. The open roof made it relatively easy for the men on the third floor to maneuver. The silo had only to drop straight to the third floor, to come to rest on its bottom half—that is, the lower half of the original silo, which had been removed in pieces and transported last fall along with the rest of the barn. When they could reach it, two men unhooked the spruce and tossed it aside.

The silo dropped below the roofline, almost completely protected from the wind by the barn's exterior walls. With the help of the museum crew, the sky-crane men tried to set the silo on its edge and then guide it into place. The silo itself was of course too heavy to support, but the helicopter held most of the weight. The men wore heavy gloves, with which they gripped the cables. Where they could, they simply tried to nudge the silo into place with their shoulders, without losing their balance and falling into the hole.

It was difficult. Resting the silo on the edge of the hole in the floor, in order to stand it up straight, meant the helicopter supported less of the weight so the silo became almost impossible to move. The helicopter was engaged in its own struggles as it contended with gusting wind while trying to maintain position. When it tried to help jiggle and lift the silo into place, the silo slid off its point of contact and hung again at an angle. At an angle, the silo would not set properly on the base below, but rolled. The men in the barn were afraid that the silo swinging around would damage the internal construction. The men in the helicopter were afraid that the silo would come loose and flatten one of the men below. They would all tell stories later.

Tuesday Bailey and the sky-crane man exchanged looks. Tuesday shook his head.

They tried a second time. The helicopter lowered the edge of silo onto the edge of its new base. The men on the floor tried to balance it there while the helicopter moved slightly backward. Again the silo slid off its mooring. One man jumped aside. A cable whipped across his arm. All of them swore.

Shit! Forget it! Fuck this!

Tuesday Bailey wanted them to stop. It was foolish to keep trying something so dangerous. But surely they knew what they were doing. Once more the sky crane lifted the silo and tried to set it down. The men struggled and pushed, the wind blew in unnatural gusts, the silo slipped dangerously.

"That's it!" Tuesday's deep voice burst from him like a spring. "Take it up!" The senior man nodded, already giving directions to the pilot hovering overhead.

"We can't do it," Tuesday said. "Not at this angle, not in this wind. Tell them to set it down just west of the parking lot. That's good enough." He wiped his face with his hand.

"Ohhhh," said the crowd outside, as the helicopter lifted the silo out of the barn once more. With speed born of relief, the crew inside scrambled across the visitors' parking lot to unhook the cables from the silo, now lowered safely into a field.

On his way back to his office, Tuesday stopped to talk with his boss, Charles Hopper.

"Well done," said Charles, with a big smile. He was a blustery, affable man. "This is an exciting time for the museum. Frieda, have you met Tuesday Bailey? It's guys like Tuesday who really run the museum. Mrs. Maxwell."

Tuesday nodded, shook the hand she offered. Had she forgotten they'd met the day before? It was clear Charles had, but that was not unusual. She looked him over as if sizing up a potential enemy.

"It's a lot of hoopla to move a large, cylindrical object, is it not?" she asked pleasantly. "A big toy." She spoke with a slight accent.

"Hope you enjoy your visit," Tuesday said politely. Then to Charles, "We'll get it moved when the wind dies down. Shouldn't be any problem."

"Of course," said Charles, taking Frieda Maxwell's elbow. "And congratulations on a job well done." They turned away to address a reporter.

"It's a beautiful barn," Tuesday heard Mrs. Maxwell say. He smiled in spite of himself. This woman in her cool silk suit and pearls had probably never seen any barn before, but it was true. It was a handsome barn.

A few others he passed also made encouraging, congratulatory noises. No one seemed to care that the silo hadn't made it into the barn as planned; apparently the event had been exciting enough on its own.

Tuesday took a deep breath. Nothing terrible had happened. When the A.P. reporter and the people from the local television station came at him, with Didi in tow, looking apologetic but in command, he told them with confidence that they would move the silo into the barn tomorrow with an ordinary crane—without danger, without mishap. He'd arrange it this afternoon.

Everything would be all right.

And then he saw Dean Allen lurking under a lilac tree, alone as always, watching the proceedings after all, proceedings he had wished to be part of, as everyone knew, perhaps even wished to oversee, the way he had overseen the creation of the circus building several years before—or its design, anyway. He looked forlorn and lonely, his shoulders hunched against the wind. Tuesday Bailey, still wound up from the morning's events, ignored Allen, but swore under his breath, awash in the sudden feeling that his troubles had just begun.

2

I wanted to see the lift-off because something told me I had to. I'd never seen a helicopter carry a building, and who knew what truths might be revealed? Even if dowsing is the path, and I'm quite sure it is, I still don't have all the answers. Besides, none of the other Fishwives were able to go, so I'll have something to tell at the next meeting. I know there is a raunchy joke about a flying silo and a round barn in there somewhere.

The lift-off was a success. But I didn't go back to the store right away. I moved the pickup from the side of the road onto the field where the silo stood—and before that the whole barn—ran my hand over the duct tape that patches the vinyl, and leaned back in the seat. *Good boy.*

I love my truck, sweet as an old dog. Old Red. The fourth one I've owned in my forty-three years. Red IV. Each one better, newer than the last, ever since the first run-down contraption I bought in high school, so proud of it I drove straight to my cousin Tuesday's to show him.

Tuesday. Why doesn't he get married? What is he waiting for? What an exasperating man. Why did he ask me whether I was all right?

Inside the truck it started to get warm, and I rolled down the window. It is too early for blackflies or mosquitoes, the nights can still bring frost. The trees that edge the field—maple and aspen, beech and ash—have sprouted bright green overnight. Beyond the field, where the woods begin, the balsam fir and black spruce mingle with the new green of the softwoods. My favorite time of year; how is it this year I almost missed it?

Damn Tuesday Bailey. All right, if he insists: I'm not fine. I haven't been feeling like myself for months. I'm tired, and bloated; I feel like I'm getting fatter even though I don't feel like eating much. If he really wants to know, I feel terrible. Since he asked. Now that I think about it. Not that it's any of his business. A person's health is personal. After all.

It wouldn't make me so grumpy if he'd . . . get married or something. Find a girlfriend, someone on the rebound from a bad marriage. Aren't there lots of those around? That concerned look on his face: agh! Why does he care so much about me, it's unnatural.

All right, then, I'll go to the doctor. Probably it's just the change of life, early symptoms, probably. Forty-three is a little young, isn't it?—but who knows about these things?

That settled—with some relief, I have to admit—I closed my eyes. Now that I was here, cozy inside my truck at the edge of this silent field with life waiting to emerge all around me, there was something else. Something more urgent, something I could hear with a different part of myself besides my ears. It tickled, tugged, like a half-forgotten memory or a half-revealed obligation. Something I needed to attend to, or do. To start, or to finish.

It had to do with the round barn, or the silo, or this field so torn up still from the work done last fall. I listened, and waited. I, Mary Bailey Daly, am not a superstitious woman. I don't trouble about black cats, broken mirrors, or God. Dowsing is different. I trust dowsing because I know it works. Something nearby, or someone, needed attention. I waited, and listened.

Across from our store, which people call Bailey Daly's, which Jimmy complains about but I don't think he really minds—across from our store is an old Congregational church people like to take pictures of. Tourists, who buy film at the store and then stand on our porch because otherwise you can't get the whole steeple in the picture. I know, because I asked a woman once and she had me look through the camera, and it was indeed picture-perfect. I grew up with it and never saw it quite that way until I looked through her camera. She shot a half a roll from our porch. *It looks like New England,* she said. *Scarlet letters, headless horsemen, witch burnings. All that dark stuff. It's delicious.*

Eustis is tiny but a lot of tourists come through.

Jimmy and I belong to this church, even though we don't go on Sundays. I go on Wednesday nights to the women's group, called the Fishwives. The Fishermen meet on Thursdays—Fishermen after Jesus, not fishing, the men around here don't fish, they hunt. Deer and wild turkey and sometimes squirrel. Not moose; it's too hard to get a license. Jimmy applies every year but they only pick a hundred or so names out of thousands that apply in the lottery. We eat moose when the warden hauls it off the side of the road after some unlucky bastard rams into one, once a year. About as often as some idiot gets shot by his best friend or brother who's had a few too many and started seeing bears.

Jimmy doesn't have much time for hunting anyway, we're so busy during hunting season. I can run the store on my own, but what for? I'm not one to dwell on the dark side, but I've always had a bad feeling about Jimmy in the woods. He survived his youth, and I say don't tempt fate—not that I believe in fate. But I'm not a dowser for nothing.

The Fishwives meet in the basement, which is damp and chilly but bright with fluorescent lights and cheery Bible scenes the kids drew taped to the walls—Abraham about to murder Isaac, Lot's wife turned into a pillar of salt, Egyptian soldiers drowning in the Red Sea—more like a bomb shelter than a place to learn the secrets of the universe. It was here I learned about dowsing.

It started as a sewing circle. We all brought our mending, and we hemmed torn seams and sewed on buttons. I'd rather take a cold bath than sew, so I had quite a pile of things I'd pulled from the closet, mostly torn stuff that I wore anyway. I'm just not that prissy. But some of the women had no sewing to catch up on—the ones whose children never ripped their jeans except on purpose—and from the beginning they brought quilting. And gradually as the rest of us caught up on our own piles of ripped shirts and worn out pants, we joined in to help with their squares.

It's true they were pretty, and I like the names—Circle of Life and Mariner's Compass. Log Cabin Barnraising. Goose Foot in the Mud. Hole in the Barn Door. And when the conversation lingered too long on babies and children, I imagined I was floating on a pond listening to the rustle of the wind in the reeds, and I made up stories to go with the patterns. I made up stories about a sailor crisscrossing the equator who missed his beloved and named dolphins for her: Happy Heart, Lovest, Sweet Breath. And about a woman with twelve children who buried them all after an epidemic, and sewed a quilt for each one, full of images of toys the child would never have. I made myself cry and had to pretend it was allergies.

We sewed quilts, one after another—for new babies, or children getting married, or a fiftieth anniversary. It doesn't matter if you don't have children of your own, everyone's got somebody to give to. Once we made a shroud. It had patterns, but it was all white. When I go, I want one like that.

Then about ten years ago someone had the idea we should bring in guest speakers. We have a committee that finds someone about once a month. I'm not on it. I'm on the Life Passages committee, that organizes meals for families in need—one week for a death, three weeks for a birth.

One time, we thought we were going to hear about knitting. Knitting! I went anyway. Naturally some of the Fishwives can knit, but no one wanted anyone from the group to be more expert than she was, so somebody's sister-in-law who won a blue ribbon at the Tunbridge World's Fair was coming to show us how to make those fancy fisherman's sweaters. I myself don't know how to make the first knot on the knitting needle, let alone knit-and-tuck, or tuck-and-purl, or whatever it is. And I wasn't the only one. You could hear the bitching clear up to Canada. Twelve women between twenty-eight and sixty-two, impatient at the slow directions, or frustrated at not catching on—some of them tickled and pleased with themselves, eager to help the dumb ones like me, some of them helpless and sighing, don't want to be helped, no way.

The visitor was a skinny, mousy little woman. When she was showing me how to place my round little fingers on the needles, she said, almost under her breath, "You'd be better off dowsing."

"What?"

"Look, you want to keep the yarn from sliding off, so hold it up, like this."

"No, about dowsing."

She concentrated on my knitting, which she now took over, to get it going herself. I had to press her. "Are you a dowser?"

"Yes." Click click click click.

"What does it mean? How do you do it?"

She set down my knitting with obvious relief. For the first time, she looked at me, and I stared back, hungry now for what she had to offer. We were about the same age. I was fat and she was thin, and she wasn't wearing a ring, but something in her eyes reminded me of me.

"Dowsing?" She scurried over to the wall and ruffled around inside an enormous canvas bag that she'd stashed under a drawing of the Red Sea, with its walls flying up like in that old movie. From the bag she drew a smooth, Y-shaped stick. All of a sudden she moved like a leopard, not a mouse. How did she do that? She held the stick comfortably and started talking to me in a low voice, and the words came out in a steady stream. I couldn't help thinking she didn't look lonely anymore. Shortly the room fell quiet. Even the Fishwives recognize a miracle when it takes place under their noses. The woman was transformed, and we listened. A few gals clicked away softly with their needles, the ones who could do it in their sleep. The visitor talked, and as she spoke the fingers of her right hand lightly stroked the stick, back and forth, back and forth. It lay in her lap, a two-pronged, cream-colored stick, a Y-rod she said, a divining rod made out of beech. It was an ancient art, she said. You could see it in cave paintings in France and on ancient artifacts in India and China. She belonged to an association; she had found amazing things—a cave, a hundred-year-old shoe, some papers stashed in an old wall—and so had most people.

But she never jumped up and showed us how it worked. She just sat, and stroked the rod with her fingertips, gently, up and down, up and down, but firmly, like it was a cat she had to hold onto because it might leap up and attack something any minute.

I told Jimmy that night. "Something wild has happened."

He worries a lot, but that night he laughed at me, and hugged me, lifted me off the ground. I could tell he was humoring me, because I'm always thinking I've found something, the one thing that is going to change my life.

"I know," I said. "But this is different. I have a feeling this is how people feel when they find God." I gave his privates a little squeeze.

"Mary!"

Later, when we got into bed, I rolled my round little self on top of him the way I like to do, but I surprised him because it was a weeknight, and we had a good time.

Next morning I drove up to Derby Line and bought sticks from the leopard woman—one stick, but I call it my sticks because you hold onto the two ends, and it's what you hold on to that matters—and I started to practice. Sure enough, I had a knack for it. It *was* like finding God—or finding something you didn't know you'd lost. Maybe I'd lost it in another life and that's what made discovering it feel so right and familiar. I don't say this kind of thing to Jimmy, he thinks I'm a bit of a kook already, but that's what I've heard. A woman came to Fishwives to tell us Jewish stories once. She said an angel teaches some people the Bible before they're born and that's why they have an easier time learning it later.

I began to learn what I could dowse for successfully and what I couldn't. It turned out I could only find certain kinds of things—like water, or an old gravesite, or a lost puppy. I couldn't find a lost diamond ring, or a rifle. It was Jimmy who noticed that everything

I found was alive, or had been at one time and therefore maybe had something of life about it still. Once the word got out, people came to me a lot. It's amazing how many people lose important things. Not me, of course. I hold onto what I've got. It doesn't count when things are taken from you.

After a half hour, I drove back to the store.

"What happened?" Jimmy sounded anxious behind the cash register.

"They took away the silo. It went fine."

"I mean what's wrong? You're all flushed. Do you want to sit down?"

I walked behind the counter and put my arms around my husband. There was no one else in the store; he wouldn't mind. I leaned against his chest. He's a foot taller than I am. "Oh, Jimmy."

"What is it?"

"I don't know."

When I went back to the deli counter, I saw that Jimmy had done the lunch prep for me—putting out the potato salad, cole slaw, pork-and-beans. I knew I should have come in before the helicopter, instead of sitting at home. But I hadn't had the energy. At least he hadn't made up any sandwiches. That was a relief. I pulled myself together. Where were the rolls? The napkins? Where was the lettuce and tomato? I needed to slice the meats and cheeses, and quickly. From under the counter, I retrieved the large bag of special rolls I'd made the day before. Shortly, with my ingredients spread out before me as on an oversized artist's palette, I began to make my famous Sexy Sandwiches.

3

Mary's never sick. But three years ago, when she turned forty, and we got insurance for the first time, she decided she needed a checkup, so she went to the new clinic here, to Dr. Smith, who is female. Mary came back and said we needed to get more exercise and were going to take walks after supper. That's silly, I thought, I'm too tired. I don't get home from the store till eight-thirty or nine o'clock. But I do what Mary wants. My life with Mary has been full of surprises and that is why I would do anything for her.

So we started walking that night, talking like we always do only this time talking and walking instead of sitting in the kitchen eating a bowl of ice cream before bed. It was summer then, too. Dr. Smith said she was healthy but overweight. She asked Mary how she felt about being fat, and Mary said fine, but she preferred to think of herself as soft and round, which is right. Did she have shortness of breath? Mary said no, only shortness of body. Dr. Smith laughed and said well, she was in good shape and some doctors thought heavier women might have problems more from the *stigma* of being fat than from actually *being* fat. Mary said everyone she knew was fat and she didn't see any special stigma in it. Dr. Smith told her to have a breast X-ray every two years.

Mary had an X-ray that year, and another one two years later, when she was forty-two. And she was fine. No breast cancer. And so I don't get it. Now she's forty-three and she's having an ultrasound. This afternoon. On something that might be cancer. Not breast cancer, but in her belly. Her abdomen. Not her breasts, but her ovaries. No one warned her about that.

She was afraid to tell me. Last Monday, a week after they moved the silo, she left the store after lunch, which is not all that unusual, she's not the most dependable worker if you want to know the truth, even if she does make the most amazing sandwiches. She bakes the bread herself to look like—well, you'd have to see them. And she fills them with things you'd never think could look like anything but what they are—bologna and cucumber slices, and olives. But the way she makes them, they're sexy all right. Tourists come to see them in the deli case, because a few years ago a guy wrote a story about her in a magazine. We sell the magazine in the store. I cut out the article and framed it and hung it in the window. I made one for the house, too. Daly's General

Store is even listed in two guidebooks because of her sandwiches; we sell those books by the register. One of our friends made a three-foot banner on his computer with the title of the article, and I taped that across the top of the window, too. It goes all the way across: World's Most Original Sexy Sandwich.

Anyway, on Monday—two days ago and it feels like weeks—she left after lunch and didn't come back. Going to do some errands, she said. It made me a little cranky, I have to say, doing her job and mine all evening, though the girl who works with us does well enough and came in on time for once. I got home after nine, and there was my Mary, meeting me at the door, and holding onto me. My wife is affectionate but not one of those clinging types.

"What's wrong?"

"Nothing. But I saw the doctor this afternoon and I have to have a bunch of tests."

"What?"

She said it again. She said she had a mass in her belly. She tried to make light of it and made a scary face: a *suspicious mass,* she said.

"Why didn't you tell me?"

"I am telling you."

"You mean—like cancer?"

"Oh, no. I don't think so. I think I'd know if it was cancer, don't you?"

She sat me down at the kitchen table and brought me a beer, set it in front of me.

"Because of the dowsing, I mean," she added. She bustled around the kitchen with her back to me, put a few dishes away. Her neck bent slightly to the side in this fierce way she has, but the way she held herself especially upright was like she would fall over if she didn't. She jerked open the cabinet door that sticks. She took special care not to bang things. She was trying so hard but she didn't know what to do with the things she was putting away.

I am a decent storekeeper, and not worse than most human beings. I'm proud to run the store my grandfather started, it's a good store and sells almost every kind of regular thing you need. I went to college for two years, the first person in my family to go; I'm proud of that, too. But watching my wife bustling about the kitchen afraid to look at me because I'd see how terrified she was, all I could think of was, *I'm the man. I'm supposed to go first.*

"I hate these chairs, Mary. They're so goddamn uncomfortable. We ought to burn them."

It was Mary who crossed the linoleum floor and sat in my lap like she has a thousand times. She stroked my back like I was the one needing comfort. I rested my head against the curve of her neck and held onto her.

I always thought Mary wasn't afraid of anything. When we were kids, she used to sing a lot. She has a loud voice, a surprisingly big voice for such a little person. One time on the bus—we must have been about ten or eleven—two older guys, maybe eighth graders, were harassing other kids more than usual, stealing lunches and throwing things out the window, that kind of thing. Mary got mad and started singing, in this enormous voice. *Oh beautiful for spacious skies*. It seems like a funny choice now, but we didn't know all that many songs besides ones like "On Top of Spaghetti," and maybe she thought a more grown-up-type song would be better. Anyway, all the other little kids started singing with her, real loud, almost shouting, the way kids do when they're being silly, and then everybody was singing, except the two guys making trouble. It was really loud, but the bus driver didn't say anything—what could she say? It was this patriotic song—and anyway the two guys must have felt ganged up on, even though it was only singing. They tried to sing something different, but you could tell their hearts weren't in it. They hunched down in their seats. They cuffed each other and laughed like they couldn't hear anything, and the singing kept going. We were having fun making a lot of noise. Maybe we sang it three or four or five times. The two guys gave up and looked out the window like they were bored. Oh, they probably stole lunches again, I don't remember. But not that day.

I fell in love with her then, because she could do things I'd never even dream of doing and not even know they were special. Things I could never even think up. She was fearless.

But she's never known what she had. She's always looking for something else. Vitamins, yoga, dyeing her hair red, health foods, even Bible study once, but nothing lasted, until dowsing. I try to encourage her, up to a point, although I think she's fine as she is. That is, she can buy whatever she wants for the house, like vitamins, but I decide what we buy for the store. I don't mean I don't take her advice. I do, but no one around here is going to pay three times as much for organic apples or some fancy potato chips when regular ones cost half as much. What's the sense in that?

I've been telling her she didn't look like herself this spring but she ignored me, said I worry too much. I should have insisted she go to the doctor. I should have made her go.

I've never made Mary do anything. It's not our way. But I should have this time.

She'll have the ultrasound today and then maybe a CAT scan, and she won't let me come with her because she says I'll make her cry. The truth is she's afraid I'll cry.

4

Mary Bailey Daly sat in the waiting room of a doctor's office for the fourth time in less than two weeks—just what she had always dreaded about getting sick. The obsession with doctors and appointments, the relentless consuming of her thoughts and time, driving back and forth to the city every other day, waiting endlessly for results. Exactly what she had never wanted, and here she was, and she was determined to see it through, to find out what she could—at least for now. She would not become obsessed with getting information, either. She would learn how bad it was, and that was it.

So far she could still think clearly, though she supposed she was in shock. She did not believe the diagnosis completely—or the tentative diagnosis, that is; she was about to hear the biopsy results in a few minutes. She did not believe the tentative diagnosis because

. . . how could she have cancer and not know it? Her whole life was about sensing forces in the universe beyond the range of ordinary people. If she had cancer, she would know. Wouldn't she?

Jimmy had come with her again this time, but if anything it made it harder. But perhaps that was not completely true; perhaps she found his worried presence more a comfort than she could admit. How odd that all her life she had taken pleasure in waiting, waiting and listening, listening to the universe for some sign. It had made her feel humble in the past, and excited, and full of anticipation of what was to come next. Always what lay ahead had excited her. But not now. Though she had always considered herself a curious soul, she wished for the first time in her life to go backward. Not forward into the future. No one in her right mind enjoys waiting in a doctor's office to hear whether she's got cancer.

She glanced at Jimmy. He was afraid, and had insisted on finding out with her. He had always encouraged her joy—all her wild searches, her silly ideas, even the funny sandwiches that she loved to make. She couldn't think about the future. She could only think how lucky she had been.

How many lives could you have? How many had she used up? Her childhood running around with Tuesday, escaping her brothers and parents; the first fifteen years of her life with Jimmy, happy enough but looking for something; and the last five years, since she found dowsing. Was that it?

When she was little, her brothers liked to keep her from doing things—they liked to tie her up, or lock her away. One of her first memories was of Tuesday rescuing her. They let her play hide-and-seek with them, but once, after she'd hid in a closet, one of them locked her in. She should have known better—they were rambunctious and unpredictable—but she was little. This time she remembered because she yelled and yelled, and then the door opened and there was Tuesday. Her brothers had all left—she didn't know where her parents were—but Tuesday had come over and heard her.

After she married Jimmy, he and she used to go swimming naked in Joe's Pond at night in the summer; it was romantic: it was where they'd first messed around in high school. From there they made a life together. Then Tuesday came back from Maine, and—she'd never tell him this, he'd take it wrong—she felt better having him around. It was as though he were a part of her.

But even then, something was missing, which was why she kept going to those silly Fishwives meetings and reading articles about self-improvement, which Jimmy said she didn't need—and trying weird things like yoga and grapefruits. And then she found dowsing. And that was it. She stopped looking. She couldn't explain it, except that after she started dowsing, she woke up every day feeling full. Not all bloated like now, but full of life. The most alive she'd ever felt. As though all the other alive feelings had been rungs on a ladder she'd been climbing, and she'd made it to the top.

One day she got to the store early—after Jimmy, but still early, before eight—and she thought, *What can I make?* The universe was pouring into her so fast and hard, like water filling a balloon from a spigot turned on full blast, that if she didn't do something, she would burst. And so she made bread.

She pulled a cookbook from the revolving wire rack of paperbacks by the front door and read how to make rolls. One thing about working in a store, it had most of what you needed.

When she read the recipe, she remembered why she didn't use cookbooks or like to follow other people's directions generally. They made it so complicated. But her mother used to say, about cooking if nothing else, *Don't worry about the directions. Trust yourself.* Her mother wasn't the world's greatest cook—trusting yourself had its disadvantages—and growing up Mary ate things like peanut butter chicken and blueberry mashed potatoes. But those meals were useful in the grade school combat that passed for conversation, when you wanted to shock.

"What're you doing?" Jimmy said, when he saw flour flying up in the air behind the deli case.

Mary told him, and he nodded, as though he'd always wanted to have homemade bread in the store, and not just the loaves they sold for the old hippies up on Lime Kiln Road.

"Look, Mary. It's raining." Jimmy took his wife's hand.

"That's good. We need rain." They watched the drops gather on the windows of the waiting room. "Remember the day I first made rolls?"

What happened that first day was that when it came time to make the buns, after she'd been kneading the warm, yeasty-smelling dough into just the right consistency, her hands light with flour, molding and squeezing and patting, enjoying the softness, the texture, so much that for the first time in her life she didn't notice folks coming and going behind her, helping themselves to coffee and Danish, and Jimmy came over and asked her if she was all right . . . after all that, her face still glowing as if she'd just had sex, then finally she made the individual buns.

She divided the dough, patted it into round shapes, and then the idea came to her. She made round circles, flattened balls really, in different sizes, different fullnesses. Just like in life. Some were longish and thin, almost oval, and some were fat and full, almost perfectly round. Some were little and perky and some were more droopy, the empty-sack look. But all of them came to life when she pulled out nipples on each one—dainty little nipples or fuller nipples. And the placement mattered, too: centered for the perky little round buns and toward the bottom of the longer, thinner buns. An older, empty-sack bun could have a full, satisfied, lived-a-good-life nipple.

When they came out of the oven, golden toasty, the nipples a little browner than the round tops, she laughed. It was all she could do not to eat every one.

"You can't sell those!" Jimmy said, right away.

She held two in front of her. "Just wait. People will love them."

"Mary, please." He was trying not to laugh, but she could see he was worried, too.

"I tell you what. I'll only use a couple for sandwiches, as an experiment, and I'll put the rest out in a bowl."

He looked skeptical. But he nodded.

So she wrote "Hard Rolls" on an index card, and set it in front of a wire basket of regular, common rolls. And on another one she wrote "Soft Rolls." But then she crossed that out, and on the other side she wrote "Mary's Specials" and set that in front of a basket of the new rolls.

There was some hooting and hollering among the regulars, but she sold every one.

"Long wait," Jimmy said.

"Don't worry."

"I never knew so many people had cancer."

"Maybe they're just naturally bald."

It wasn't long before she expanded her repertoire.

It was a Thursday, the day fresh produce was delivered. She came in early as usual, stacked the crates of lettuce and tomatoes, cucumbers and cabbage. She mixed the dough, and set out the day's batch of potato salad, cole slaw, beef stew, and macaroni and cheese. She made her special rolls—laughing at herself, smiling at each one, as if she were in love. She didn't think about women, not specific women or even imaginary women. Rather she thought about shapes—earthen mounds, and stones below waterfalls. Clouds. While the rolls baked, she washed the lettuce and sliced the meat and cheese. When the rolls were done, she admired them as they cooled for a moment, and then chose one and sliced it open. Steam rose from the soft interior.

She smoothed the mustard over the bread in small, gentle circles. She slid bologna slices in place so that they drooped just a tiny bit over the edge of the bread, as if peeking out from between covers. She adjusted the lettuce and the tomato slices so they, too, peeked out. Enticing, beckoning.

"What are you doing now?"

She'd felt Jimmy watching her, but hadn't looked at him, though she couldn't keep from smiling to herself. She licked her lips. She raised the sandwich as if offering it to him, then held it against her like a breastplate.

He shook his head, just as the door jingled open and a customer came in.

For the next half-hour she made ham and swiss, smoked turkey, corned beef, and tuna sandwiches and wrapped them in cellophane, which bound the ingredients unkindly and hid their true nature, and so she stopped. But when at lunchtime she also made sandwiches on demand, she began again. The cheese slid over the ham like a tongue. A tomato dripped a delicate line of juice down one side of the bun. The turkey slices fell into delicate folds of skin barely covering a small, round pepper slice in the center. One woman she knew, watching her make her sandwich, winked at her; another raised her eyebrows. A local man laughed when she handed him his; a man she didn't know got red-faced, as though he would have preferred macaroni. She smiled and told them all to enjoy their meals, as she always did.

Her cousin Tuesday stopped by, which he didn't do very often. She teased him: *you need a wife!* She started to make him a sandwich, on the house even, but he left abruptly. She made it anyway, for him, a fat bun with soft white insides, slathered with tuna, topped with crispy red-tipped lettuce. She sprinkled red onion bits on top, and something about it—the onion, her lonely cousin who didn't want her sandwich—made her eyes well up. *Well,* she thought, *I did what I could.*

Her bosom sandwiches were only the beginning. She tried making flatter, circular rolls like butts. She made two smaller rolls attached to each other, with a hotdog in the middle. Butts, breasts, balls, they looked too similar. She began making rolls vaguely in the shape of a woman, and these became her favorite, and her trademark. Women's bodies come in endless, delectable variety. She wrote that—*delectable*—on the signs she set in the window: Mary's Delectable Deli Sandwiches. Mary's Luscious Lunch. They came from the paperback thesaurus that never sold but that they kept on the bookrack anyway. She sought ideas there, even though you couldn't count on it to make sense. Like who would ever say "toothsome" when they meant delicious?

"Jimmy, do you think I'm toothsome?"
"What?"
Mary smiled. "Never mind."

She made fat women, skinny women, lumpy or smooth, with small pointy breasts or large droopy ones. It was hard to control the dough and she never knew exactly how they would come out. She left off the heads and usually the legs. She was an artist creating torsos, only instead of plaster casts, hers were edible. She was delectable.

Less than a year later, a man who wrote for a magazine Bailey Daly's sold to tourists and summer people who wished they lived here year round came to do a story about Mary's sandwiches. A photographer took pictures of her behind the counter, and of Jimmy and her in front of the store. Two months later, it arrived, with the words "The World's Sexiest Sandwiches" on the cover. And inside, a picture of Mary with one hand at her forehead brushing hair away, and a little white smudge on her cheek, the perfect image of a happy, round little cook, except for the wire basket of bosom rolls in the front left corner of the photo, with the nipples poking out just begging for a little lick. Jimmy blushed when he saw the picture, but Mary tore it out and taped it to the front of the deli case. She had to post it; nobody around there would see it otherwise. She tore out a second one and taped it to the inside of the store window—to Jimmy's embarrassment and pride. Later he framed it for her birthday. They both thought it brought in customers. Mary said the tourists came in expecting to find her naked and bought a sandwich because they were so relieved she wasn't.

Mary and Jimmy were shown into a warm, carpeted office full of bookcases, filing cabinets, and a cluttered desk on which sat a computer and printer amid stacks of untidy papers. Framed certificates and pictures of children hung on the walls. Mary and Jimmy sat in wooden chairs in front of the desk, without speaking. The rain came down harder and lashed the window behind the desk. Shortly the doctor came in. He offered them coffee, which they refused.

He was not overly sympathetic or falsely cheerful. He told them simply that the tests so far indicated that Mary did indeed have ovarian cancer, that he believed it was in a fairly advanced stage, but that a few more tests needed to be done to determine exactly how advanced it was before the proper course of treatment could be recommended.

What kind of man wanted to be a gynecological oncologist, Mary wondered.

What would the treatment likely be, asked Jimmy.

"We might want to take it out, but we should have a bone scan before we discuss treatment options. That's the next step."

Mary looked out the window. Rain was good. They needed rain.

"How—?" Jimmy looked at Mary, fumbled for the right words. "How bad, how much . . . ?"

The doctor directed his answers at Mary although she didn't appear to be listening. "I'd like to be able to tell you how extensive it is, but I don't know at this point. From all indications, as I said, it appears to be fairly advanced, which is why you haven't been feeling well. You can have cancer for quite a while and feel just fine."

Mary glanced at him sideways. "Have you ever known a dowser?"

He blinked. "No."

Mary nodded.

"The receptionist will make the appointments for you for later this week. I'd like to see you again next Monday. The sooner we get started, the better."

5

Mary loves water. This morning I came out of the shower, in a big cloud of steam, and she was sitting where I left her on the couch, wrapped up in that blue and white quilt the Fishwives made for her. The newspaper was in her lap and she was staring out the window over her shoulder looking morose.

"Typical paper. The headlines say one thing . . ."

"What?"

"It says 'Breast Cancer Detection Rate Up.' Right here. Then it says that the rate of deaths is the same. That means early detection doesn't help. It means treatments don't help. It's like I thought."

"You don't have breast cancer. And it's got to be more complicated than that." I try to be reasonable. One of us has to be. Mary flies off like a hot-air balloon sometimes with her ideas. I'm afraid of her getting some crazy notion, like treatment doesn't help. Of course it helps.

"Maybe so, Jimmy, but how can I tell from this *fucking* paper?" She threw the paper on the floor and struggled like crazy with the quilt, because it was caught around her short legs. "Are you finished in the shower?"

"Sure, sure."

She comes up to me, then, and leans her cheek against my damp chest. I'm still warm, I like a hot-hot shower, and her cheek is cool. She says, "Are you clean enough?" She tugs at my towel.

"What are you doing?"

"Come take a shower with me."

"I just took one. I'm still wet."

She pulls off her nightgown, right there in the kitchen in front of God and everybody. She holds her belly like there's a child in there and leans against me. "Take a shower with me."

6

Speed limit: Horses at a Walk, Motor Vehicles 10 miles an hour, read the sign over the entrance to the covered bridge. No longer used as a public entrance, it led from the staff offices to the museum grounds. Didi Jamison had worked at the museum for ten years, and though it had lost a bit of its mystery, she had only to thump through the covered bridge on a foggy, drizzly day when the museum was closed, listening to her muted footsteps on the thick boards like thousands of footsteps before her—and the old feeling returned. The sense of possibility, of things hidden and unexpressed, the invisible presence of all the unknown ancestors, all the previous inhabitants of the buildings, the creators of the artifacts, the ordinary and extraordinary people who built the houses, patronized the general store, sought out the dentist, attended the schoolhouse, rode in the carriages, sewed the quilts, carved the circus figures, sailed the steamboat. On the quiet, empty days, the commotion of all these boisterous lives pressed against her skin. Their spirits slept in the shadows.

It was always a relief to Didi that she could tell the truth about the museum. It was her job. Tell the truth, be accurate, just say the way things actually are, to the best of your knowledge. Even now, calling it a history museum rather than a folk art museum because of this latest flap . . . well, that was truly what it was. She did not like to exaggerate. She believed in truth. She knew her friends considered this an extreme trait, but she couldn't help it. It might be why she had such a hard time writing poetry: *Tell all the truth but tell it slant,* wrote Emily Dickinson. But what did that mean? Still, she had made a lot of progress over her lifetime; when she was in college, she could hardly answer a straightforward question. *Where are you from, what do you like to do, what is your family like, do you have any brothers and sisters?*

"I think I have one sister."

"What? Don't you know?"

"I think I know. I mean, I didn't grow up with more than

that—only the one sister—but how would you know for sure? How can you be positive your parents didn't have other children before you were born, or secretly by someone else?"

The questioner tended to drift away with raised eyebrows, shaking his head.

She wasn't being difficult. It was a matter of being scrupulously accurate.

What do you like to do?

"I think I like to do most things."

"Like what?"

"Like everything, you know, except that I haven't tried a lot and I don't know about those things because you never know until you try, you only think you do. Know what I mean? Like Eeyore, you know, he loves to eat everything, he thinks, until he tries things one by one and discovers finally there's only one thing he likes after all, and that's thistles."

"Thistles?"

"Yes. Didn't your mother read you *Winnie the Pooh* when you were a kid?"

"Who knows? I might have seen the video."

"But if you don't know, who does? Who knows the truth of your experiences better than you?"

Not everyone ran from Didi. She had a number of sexual and romantic liaisons with men, some of them even lasting a year or more. But at twenty-five she met Maude.

They were introduced by a friend. "This is Mad Dog," said the friend.

Maude rolled her eyes at Didi. "I pick up strays like her," she said, indicating the friend. "Maude Dodge Lake," she explained, and offered her hand, "named for Mabel Dodge Luhan. I'm the kind of person who picks up nicknames, too. They wanted to name me Dodge Lake but that sounds too much like a resort, don't you think? For old people. They knew I wouldn't be the kind of person who'd want to sound like a resort."

Didi and Maude went out for dinner a few days later, and the next night and the next, to a small but inexpensive place that suited them both, with an eclectic, vaguely Old World décor—paneled walls, peacock feathers standing in every corner, painted wooden fish on the walls, a piano bar, ornate tin Mexican candelabras, and famous newspapers with screaming headlines: Dewey Defeats Truman.

"I'm the kind of woman who knows who she is," Maude said, but she spoke so shyly, so uncharacteristically softly, and there was such an unspoken appeal in her voice, that Didi laid her hand gently over Maude's across the small table. Maude interlocked her fingers with Didi's and wouldn't let go even when the waitress approached. But Didi was not at all sure of who she was and pulled her hand away.

Didi and Maude made love for the first time on a clear, moonlit night.

"Are you the kind of person who turns into a wolf at the full moon?" Didi whispered into her new friend's ear.

"Yes. Make friendly noises."

Didi growled and nibbled and laughed so freely that she thought perhaps she did, after all, know the kind of person she was.

They became inseparable, and had stayed that way for almost twenty years.

Maude was at her drawing group this evening, and soon she would leave for eight weeks at an artists' colony, leaving Didi the company of the two cats, the laundry, the cooking, the dishes, the errands, all whining at her. Didi hated errands.

But Maude was happy, Maude was excited, Maude had worked hard for this chance and of course she deserved it, and that was all that counted. Of course. Maude was a talented painter. No, she hadn't made it big, hadn't succeeded in financial terms perhaps, but Maude didn't measure herself that way. She would have liked more recognition, yes, who wouldn't, said Didi, but Maude was clear about her commitment to her work, knew its place in her life and knew what she was willing to give up for it. She was willing to give up Didi for two months.

But that wasn't it. Didi wanted Maude to go. Truly. Jesus Christ, this kind of chance didn't come up very often. Or it came but you couldn't take advantage of it because of jobs, sick mothers, ailing pets. Although some people never let their families get in the way even when they should. But that wasn't the point. The point was that Didi never ever wanted to be that kind of partner, the crazy wife of the gifted painter. She would kill herself first. Yes she would.

But . . . why did Maude have to go now? Didi had been working her buns off getting ready for the opening of the museum this year, which included the dedication of the museum's million-dollar restoration project, the round barn. The delivery of the interior silo had come off without a hitch in the end, when the crane lifted it into the barn. A day late, yes, but with no smashed hands, no broken silo, no deaths. It had slid into place easily. "Made for each other," Adrian said in his usual teasing way. Adrian, her new friend. He'd missed the adventure of the flying silo the day before because he'd covered a barn burning, but he managed to write a small follow-up story the next day. All in all, the news media, her allies and foes, had treated the move well. It looked like the round barn would be ready by the opening, and all was in order.

But even as the silo eased into place, Didi found herself caught in the middle of a national uproar about something she should have seen coming—not exactly in the middle perhaps, but caught nonetheless and dragged along flapping and bumping like a seat-belt hanging out of a speeding car door.

It was true that no one else had foreseen the reaction either, but Didi berated herself for not having attended to her own intuition. She'd been afraid they would have problems selling off some of the paintings, but everyone else was so confident, she'd all but forgotten her own initial reservations. Besides, her instincts were confused these days. And after all, what was wrong with selling off a Manet or two, a small Degas dancer, and a few other paintings in order to put the museum on a sound financial footing? And the museum had been careful. The board had reviewed the museum's policies, and wrestled with questions of professional ethics, and the staff had checked out the board's recommendation with various professional associations. All seemed okay.

But *no-o-o,* said the leaders of those same associations now, now that the heat was on. You never checked with *me. I*'d never have given my blessing to such a worthless, materialistic, shortsighted plan as this. Articles in all the major newspapers and all the major art journals made the museum look bad—hasty, unethical, as if they didn't care about professional standards, art, or the future of their own museum. And how the museum looked was Didi's business.

And in this matter, Adrian hadn't helped. He had been neutral perhaps, but he hadn't helped.

But what did they want, these outsiders? The board had to find financial resources somewhere, and it was bound and determined the museum would not go the way of other outdoor museums that had become nothing more than glorified theme parks.

Was that true? Yes, it was! Didi would not exaggerate.

It was odd anyway that an outdoor folk art museum—no, a history museum—had a collection of fine art in the first place. But it did. The founder had collected cigar-store Indians and duck decoys, but her parents before her had collected what was then considered the only "real" art. The building called the Gallery housed these ancestral works, and the truth was, the Gallery was Didi's favorite building. At least once a week during the long months from November to May when the museum was closed to all but school groups, she ate lunch there—nothing crumbly that could attract bugs, only her usual pasta salad. She let herself in, and usually wandered through the building alone, unless she ran into Tuesday Bailey. The first time that he greeted her as she came in, she jumped. He was sitting on a bench in the vestibule, across from a large Manet, a "satiric pastoral," an outdoor scene of young people around a table, laughing and drinking.

"I hope I'm not disturbing you," she said.

He shook his head. "Is it innocent, or subversive?" he asked solemnly.

She smiled. He was quoting the catalogue, which she had written. She didn't explain what she was doing there, nor did he. She liked that. Sometimes she found him in other rooms; a few times she met him on her way out. She surmised he was taking a late lunch, or simply stopping in for a restorative ten minutes after an encounter with Charles Hopper or Dean Allen. She didn't know. They never spoke much, beyond exchanging pleasantries. If they silently enjoyed sharing their love of the paintings, neither ever said.

Adrian was different. He talked too much, about things that were better left unsaid. Because of all the recent hubbub at the museum, the tenor of their casual colleagueship of the last two years had changed. He called her every few days about something. First it was the round barn, and moving the silo. When the museum opened on Lilac Sunday in a few days, the round barn would offer museum visitors a spectacular introduction—to the barn, and farming in Vermont, and the museum as a whole. She'd told him everything she knew. Now he wanted to know more about the paintings. And sometimes he just wanted to chat.

And his voice on the phone . . . It was too sexy, it made her feel . . .

Today Adrian called again. After a moment, he said, "You seem curiously detached from all this somehow. Are you all right? I know you like the paintings."

Didi hesitated. What was the truth? "I didn't want to see them sold at first because I like seeing them. I—love them." Why did she feel shy using that word around Adrian? She became impatient with herself, more aggressive. "But the reasons make sense. I don't really understand all the uproar. It's not as if we're burning them. So we sell them, and someone else owns them. So someone else cares for them and displays them. So what? Does it really matter who owns a painting? What's really important?"

"You don't believe in what the ArtNews fellow called 'the integrity of the collection'?" He was teasing her. She didn't laugh.

"He was talking about collections as if they're static; how can a collection have integrity in that sense? In real life, collections are fluid, they change all the time. What has integrity is the way an institution makes its decisions, meaning the way the people who run it abide by their guiding principles—or don't. I keep trying to get to the heart of this—"

"The heart, yes."

She ignored him. "Is it about possession? Is it about holding on to what you have no matter what? Or is it because the works are so valuable? In other words, sheer materialism? Or is there maybe some fear that the museum doesn't value the paintings, which threatens everyone because art *isn't* valued highly enough. Or consistently anyway. The public is fickle—" She broke off. "Wait. You're not taking notes, are you? This is off the record."

"You didn't say so."

"Adrian!"

"Didi, trust me."

"I don't trust you."

"Off the record," he agreed. "My feisty friend, I understand you very well. We are related under the skin, you and I. Off the record, have lunch with me next Thursday after I interview Charles."

She wished Maude weren't going away.

7

May 20
Cynthia Allen
New Zealand
Dear Cynthia,

I've come back to the museum where they have the wagons and carts and the old schoolhouse and the steamboat up on risers like a dinghy taken out for the winter. My favorite still is the circus building. I love that endless procession of tiny elephants and horses and lion tamers and clowns, like the magic will never end. Do you remember when we went to the circus? I loved the circus. This museum is worth preserving if only for the circus, and the steamboat, and the stocks. Did I ever tell you there were stocks in front of the schoolhouse? Or is it the jail. Children are always sticking their heads and hands in the holes and pretending to be 18th-century miscreants. They can't imagine the true humiliation of people throwing rotten food at you, of course. Only I know things like that.

I wish you would write to me, I am lonely here. The circus figures are good company but not good enough.

Dean

8

Was it minor vandalism or simple sloppiness on the part of some of the crew? Tuesday came in early on Wednesday morning. He had assigned double shifts in order to finish the roof by the museum's opening this weekend, but no one was scheduled to be working at six, nor did he see anyone around. He walked quickly through the round barn as was his habit, before attending to other duties. On the top floor, tools were scattered around as if the workers had been called away suddenly in the middle of a project—and never returned to clean up.

He mentioned it briefly to his restoration crew chief later that day. When he stopped in for a quick look the next afternoon, the crew chief said, "By the way, the guys all say they left their tools like they always did. They were a little pissed off to come in and find them strewn around like that, actually. Like their kids had been playing with them and left them on the driveway. We all see plenty of that. Maybe you got a hole in security. Thought you'd like to know."

It was puzzling, but Tuesday thought little more about it. Indeed, the reconstruction of the round barn was going well, though behind schedule, naturally. But they would be ready by Sunday, when the museum opened for the season. The curators were already setting up the new farming exhibit on the second floor and hanging the new introductory panels upstairs. Eight thousand square feet's worth of cedar shingles would be in place by the end of the day, and the louvered cupola would be lifted onto the very top by crane tomorrow. The outside had been repainted the traditional deep, barn red, the window frames white. The sprinkler and security systems had been tested and retested.

Visitors would enter on the top floor, an open, airy space with several information desks, benches to watch a short film about the museum, and ten-foot-high posters hanging overhead like banners in a cathedral which highlighted some of the museum's offerings. On the floor itself, a few selected artifacts suggested what lay ahead: a carriage, a collection of antique dolls, a gruesome arrangement of primitive dentist's tools.

Below, on the dairy floor, only a sampling of the original stanchions remained as an indication of the barn's intended use. Within a large pen, the pillars of which were left with the paint chipped and worn, were two large papier-mâché Holsteins—one standing, one lying on its side—surrounded by hay. The rest of this floor was given over to a display about Vermont farming, with a focus this spring mostly on maple sugaring, dairying, and growing apples. The core display was augmented by additional tools placed here and there. Two curators were still installing panels of tools against the walls. Other artifacts were clumped together on risers or stood alone, artfully arranged throughout the space—a butter sink, an ox yoke, milk cans, a grubbing hoe, sheep shears, a spade plow.

Tuesday Bailey observed everything with pleasure, noting what still needed to be done—a safety bar needed to be installed across the hatch into the silo, which was left open so visitors could see inside, a cracked window on the bottom floor needed to be replaced, exit signage in the basement needed to be better lit before tomorrow. Several inspectors needed to sign off on the project tomorrow afternoon.

He paused at the silo. He had argued for leaving the hatches open. So what if kids threw things down into it, it could be cleaned out. How else could visitors get a sense of scope, of magnitude? Of the less than two dozen round barns that had been built in Vermont, eighteen had burned or collapsed. A few others had been extensively modified. This one, this beautiful structure, which had probably remained standing for so long precisely because of the great strength of the silo, gave him shivers. He would oversee its well-being as long as he could.

Sam Desautels, the museum's head of security, had been Tuesday's right-hand man since Tuesday hired him years ago. They'd grown up together in Eustis; like Tuesday, Sam lived there still, though perhaps with better reason, since he had a wife and family. His four children had over seventy cousins within the county.

On Thursdays, the two men ate lunch at a table outside the security building.

"It's sad about Mary," Sam said as he unwrapped his sandwich. "A damn shame."

Tuesday's own sandwich was halfway to his mouth.

"What's that, Sam?"

"The cancer. Shit, I guess you didn't know. I'm sorry, man. I didn't mean to—Anne Marie . . ." He trailed off helplessly. His wife, Anne Marie, was Mary's best friend.

"I didn't know."

Tuesday's hands, sandwich still held between them, rested on the paper bag on top of the picnic table. He waited.

"I guess she's got it pretty bad. Ovarian. Anne Marie's cousin Ruby had it, you know, the one in Rutland. She had a bad time of it, too. She had radiation, chemo, all her hair fell out, she was real sick. Bad way to go. Hey, bud, you all right? Hey, don't faint on me." In one motion, he leaped to Tuesday's side of the table, pulled out the bench, and forced Tuesday's head between his knees.

"Jesus, I'm an asshole. Sorry, man. You all right now? I shoulda let Mary tell you, I guess."

A half-hour later Tuesday was on the road. He saw her watching the silo, rosy-cheeked and windblown, and he railed at himself. She had been thinner. She didn't look well. Why hadn't he said something more? Why hadn't he called her the next week, or the next?

Because he never called her. They never spoke on the phone, they only ran into one another, usually at the store. That is, he stopped by the store and saw her there. It was more than twenty-five years since she'd last come over to show him something she was excited about—her first truck. For twenty-five years he'd remembered her profile as they drove around that afternoon, another time the wind blew her already wild hair and reddened her cheeks.

She was still Mary Bailey then. A few months later, during her junior year in high school, she would start going out with Jimmy Daly, but that summer she was still unattached. Still nobody's but his. That Saturday in August, Tuesday had been outside doing some chore, when he heard insistent honking on the road, and then there she was, clattering up his long gravel driveway in a red truck with big bites of rust out of the sides and rear, beeping all the way. She made a tight circle on the grass and headed the truck back down the driveway. "Reverse don't work too well," she called out to him cheerfully.

Tuesday didn't have a truck of his own. He hopped in without a word, banging the door after him. It didn't close, but he swung it again, lifting it as he did. This time it stayed shut. "Nice," he said.

Through a hole in the floor the size of a fist he could see the ground. "How's the rust underneath?"

Mary shrugged. "It's just for fun. Nothing lasts forever." She grinned at him and smacked the outside of her door. "My truck!"

They drove over the back roads up to Troy and North Troy and over to Derby Line on the Canadian border. They drove through Island Pond and West Burke and Barton. They stopped for gas and Tuesday bought two dollars' worth—all he had. The truck had borrowed plates, and nearly two hundred thousand miles on it, but it was red, and it ran. She'd driven straight to his house. She didn't talk about how she was going to fix it up, the way a guy might have. She simply loved it as it was, rust and all. The vinyl seat was torn in the middle and along the edges so the foam peeked out, where it hadn't been dug out altogether by bored fingers. The passenger-side window wouldn't close or open all the way. Holes the size of grapefruits gaped all along the frame, and the shocks were worn. The seatbelts worked because they'd never been used. Mary drove fast, and laughed at every bump in the road that lifted her out of her seat. Tuesday, nearly a foot taller, hit his head the first few times and then slid down in the seat for protection, but he couldn't help smiling. He held his arm out over the stuck widow and felt the wind. They didn't talk much. The radio didn't work; Mary sang loudly and banged the side of the truck with her hand. It was hot; her face was flushed from the heat and the wind. Tuesday was happy.

They stopped at the boat ramp at Joe's Pond. Quiet now, they sat in the truck, in the late afternoon shade of hundred-year-old maple trees. Kids played in the pond, splashing and laughing. "Go?" Mary said. Tuesday smiled. The truck started right up, but the gears screeched when she tried to set it in reverse.

"Goddamn shit fuck for crying out loud." Mary got out, slammed the door, kicked the front wheel, spit.

Laughing to himself, so happy to be with her, Tuesday wandered down to the shore. He heard her behind him, cursing and fuming. Everything was right with the world. He didn't care if the truck never moved. He could have lived there at the edge of Joe's Pond forever. They could catch fish and make love by the water. The heat rose to his face as he thought of it and he rubbed the back of his neck. He thought the kids in the water were like him: they could play and play and play and never get tired, not stop even when they were exhausted, they loved it so much, yelling and screaming and diving in and out of the water. That's how he was with Mary.

When he returned to the truck, Mary was unfazed, as he knew she would be.

"We have to push it backwards," she declared fiercely.

They began shoving and rocking, a happy together job for Tuesday. Mary wanted to stand on the driver's side so she could turn the wheel, but she was so short, she couldn't get a good grip on the door and the wheel at the same time.

"Trade sides," she commanded. He obliged.

He never laughed at Mary. He never felt like laughing at her; he laughed out of delight. How could she not see it, he wondered for years? But maybe she had. Maybe she always knew and it didn't matter.

He thought of her that way for years, straining against the truck, short and round but strong and fierce. So determined, as stubborn as any damned truck without reverse. Red-faced and outraged, but able to move with a moment's notice into joy once they got the truck turned around and maneuvered up the ramp, announcing with a shout her triumphant arrival back on the main road.

"Way to go!" she yelled, and they took off.

Mary's current truck, Red IV, was not in front of Daly's General Store, nor was it parked in her driveway. It wasn't at the Desautels' or in the church parking lot or anywhere in the village or anywhere in Eustis that he could see.

Tuesday drove home. What was he doing tearing all over kingdom come anyway? He'd about run out of gas. She was probably at the doctor's. He was overreacting. He had panicked. It was unlike him. He was usually so level-headed, good in a crisis they always said at work. She'd probably be all right. In the long run. But—

I've got a feeling, he and Mary used to say when they were kids, pretending to see the future. His first two years in high school, he'd bought lottery tickets at Daly's Store, when Jimmy's father still ran it. *I've got a feeling,* he'd say to Mary. Once he won five dollars and gave it to her, saying she'd earned it with her doubt.

Now he had a bad feeling.

9

This morning I looked out the living room window and saw Mary hunched over the ground like a child. She stayed in that crouched, folded-in position for a long time, watching something. The dew must have soaked into her slippers and the chilly morning eaten through her thin housecoat—but Mary doesn't feel the cold, of a May morning or a January night. She is round and warm like the sun. When she came in, I asked her what she was staring at. She said maggots.

"I read they're starting to use maggots again in hospitals. I forgot where. Maggots are amazing; they only eat the rotten flesh and let the good flesh be, so say you have gangrene, the maggots will eat the gangrene off your leg. They're really thorough, that's the main thing. Doctors can never be as thorough as millions of little bugs."

I couldn't say what I thought of that, Mary thinks I'm too soft already.

"You should've seen them on the bluejay carcass. No sound—just millions of maggots, silently swarming." She laughed at herself, repeated the words. "Then when they're done, they disappear into the grass. Just like that. No sign of them. It's all natural, Jimmy. Maggots need to eat. And nobody has any need for that gangrene on their leg, the maggots might as well have it. Now if maggots would eat cancer."

I collected the Sunday paper that was strewn around the floor. My Mary is not the neatest housekeeper.

"Oh, don't look so stricken." She puts her arms around me. The top of her head reaches my armpits. After nearly twenty years I'm still surprised at how little she is. Little and round. But even now, it feels like she's the one folding me in her great wings.

"I'm not afraid of death," she says.

"I know," is all I can say.

But I think she's saying it for my sake. Tomorrow she meets with the oncologist for the second time. She's had all the tests. She wants me to stay home—at the store. She wants to hear the recommendations by herself. I don't know what she's thinking. When she's kidding around, teasing me, like when she wants me to give her something, Mary says, *I've got a feeling.*

Well, I've got a bad feeling.

10

Mary Bailey Daly paused in the parking lot outside Dr. Smith's tiny clinic in Eustis. It had a comforting feeling, this pleasantly nondescript old house that had been altered already several times over Mary's lifetime, and no doubt a few more before that. Most recently it had been a hairdresser's shop in the front and a used clothing store in back. Now a long ramp led to the new automatic door, and the two wide front windows were framed with bright, interior curtains. Would Dr. Smith understand? A flurry of grackles rose from the trees behind the clinic and flew across the road to other trees. Maybe they were a good omen.

In the past three weeks, Mary had seen three doctors—Dr. Smith, the surgeon, and the oncologist twice—and several technicians. She had seen five different waiting rooms full of frightened, unhappy people in various stages of decay. She had read the small print on posters of food pyramids, skin cancers, and methods of birth control. She had had an ultrasound and a CAT scan, blood tests and a bone scan and a chest X-ray. She had begun to learn the special language of cancer patients: she had a CA-125 of 5,000. Now she was meeting again with Dr. Smith—the one doctor who, as a general practitioner, couldn't help her anymore, in theory. In any case, Mary wanted to talk to someone who knew her as herself, not as a body with cancer.

"Thanks for seeing me," Mary said, when she was shown into Dr. Smith's office. "I know you're not exactly my doctor anymore."

"I'll always be your doctor, until the insurance system forces me out of practice. You've seen Dr. Isenberg?" One of the best oncologists around, Mary had been told.

"I don't think I'm going to do it."

"You mean—"

"I mean undergo treatment. It's not worth taking out the tumor, because it's so big, and besides, it's metastasized. To my lungs and liver. Maybe you know this already? Anyway, they think the best bet is to do some heavy duty chemo." She paused. Dr. Smith waited.

"I said, what are we looking at here? He said—Dr. Isenberg—*prolonging your life.* Not saving it, you understand. Prolonging it. I guess I have stage four? I said, *what're the chances of my life being prolonged?* He said everybody's different, blah blah blah, but what it came down to was eighty percent. All that torture to maybe prolong my life. I said, *okay, prolonging it how long?* He said he didn't know. Why do they make you beg for information? I said, *Come on. Months? Years? Weeks?* He said he really couldn't tell me, but he'd guess months. At best."

"Can I get you a cup of coffee, Mary?"

"No. Thank you."

"I gather you told him you'd think about it."

"But there's not much to think about, really—is there? I've seen people go through chemotherapy. The sicker you are to start with, the worse it is. I always said if I got breast cancer, they could take my breasts, but I wasn't going to spend my last years getting poisoned, and worse, obsessing over my symptoms. I just don't want it. Would you?"

"I don't know. I'm trained to value life at any cost, so yes, I probably would do anything I could just to get a few more days."

Mary retreated. Outside the window, aspens bent in the wind.

"You understand that by having no treatment, you'd be hastening your death?"

Mary frowned, her disappointment clear in her face. She had hoped for something else. "I guess I don't see it that way." She stood up to go. But Dr. Smith was not the enemy; and she would need her help in the end.

"Do you like to garden?" Mary asked.

"No, not really."

"Neither do I. That's funny, don't you think? Two women?" She walked to the window to compose herself. She didn't want to cry. "You have a nice view."

"Do you want me to talk you out of it, or have you made your decision?"

"Do you know what's most important? It's not a rhetorical question. I mean do you know?"

Dr. Smith didn't answer.

"I know what you learn matters, and I don't want to spend the rest of my short life learning about drugs and hospitals. Can you understand that?" Mary sat down resolutely. "But I didn't come to talk about that—or maybe I did. Anyway, look, I'm asking for your help. I want you to tell me, straight, what my dying is going to be like."

Instead of going home, Mary drove to the top of East Hill, her favorite thinking place ever since the round barn was moved. She pulled into the meadow that still bore the imprint of the barn. What was it about this place? It wasn't that she found it relaxing; in fact, the opposite was true. Something about it was unsettled, and its very unsettledness soothed her. All that activity, all that commotion, diminished her own noise.

She turned off the engine, which sputtered and clicked and sighed—would she go that gracefully? She would not. How wonderfully quiet it was up here. The wind rustled the new leaves and the insects buzzed interminably. Of course, no single insect was interminable, only all the insects together. That's how it was, only life itself went on, not your own life.

It was the end of May. The discomfort she'd been feeling in her gut, the all-around crummy feeling she had attributed to mid-life, was cancer.

Do you have pain in your abdomen?

I always have pain in my abdomen. My gut doesn't like all kinds of foods and I eat them anyway.

Have you lost weight?

Well, yes, as it turns out, but I didn't notice. I'm not one of those women who weighs herself all the time. My overalls fit like they always did, except I thought maybe they'd gotten stretched out.

How could she have lost weight when she wasn't hungry? She used to try to lose weight in high school, and then she was hungry all the time.

So, she'd been wrong. She had cancer after all. It had taken nearly a month to get from there to here, but here she was. Now what? Mary climbed out of the truck and onto the hood. She wanted to feel the afternoon sun on her face. At first the metal felt uncomfortably hot on her legs through her overalls, but she got used to it. She leaned back against the windshield.

Her conversation with Dr. Smith had drained her. She'd wanted to appear strong, firm, not hysterical or grief-stricken. But now that this last conversation was over, now what? What she referred to as the Other Problem came floating to the surface, and there it was now, staring her in the face, leering at her, monstrous and mocking. The secret problem no one else could understand. She was a dowser? Hah! She was attuned to some secret flowings of the universe, the water beneath the continents, the lines of power beneath the earth? What a joke! Her crazy vision of the world, ordered by a grid of energy that allowed her to listen, and hear, and know things . . . how stupid. It was an illusion. She had been wrong.

And probably there was nothing actually unsettled about this place, either. Probably she had imagined it, mistaking her own confusion, her own unconscious worry about the pain in her belly for something outside herself. Who knew? She certainly couldn't trust herself anymore. It was clear she had lost her gift—if she'd ever had one in the first place.

She was not fragile, not sickly, not easily wounded or diminished. She was not, even now, crippled or weak. She had never been frail or sluggish or helpless. She was strong! She was mighty! She was vital and lusty, round and ravenous. She was a dowser who listened to the world and sensed when a child had fallen behind a boulder, and where water rumbled beneath the earth. How was it possible she could not have known?

Mary closed her eyes. The wind blew softly over her skin. Would her soul blow away when she died, like pollen on the wind? Or would it dissolve and float upward toward the sun? Or simply dissolve into the universe in no special direction?

She had told Dr. Smith she wanted to learn about life, and that was right, but . . . what if it took dying to find out what really mattered?

Last Monday afternoon, after Mary and Jimmy had met with

the oncologist for the second time, they drove home in silence. They sat on the couch in the kitchen, against the Eternal Triangle quilt covered with cat hair, holding onto each other, and they cried. Jimmy rocked back and forth. She told him she didn't understand how she could have cancer all through her and not know. She told him she felt tricked. The red cat jumped in her lap and she petted him, patient with his needs for once. Jimmy never let go.

"I'm not scared," she had said. "I've never been afraid of death, you know that. Remember the dead mouse?" She tried to tease him.

"You can't die." He rocked.

"No," she said. "I won't."

If she wasn't a dowser anymore, what was she? It was more urgent than ever that she live her life in the right way, but what was that? If she couldn't trust herself . . .

Her mother used to talk about a blue funk, Desolation Sound, the Slough of Despond. Mary fell into the Slough of Despond, and could not find her way out.

II

It was during the ribbon-cutting ceremony outside the round barn on Lilac Sunday two weeks before that Didi had conceived of inviting her nephew for a long visit while Maude was away. He'd always liked the museum, and with his fascination for unusual structures he would love the round barn, and she would love his company.

Was that true? Why hadn't his enthusiastic acceptance made her feel any less irritable? And now he was coming tomorrow. Which was fine. Which was great. She loved her nephew. He was probably the one male in her life she loved unconditionally. It would likely be the last time he'd visit for any length, since he was going to college in the fall. New worlds would open up to him, new experiences that would help him find himself, help him spend his life energy on what he really loved, his heart's desire and all that. Great. More power to him. He was an artist and he'd find his way. Hadn't helping David find his own artist's soul been one of Didi's life missions? Hadn't she drawn, painted, made things with him all his life for just this reason? David was the artist in the family; Didi and her sister, David's mother, had no such aspirations, unlike their father. Perhaps that kind of talent skipped generations.

Didi scowled at the mirror across the room; she didn't like what she saw, but then her father always said she didn't know how to see, how to look in order to see.

She scowled at the pad of paper in front of her on the kitchen table, full of crossed out phrases. When the cat jumped onto her lap seeking comfort, or seeking to comfort, you could never tell with cats, she thrust him aside. The wadded up paper followed.

In her restlessness, Didi prowled the house, fussing from desk to refrigerator to living room. She couldn't find what she wasn't looking for, so her search was as futile as it was relentless.

It was windy and unpredictable outside, but Didi gave up on the vague idea she'd had of trying to write a poem and changed into her running shorts. While it was still light, approaching the longest days of the year, she would run to the lake, and if she were hot enough, jump in, shed her anxieties like a sealskin and come home refreshed and pure and ready to write late into the night. Maude had been gone less than a week, though it felt like longer, but Didi was determined to use Maude's absence to spur her to act like the poet she hoped that she was.

In the drawer where she kept her shorts and T-shirts, Didi found a poem handwritten on a scrap of white paper.

after say a night away / comes / pure surround / a delicious devouring

It was the third little poem she had found since Maude left. How did Maude do it? Didi had found the first one in her wallet as she left the parking garage after delivering Maude to the airport.

a thousand hot mornings / beg the day / for a wave of you

Didi had laughed out loud at this one. She recognized it as the first poem Maude created out of the romance poetry kit on the refrigerator. Last Sunday, when Didi came home from the airport, she'd found the second one neatly written on a small square of yellow paper stuck to the bathroom mirror.

each kiss of light / touches your neck / this musty evening / take my gifts

There were no capital letters in the world of refrigerator poetry. Only a few days ago, Didi had felt only delight at these gestures. They were loving, thoughtful. Maude gave her the kit for Valentine's Day this year, and she and Maude had had fun creating silly love poems, especially Maude. So what was wrong with her today? She had no idea.

Except that she'd talked to Adrian. Adrian! Why didn't he go away?

It was hard to run against the wind. But she liked to move her body, graceless as she believed it was. She liked being outside, liked the way the light changed the way things looked, though she had passed the same scenery a hundred times. She couldn't name what she saw, she was actually terrible with words, knew this about herself, had long ago given up trying to describe the physical world—but how else could she respond to the powerful impulse to do something with her vision? So she ran and looked, and it pleased and grieved her in equal measure.

Look at the colors of the leaves, new-summer green turning and flapping. Look at the shapes of the shadows dancing wildly on the sidewalk, chaotic shape-shifting in the dusk. Look how everything moves, and look, look at the shimmering spaces between things, between trees and their long shadows, between hedges and parked cars and cats, between the iron bars of the fence leading to the park.

Adrian played jazz clarinet; he didn't care what things looked like. Dark and light for him were forms of sound, which he described like a connoisseur of fine wine—dry and light, moist and fruity. Naturally he preferred the dark, wet, juicy sound, being Adrian.

Why had Maude left now of all times?

Didi puffed through the park down by the lake. She was hot, but she didn't want to stop. She rounded the pavilion in the park and headed home. Adrian had told her recently he'd seen a dancer who reminded him of her, the easy way she moved. Maybe she wasn't graceless after all. But that was ridiculous, he was just flirting, pure and simple. Was she that gullible?

Thank God David was coming.

Maude had been present when David was born, eighteen years ago. Not at the birth itself, not in the room, any more than Didi was. But in the picture. Maude loved David from the beginning; they had a playful connection that Didi sometimes envied. Exuberant Maude, robust and easy, used to swing David into the air and hold him upside down, wrestle with him on the floor, tickle him and play Monsters with him, grunting and shrieking and chasing him around the house. Still, Maude the artist never made art with David. That fell to Didi, who desperately wanted David to have childhood experiences different from hers.

She wanted to imagine David sitting down to make art, of whatever kind, in a pristine loft or a cluttered office, it didn't matter, with that intensely focused look that an artist got—that she used to get, she saw it once in a photo her mother took—when working.

When Didi unfolded a fresh towel after her shower, a slip of paper fell out.

angel soaks here / trust skin / bring love

She missed Maude. The two of them had showered together nearly every day all their life together. How many showers was that? Twenty, times, say, three hundred and fifty—subtracting a handful from three hundred sixty-five because there must have been some exceptions. She did not want to exaggerate. Still, that made at least seven thousand.

Adrian knew she lived with Maude; he, too, was happily married, as far as she knew. Wasn't he? Why did he speak of channels of communication open between them like a passage beneath the waves? They were just friends. But maybe special friends, closer than was usual between . . . friends. Maybe more like . . . siblings. At ten years older than she, he could have been the brother she never had, the generous father she might have wished for.

That was the first lie.

Was she falling in love with him? Or was that the second?

She did not think of the seven thousand showers. She would have lunch with him again this week.

12

Saturday, June 12
Dear Cynthia,

I think they are trying to get rid of me. I have a nice office though, with a view of the employee parking lot so I can watch people come and go. The new building that came this spring is a round barn. I told them how to move it. But they laugh at me behind my back. Something peculiar is going on.

D.

13

On Saturday evening Didi picked up David at the airport. He was as tall as she remembered him but more filled out. A slim, eighteen-year-old man with a boy's sweet face.

"I'm a virgin," he announced sadly.

"I'm sorry. I guess. Is that the right response? Maybe you'll find a good, safe lover on this trip. Moonlight in Vermont and all that."

He kissed her cheek. "Thanks, auntie."

On Sunday, David wanted to explore Burlington. He would spend most of the next five weeks outside in natural places, when he wasn't at the museum drawing its buildings. Today he wanted to walk around Church Street where the outdoor vendors and musicians congregated and kids his age stood around looking bored, smoking, sizing up one another's ratty clothes and even rattier hair, jostling for position, teasing, trying desperately to connect without getting hurt. Didi dropped him off and headed gratefully for the Farmers' Market, where what was for sale had a price.

After buying two bags' worth of organic vegetables and making two inconvenient trips to the car—why hadn't she asked David to help, she wasn't here to wait on him—she found herself in front of the art supply store. As a child, she loved going to art supply stores with her mother, loved the colored pencils and tubes of paint, the blank canvas boards, the empty pads of paper. She knew this store as well, had often bought presents for Maude—a new brush, an extra canvas, a differently shaped palette knife. She loved the store's promise, the implicit suggestion that if you picked up that pastel stick and applied it to paper, something magical would happen. Something unexpected. Something that had never happened before that moment that would, or might, take you where you'd never been. She fingered a tube of paint, then replaced it roughly. It didn't pain her to buy materials for others. Why should it?

She wanted to get something for David. He didn't call what he did "art," but he was an artist nonetheless. An artist was someone who saw a certain way, she has said to him impatiently.

"Look at you, of course you're an artist. You always have been, and you always will be, no matter what you do!"

He always nodded solemnly. Even during his supposedly difficult adolescence, he always listened to her. Or he was a good pretender. It made her feel humble—and today, inexplicably irritable. What would he like? Look at all the different kinds of drawing pens, of varying thicknesses, from .08 to .5 millimeters. Would he like that? Maybe she should get herself one, to write with!

"What is your art, Aunt Didi?" he had asked once, when he was about eight.

"I'm a poet."

He accepted this. But it wasn't true.

Didi replaced the pen. What would David like? A glue gun? No, his constructions held together naturally. Some special paints designed to adhere to wood and other materials, in order to experiment with color? She lingered over the oils, attracted to the subtle change in hue from tube to tube. Maybe when she retired, she would work in a paint store and just arrange things.

She left the store empty-handed and dejected. Maybe she'd come back in a few days, when she had a better sense of what would suit David right now, in this time and place so full of inexplicably opposing pulls.

On the drive home, shielding herself from the sun, Didi found on the visor another poem. *Does she want me to have a wreck,* she thought grumpily. It was only lightly attached and came off when she tugged.

baby that life shall blaze / in this too airy world

Right, she thought. *Whatever that means.*

Didi began drawing with David when he was less than two. "Paper," he demanded. "Paper. Write." He loved to scribble over one page after another. By the time he was five, he had discovered you could make something unusual by putting familiar things together. He cut out unrecognizable shapes from magazines or newspaper and glued them to the table, or to his arm, or his shorts. "Look, Didi!" he'd shout. "Look!"

He glued other things together, too—sticks and leaves, string, a paper clip—and glued the new creation to the kitchen counter or his mother's desk. The day he found the patience to glue something to a vertical surface—you have to wait a really long time, he told Didi on the phone that night—he insisted his mother take a picture of it.

All of this made his mother cross, and she blamed Didi for encouraging him, even though Didi lived five hours away. "Can't you do something else with him once in a while?" she asked, on Didi's next visit.

"Sure." Didi knew her sister's limits. She took David to the park to play on the swings. Afterward, they collected leaves and acorns to make something later.

"I'm trying to be a good mother," Saskia said.

"Of course you're a good mother! Much better than I would be."

"I buy him markers and paints and scissors and glue and all that stuff—but I can't do it with him."

"I know."

"It's just that I'm not artistic."

"I know, Sas. Neither am I. But he is."

"Right." Then, "But I don't want him to grow up to be an artist."

Didi didn't respond.

"They're mean, nasty shits," Saskia burst out.

"Maude is an artist."

"She doesn't count. She's a lesbian."

"Saskia!"

"Didi!"

Didi reached out to pinch her sister. Saskia jumped away, laughing. "You trying to pinch me itty bitty?" She grabbed Didi's arms and held them together. Then she embraced her older sister, who felt like crying.

"I love my sister."

"Me, too."

14

David Michaels wanted to be an architect so he could build tall, hard structures that towered masterfully over cities. But in the meantime he made birdhouses—small, original, delicate constructions, each one inspired by a particular person or place and created with exquisite care, from the first clumsy attempt in honor of his third-grade friend, John Barenholz, to the latest testament to Mr. Marcus. David Michaels wanted to be loved.

He'd come to Vermont to spend a few weeks with his Aunt Didi who worked at the museum. As practice for his future career, he would draw the museum's many buildings—the sawyer's cabin, the stone cottage, the old schoolhouse, the jail, the railroad station, the horseshoe-shaped building housing a collection of circus figures he loved. The first time he'd seen the circus building, the summer he was ten, when Didi and Maude took him to the museum after hours, nothing could stop him from running up and down the horseshoe-shaped hall in his joy. Then he had spent an hour gazing at the rows upon rows of figures—clowns and trapeze artists and ringmasters and lion tamers walking in a procession. Brightly painted cages on wheels with tigers thrusting their heads through the bars. Horses with carefully carved plumage, manes flowing forever in the wind. Elephants waving their trunks in salute. Musicians of all kinds, playing trombones and trumpets and drums. Who had assembled all these figures, who had made them? One man! One man who spent his entire lifetime carving pieces one by one. David pressed his face against the glass separating him from the figures as if trying to remember every detail. In fact he was: David saw with new eyes during that visit because he had a new best friend, to whom he wanted to tell everything, because his friend couldn't see for himself.

David had always liked sketching here at the museum because he could get far enough away to really see the buildings, as if he were a giant and they, tiny toy houses. Otherwise he could not get close enough to see. It was a paradox he didn't quite understand. He was especially eager to draw what his aunt called the goddamned round barn, and to find out what was wrong with it, though she said it was an impenetrable mystery.

When not drawing, which would be most of the time, he would scour the woods for materials for his birdhouses. He wanted to see how his latest idea would turn out using the sticks and stones and misshapen pine cones of the northern forest. He wanted a sprite to emerge from the shadows, like Puck in *A Midsummer Night's Dream*, and jump his bones.

David had visited his aunts, Didi and Maude, every summer by himself the past eight years. When he was very little, so the story went, David asked his mother why Didi and Maude didn't have the same last name, like other couples. His own mother and father, divorced since he was six months old, did not have the same last name; the point of the story was his precociousness: *Look how my brilliant son understands the world!* But he didn't understand it, not really.

At the museum on Monday morning, Didi reintroduced David to Tuesday Bailey, head of buildings and grounds, and his security staff, those she could find. David had met most of them in previous summers, but now that he had graduated from high school, he was not just a kid to be tolerated, watched with suspicion to make sure he didn't steal or break anything. Now he was an honored guest who might come and go at his leisure. He knew he was not the first person in the world to graduate from high school full of secret longings and equally intense urgings to power, but he couldn't help the feeling of anticipation. On his own for five weeks, who knew what could happen? He'd written a guilty postcard to his mother last night: *I'm happy and life is good.*

David was disappointed they couldn't find Charles Hopper. Charles had always treated David warmly and made him feel special. It was true Charles was old, older even than his mother, but he had beautiful gray eyes. And weren't the souls of beautiful men ageless?

Instead, they met Dean Allen sitting on a bench across from the schoolhouse. Didi introduced the two.

"Dean designed the circus building," Didi said. "And consulted on moving the round barn."

Dean Allen smiled sadly at David. In a burst of sympathy and curiosity, David made an appointment to talk with him the next day.

"Why haven't I met him before?" David asked as soon as they were out of earshot.

"He just got here. That is, he worked here years ago, but he went off to do something else."

"He's wonderful looking. That sad, dark face."

"Really? I guess. The curly black hair." Didi considered. "Don't get any ideas. He's too weird."

"I'm just going to talk to him."

They strolled through the covered bridge in a companionable silence. Their footsteps resounded against its sides. David ran his hand lightly along the diagonal wooden trusses, thick square beams wider than telephone poles. "This bridge is amazing."

Didi smiled. "He's a fount of information about the museum, I'll say that for him—if you catch him on a good day. Just hold onto your hat."

15

Didi looked for David at lunchtime, and when she couldn't find him, she wandered over to the Gallery. During the season, she preferred the building after hours so she could sit and think. During the season, the docents ruled, as austere and disapproving as nineteenth-century British private servants. No one could sit in their chairs or stand too close to their velvet ropes marking off the public walkways from the exhibits. During the season, the Gallery became their dominion. They hovered, guarded, informed with repressed ardor. The fiercest, sternest docents were sent to the Gallery, she supposed, because it contained the museum's most valuable holdings. Didi leaned against a wall, in her own private staking out of territory.

"Everyone has secrets," Didi's mother used to say, often when Didi found her doing something odd, like hanging the one painting in her bedroom upside down for the day. She would change it back before Didi's father came home.

Didi hated secrets, except those found inside paintings. In such secrets she reveled. From a young age she knew that paintings held secrets, secret truths, and she discovered those secrets when she went inside the paintings. It was less a trick than a carefully executed, almost religious act. Even as a child, she simply stared without blinking until the landscape or abstract or even figure painting grew in front of her, bigger and bigger until she felt herself falling into its interior. At that precise moment she closed her eyes. She knew the painting now by heart with her eidetic memory, and she walked around inside it. Within the painting, she reached out to touch her surroundings with a childlike gesture, the sensation of which had remained with her all her life.

If she let herself, as she rarely did now, she could still gaze at a painting until she knew it, could feel herself physically falling inside it, and close her eyes and find herself within it, and reach out her hand and touch the colors that surrounded her. She could not explain this any better at forty than she could at five, and it gave her more pain than pleasure now. For better or worse, it was one of the things she had left behind.

She did not allow herself to fall into the paintings in the museum's Gallery, no. But she had befriended them even so. In their company today she thought about her father's studio, lined with paintings she never got to know. It was perhaps odd that she had not done so before, in this setting. Or fortunate. She supposed it was David's coming, and Maude's absence. Who knew.

As a child she was allowed to visit her father's studio by special invitation only. It was a mysterious place, full of the strange smells of paint, linseed oil, turpentine. It was quiet; people spoke in hushed voices, unless they were her father's special painter friends, who were exuberant and boisterous, surprisingly benevolent. The large open space made her want to run and skip. Of course she didn't. Upon the rare occasions when her mother took her to the studio when she was very small, before Saskia was born, Didi learned quickly to be as still and quiet as a mouse, as her mother told her. She was not allowed to touch anything but the old rags her father used to clean his brushes. They became the things she headed for when she came into the room, trotting on her short legs over to his pile of old, soft shirts, sorting through them, looking for the one that was the most beautiful, most wonderfully splotched with color. She touched the dried paint that was thick and cracked in some places and thinly smudged and soft in others. She pressed her face happily into the cloth and breathed in the smells: these were hers.

As she got older she learned not to touch even the rags. She learned that her interest in the rags rather than the paintings was a source of humor and scorn for her father. He introduced her to his artist friends as his daughter the ragpicker, and she could tell from their embarrassed reactions that this was not a good thing to be.

What was her father's secret? Did he have too many, or not enough?

A rambunctious group of students on an end-of-year trip trooped into the Gallery, and the docents sprang into action, proffering helpful information with stern looks. When Didi stepped outside into the June sun, the wind caught the door and banged it open.

"Sorry," she called over her shoulder, but she wasn't. What was getting into her?

16

June 14
Dearest Cynthia,

I am thinking of another exhibit for the barn, but no one seems to listen to my ideas. I am like the Invisible Man I had as a child. Remember how we played with that pink plastic man whose organs came out? The woman outside my office paints her fingernails when she thinks I'm not looking. I hate that kind of female affectation. I hope you do not paint your fingers—or worse, your toes.

17

David waited until his second day at the museum to explore the round barn. He entered on the top floor as an ordinary visitor would. From a distance it had seemed to him merely a barn, though round. But no. The interior took his breath away—the high ceiling, and the enormous roundness, like being inside a mosque, or a cathedral, or a huge cave. Not a cold, damp, scary cave, a den of brigands and thieves, but an immense treasure trove, round and comforting, suggesting something going on forever, around and around—ageless, a merry-go-round, a Ferris wheel. And the massive silo at the center was a masterpiece, any fool could see that. It would take, what, probably twelve or fifteen people to reach around it, touching fingers. And bending the wood siding around the silo—and on the outside of the barn itself—how did they do that? And the interior construction, with no supporting pillars, nothing holding up the roof except the silo in the center, and the ceiling beams longer than telephone poles.

David meandered through the lower two levels of the barn, admiring the stonework on the bottom level and the beautifully hand-hewn beams on the dairy floor above. He admired and observed for a long time—too long. Dean Allen did not come. They had planned to meet here. Where was he? David checked the barn's lower two floors once more. Now he observed that the second floor was overly cluttered with artifacts. They obscured what was important, but what did that mean? Now he felt irritable, as if something were not right. Something was out of place. Something was not clear that should be, something that mattered, something about the barn, some story that should be told that went beyond the mere structure of the barn itself, magnificent as it was. Or was he mistaking his own wish to know a building's human story for his discomfort at being stood up? For it was clear he had been stood up; there was no point in trying to disguise that fact with any convoluted imaginings.

At another time he would like to examine the barn's structure more closely, to determine what was original and what restored, but not today. He no longer felt like an honored guest but like a child people consider a pest, unfairly.

Fuck the museum.

He borrowed his aunt's car and drove fifteen minutes north to Red Rocks Park, a wooded refuge in which he had found solace in years past. Here he knew who he was and what he could do. No one would fail him.

It was David's childhood friend John Barenholz who had introduced him to nature, because John had to look at things up close. John Barenholz was a thin boy with glasses whose scientist parents talked in loud, excited voices and laughed inexplicably. John's mother said things like "I'm exploring the properties of coffee this morning. Would you like some?"

John Barenholz was quieter than his parents but like them didn't seem to care about ordinary things.

"I'm legally blind," John said on the first day of third grade.

"If you're blind, how can you see?" Because it was obvious John could see, or why did he hold things up so close to his face? Why did he bend over his book so close it looked like he was sniffing it? Why did he wear glasses? If he was blind, why didn't he have a cane?

"It's a legal term. It means I can't drive."

"Nobody in third grade can drive," David pointed out.

"I mean ever. I have glaucoma."

John was interested in fire. That was how he put it.

"I'm interested in fire. I've been exploring its properties. Doing experiments. Don't worry, I'm not a pyromaniac. It's okay to do experiments with fire, you just have to be careful."

David, whose anxious mother hovered excessively, was won over at once.

"I like to burn different things," John said. "I'm allowed to burn anything that's in the garbage. But not everything burns."

The aluminum garbage can in the corner of the kitchen had a step-on lever that opened the top, which David played with a few times before John nudged him aside. John rooted carefully through the garbage. David looked around the kitchen, at the untidy stacks of books filling the corners, and the clumps of unlabeled jars crowded together at the back of the counters—fat jars of colored, curly noodles and small jars of bright powders and tall, oddly shaped bottles of amber liquids with seeds and leaves drowning in them. Newspapers covered half a small table, and had numbers and diagrams inked in the margins.

"How come there's two garbage cans? What's in this one?"

"Stuff I can't burn. It might be toxic."

"What's toxic?"

"It means it can kill you. A lot of things are more dangerous than you think." He handed David a cereal box, splattered with coffee grounds, a grimy piece of wax paper, a wadded up plastic bag, and some orange peels.

"Those won't burn, I don't think—lemon peels don't—but I want to smell them."

John led the way onto the balcony. David followed with the armful of scientific material. "Never throw anything burning off the balcony, no matter what happens. If it won't burn out by itself, or if you get scared, you can pick it up with these tongs and put it in that pail. It's steel. The top is heavy."

The cereal box did not burn at all, only smoldered at the corners. "Too wet," John pronounced. The oily wax paper burned well, better than the cereal box. But the plastic bag! It was to be the beginning of a week of experiments.

John wiped off the bag with a towel. "It's kinda gross," David agreed. Who knew what disgusting thing had been in the plastic bag. Its wet folds stuck together stubbornly. John shook his head. This was science, he explained patiently.

David held one corner of the bag with two fingers. John brought the box of kitchen matches close to his face to locate the sandpaper strip, then struck the match. He held the match under the plastic bag, which hung like a rope. The plastic caught fire, the flame flickered upward quickly, and suddenly—

Zoop! A drop of melted plastic fell to the cement floor. The boys looked at each other, caught by surprise.

Zoop! The strange whizzing sound happened again. They hooted with delight.

"Hold it up, hold it up!" John shouted.

Zoop! Zoop! But David had to drop what was left of the bag onto the cement floor.

They looked at each other; John's magnified eyes were wide and bright. He raced into the kitchen. David followed. John yanked open a drawer that scraped and stuck halfway, peered into it from two inches away, grabbed a box and ran. David banged the drawer shut and raced out to the balcony after him. John, still excited but methodical now, unrolled a long strip of plastic bags, counted fifteen bags' worth. He frowned; the strip was broad and flat.

"Crinkle them up and tie knots," he urged. He began at one end and David at the other. They worked with fierce concentration.

"Wait," said John.

He returned with a kitchen chair. "I'll hold it. You light it this time."

David understood the generosity of this act. John held the twisted rope of plastic high over his head. It was several feet long even with all its knots. David lit the bottom.

Zoop! Zoop! Zoop! Zoop! dripped the melted plastic. The boys laughed and whooped.

"It's singing," David cried.

"It's an apple of mystery," said John.

Not long afterward, David had dinner at his new friend's apartment. It was Friday night, and John's mother waved her hands over candles after she lit them. Both John's mother and his father chanted strange words in a language David didn't understand, convincing David that the entire household worshipped fire and had the ability to perform magic at will.

Over the next year David learned to hold things to his face and turn them over with both hands, to feel their contours with his eyes closed and breathe their smells. This was how you really knew something. David made his first birdhouse for John Barenholz shortly after John moved away in sixth grade and called it, proudly, Apple of Mystery.

David already had an image of the birdhouse he would build in Vermont this summer. He needed a solid wall of straight sticks, alike enough to fit together but each one with special markings. It would look like a prison in the process of transformation; that was how he felt upon graduating from high school—released from prison. Through the sticks, he would intertwine gnarled and twisted twigs and vines to give the walls character. Because after all, it hadn't been a sterile, all bad prison. Even prison had its moments. But it was confining. Everyone was so similar. Well, not exactly similar. He knew what he meant.

Comfortably, David wandered off the path among the trees. *If you go among the trees, the children of night will change your spirit.* Mr. Marcus had said that; he was always quoting poets. But when, David wondered. When will my spirit change? He collected some feathery-soft, gray lichen from a rock. It might give his house the look of a Scandinavian hut, the kind of remote prison one might be exiled to if one lived in Norway. Birds called and chattered around him; David had no interest. He didn't know anything about birds. He was drawn only to make tiny houses, which other people had called birdhouses from the beginning—adults, that is. John Barenholz, to whom he still wrote on occasion, never thought they were anything other than what they were: tiny houses. They had a purpose, only it wasn't to house birds.

Still, he liked the idea of working within a tradition. When he learned that other people had made small houses before he ever thought of it, the thought anchored him. He did not otherwise feel part of a lineage. He had no ancestors he could point to and say, *There I am. I'm like that, too. What is in him continues in me.* Except his Aunt Didi, and Maude, who wasn't even a blood relative. Well, there was his grandfather, the painter, who might have stood for something in an ancestral line-up—*do you recognize any of these suspects?*—but his grandfather was too mean. In David's ongoing attempt at self-definition, he worried about meanness and creativity, feared he was not hard enough. Did you have to be nasty to be creative? He would do anything to be a great architect. Or would he? He stretched out on a patch of rock in the sun. Voices approached on the nearby path, a dog bounded through the bushes and sniffed him, then bounded away. The voices retreated. David wished again that a handsome stranger would step softly from the shadows and fall madly, wildly in love with him, with a blind and searing passion like that of Odysseus who had to be chained to the mast. Only this fellow wouldn't have to hold himself back. David would welcome him with open arms. David imagined what the man would look like, and what kind of small house he would live in. What kind of house did Dean Allen inhabit? Or Charles Hopper? But now David could barely call up these men. It was only the imaginary characters who populated his small houses, imaginary characters who resembled closely the people he had loved—only his imagination and the sun licking his skin warm—that kept him from dying of loneliness.

In his senior year, David had fallen in love with Mr. Marcus. Mr. Marcus wore a jacket and tie when most teachers dressed much more casually, as if sloppiness were a way to reach disaffected teenagers. And Mr. Marcus didn't use the latest kid slang like a lot of teachers. Rather, he spoke carefully, made jokes half under his breath as if for himself alone, for the pure pleasure in expressing himself, not trying to please students at all—in fact, as if he didn't particularly care what students thought of him one way or another. When Mr. Marcus alluded to the Bacchae, or Ancient Rome, or Luther's revelation on the privy, or Bloomsbury, it seemed all the same to him whether students understood the reference or not. Some rolled their eyes at each other. David wrote down the references on his palm, and later looked them up. After Mr. Marcus mentioned Ovid, David discovered that his mother had *The Metamorphosis,* and he read the first fifty pages. (His mother insisted you couldn't tell about a book until you'd read the first fifty pages; it was how you kept an open mind.) It puzzled him, but he had no time to feel discouraged. He was busy looking up Schiller, and Dante, and Milton—who were these guys, anyway?—and doing his homework, weekly essays about Wallace Stevens and D. H. Lawrence and Langston Hughes. Mr. Marcus let them choose their author-subjects, and David, whose mother gave him Alice Walker, Toni Morrison, Penelope Lively, Eudora Welty, "to round out your education," chose men.

By Thanksgiving, David felt more at ease in Mr. Marcus's class, and wanted to please him more. By January, he had replaced his admiration for the teacher with a growing fondness. That was what he called it to himself, using a word his mother might have used: *Oh yes, the Smiths are very fond of each other,* spoken with irony, as if it wouldn't last. His mother didn't have much faith in traditional marriage.

In his imagination he traced the wrinkles around Mr. Marcus's eyes with his fingers, and felt the firm warmth of Mr. Marcus's skin. He laughed quietly at more of Mr. Marcus's jokes and smiled to himself even when he didn't understand them: it delighted him to see Mr. Marcus enjoying class. It secretly pleased him when a classmate disappointed Mr. Marcus. He himself tried hard not to disappoint his teacher. He had never worked so hard. He thought about poetry a lot. He thought about Mr. Marcus. Mr. Marcus, though aloof in a strange way David couldn't account for, seemed at the same time to take pleasure in David's accomplishments. David thought Mr. Marcus liked him, but he wasn't sure.

That spring, his Aunt Didi, observing his new interest in poetry, had sent him a new biography of W. H. Auden. W. H. Auden had lived with Chester Kalman. As a lover. Loving each other openly. David wondered whether Mr. Marcus knew this, and what he would say. He dared not ask.

David took to visiting Mr. Marcus after school—something he had resisted until now, though he couldn't have said why. One warm spring day he arrived just as Mr. Marcus was locking the door.

"David! How nice to see you. I'm afraid I'm just going out. *Oh frabjous day, callough callay, he chortled in his joy.* I've got to walk to clear my head or I might start barking at the door."

He had no objection to David's walking with him. They walked for an hour, into town and back again, talking about Greece and Turkey. David had seen a television show the night before about ancient Greece. Mr. Marcus had lived in Greece for two years. David had written a paper on Cycladic art once, inspired by the smooth, oval head with no eyes that sat on his mother's desk. Mr. Marcus spoke to him of Greek poets—Sappho, and Rita Bounci-Pappas.

"You must travel, David, whenever you can. *If you go among the trees, the children of the night will change your spirit.* Rudyard Kipling said that. You must have read *The Jungle Book* when you were young. The Connecticut woods are beautiful, don't you think? *Now he is scattered among a hundred cities and wholly given over to unfamiliar affections, to find his happiness in another kind of wood.* That's Auden's elegy for Yeats. What do you think he meant?"

His teacher knew Auden, too. What did that mean? "That different people would love him when he was dead than when he was alive?" David almost whispered.

One night in March, David accompanied a friend to a basketball game at school. An important home game, a full gym, bleachers creaking and shaking, everyone yelling and stomping, everyone caring deeply about the outcome—except him. Or maybe not, he reflected. Maybe no one else did either. Maybe they were all pretending. Maybe it was the weather, as his mother often said. The moon. Maybe so, but he didn't think there was a moon, just an unusually warm spring night. Inside the packed gym, people were pressed too close together, the light was too bright, David could hardly breathe. A few minutes into the game, Mr. Marcus appeared in the doorway to the gym.

"I'm going to say hi to Mr. Marcus."

Impatiently David climbed over knees and slapped hands raised to him until he reached the aisle. Impatiently, but without a glance toward the door, as if he were going out for a soda or a smoke, afraid lest his teacher disappear at any minute, impatiently he made his way to the entrance. If he could talk to Mr. Marcus, the evening might be saved.

"Hey, Mr. Marcus. Do you know any poems about basketball?"

"No, but I'm sure there are some." Mr. Marcus smiled at David, uncrossed his arms and shoved his hands into his pockets. He leaned casually against the gym wall but his eyes darted about, following the players.

"I have known the inexorable boredom of basketball," David said, and he felt gratified by Mr. Marcus's smile. Did Mr. Marcus hold his gaze a second longer than necessary?

"Look at the challenge, the fight, the extraordinary energy of youth. The sweaty, banging bodies." Mr. Marcus didn't seem happy.

They stood shoulder to shoulder, not touching but nearer than they were in class, nearer than in Mr. Marcus's office. It was noisy in the gym, and Mr. Marcus tilted his head slightly toward David when he spoke. "I had a close friend who loved basketball," Mr. Marcus said suddenly.

"What happened to him?"

"He died. Like so many others."

Soon Mr. Marcus left, to finish grading papers, he said with a wistful smile. He had only stopped in for a moment. David returned to the stands but could hardly sit still. He clapped and shouted with the crowd, felt the bleachers tremble beneath his feet, and it wasn't enough. At half time when the crowd spilled into the lobby, he excused himself. He had no plan but felt restless and itchy and needed to be outside. How sweet the air was, after the gym. How warm and soft on his skin. He spread his arms. He wanted something to happen. He jogged around the outside of the school, away from the gym and the theater and the cafeteria, toward the one-story, white clapboard classroom buildings. A soft light spilled from Mr. Marcus's open window onto the brick path and the flattened grass that surrounded it. A few minutes later, David knocked on Mr. Marcus's door.

"David! Game lost your interest again? Do come in."

David shut the door behind him. The small, book-lined office was half in shadows, lit only by the lamp on the desk, green glass that gave off a warm glow. "Am I interrupting?"

"No, no, I'm just finishing up. That is, it's too lovely a night to work. I've been sitting here thinking about life and death and other mundane things. *The rule of earth is attachment.*" He'd come from behind his desk to look out the window. He moved quickly, as always, but when he leaned on the windowsill, David observed the outline of the man's body in his slacks, sensed his quiet strength, and took courage.

"I have a present for you. Would you like to hear it?"

Mr. Marcus hesitated only a second. "Of course." He sat on the edge of his desk with his arms folded across his chest, as if trying to contain his own restless energy. David stood near the door, sensing the wall holding him up the same way it held up the ceiling. He waited. Finally Mr. Marcus looked at him. David recognized the usual friendly encouragement, the seriousness, and yes, something else. He closed his eyes.

Oh sweet spontaneous
earth, how often have
the
doting

fingers of
prurient philosophers punched
and
poked

thee
,has the naughty thumb
of science prodded
thy

beauty .how
often have religions taken
thee upon their scraggy knees
squeezing and

buffeting thee that thou mightest
conceive
gods
(but
true

to the incomparable
couch of death thy
rhythmic
lover

thou answerest

them only with

spring)

"Yes!" Mr. Marcus sprang from his desk and embraced David. His strong arms squeezed David's shoulders. His quick, light breath warmed David's neck. His firm chest, his taut thighs pressed against David's chest and thighs—hastily, only the lightest touch, lasting no more than a second. In two steps Mr. Marcus was at the window. He leaned outside. "Yes!" he shouted into the night. He turned quickly back to David, face flushed. "You are a delight, passing stranger. It's perfect." He grabbed a volume from the bookcase. "Here is another tribute to spring. Read Whitman tonight when you can't sleep."

David laughed along with his teacher.

The next Thursday David went to Mr. Marcus's office at his regular time. The wait had nearly killed him; he'd bitten his fingernails, a habit he thought he'd left behind years ago.

"Ah David, how nice to see you. Please come in."

Mr. Marcus shut the door behind David. He spoke slowly, unlike his usual, slightly rushing mumble. "David, I'm sorry that I embraced you the other night. It was inappropriate."

The words hung in the air between them. David couldn't breathe.

"Why?"

Mr. Marcus sighed. "Because I have a partner. Because you're a student. Because I'm gay and you'll get the wrong idea."

"What's the wrong idea?"

Mr. Marcus didn't answer at once. "*Honesty isn't so simple; a simple honesty is nothing but a lie.* Denise Levertov." He smiled slightly. "Sometimes it's better not—some things are best left unsaid."

What things, David wanted to know. But he didn't ask. He could barely think, let alone talk. He wanted this moment to go on forever.

"Can't we be friends?" he asked finally, in spite of himself.

Mr. Marcus started shuffling papers. "Shall I say yes, of course, we are friends, and let you be slowly disappointed when you find out that things aren't . . . as you want them to be? Or shall I tell you the truth and say no, and disappoint you now?"

Say yes and mean it, David thought. But he didn't say it. Mr. Marcus was leaving him his dignity. In response, David felt such a rush of longing, he could barely stand up. "I gotta go."

A week later, David came to Mr. Marcus's office for the last time. Mr. Marcus greeted him as he always had, with formal warmth.

David didn't sit. "I have a question for you, Mr. Marcus." He took a breath. "I'm gay, too. Did you know that?"

"Yes, I know."

They regarded each other in silence, each waiting for the other. David waited to see whether anything would come of the slight shift in power he felt at that moment, now that he had said aloud, and with pride, something he had never said before. Even with his Aunt Didi, it was simply understood. But nothing happened.

"Thanks for lending me the book. I liked it." He held it out to his teacher.

"It's a good thing to be gay," Mr. Marcus said carefully. "Do you want to talk about it?"

But David didn't.

He might love other men during his life—maybe—but surely he would never, ever feel the same acute longing he felt for Mr. Marcus.

18

After lunch on Thursday, Didi and Adrian stood in the parking lot talking. They stood close together. Since Adrian had first become interested in the round barn last fall, and they shared a meal together and laughed with the tingling pleasure of new friends, and Didi hugged him spontaneously in a burst of warmth and excitement afterward, they had embraced after every visit—visits that had become more frequent. These were friendly embraces, bear hugs such as old friends might enjoy, Didi told herself, which was what they felt like, old friends. And lately, in the past two months, he had taken to kissing her lightly on the mouth when they left each other. It was a soft, almost butterfly kiss, the way she might kiss a woman friend she had known for years. But he was not an old friend. He made her juices flow.

They stood together today, and finally Didi slid her arms around his neck. They held onto each other, their bodies pressed together for a borderline minute. He kissed her, slowly, lightly. They drew apart, looked at each other. "Friends for life," he said softly. She kissed him.

They were just friends. She wanted to sleep with him. She drove back to work.

Didi finished up work in a distracted state. She returned a dozen phone calls, relieved that most people weren't there, edited copy given to her for a brochure about a symposium in September, wrote a quick memo to Charles Hopper, the director, about a different symposium still in the planning stage. She had a typically unsettling encounter with Dean Allen, and finished the day by checking her messages. She wrote the necessary responses choosing her words carefully to make sure that what she said about the museum was accurate and at the same time conveyed the right tone. The choices didn't come easily. She struggled. Was the new quilt exhibit a "vigorous reinterpretation" or the expression of an "original vision"? Which was right? As much as she wished she didn't care, Didi couldn't act as if it didn't matter. It mattered. The world was so uncertain, so confused, so goddamned confusing, that she had to be as careful with words as possible. The words determined how you saw things. So she reexamined them from every angle, imagining responses, unknown consequences, and finally settled on one phrase, her anxiety not the least diminished by all the effort she put into the choice.

What were "friends for life"?

Maude had no such qualms about words, labels, perceptions. She saw what she saw, thought what she thought. At first she called Dean Allen the Village Idiot.

"He's not an idiot," Didi clarified. "He's some kind of brilliant, creative . . . something, who's fallen from grace. Gone over the edge. Schizophrenic maybe. He was here years ago and did some good work. He designed the circus building. I don't know the whole story."

"Why don't you just ask Charles?"

"He wouldn't tell me. I think he's afraid of him."

"A man with a past. A man of disguises. The Phantom of the—"

"Stop. He's related to someone, one of the founders, but I don't even know who. Shouldn't they tell me things like this? What if something happened? It makes me cranky. He hangs around the photocopier without ever copying anything. He watches you out of the corner of his eye, while he's pretending not to. And sometimes out of the blue, like a light just went on, he starts talking a mile a minute in this wild monologue full of literary allusions and little self-deprecatory jokes—not to me, he doesn't like me. But I've heard him. It's kind of charming—he probably is some kind of genius—but . . ." She trailed off.

Since then Maude had called him The Lurker.

On her way out, Didi passed his office, a small room off the entry presided over by the museum's receptionist. He sat at an empty desk gazing out at the parking lot. His face was blank. If Didi were to paint him, which she never would, she would use browns and blacks, sepia, maybe show the light Vermeer-style streaming in the window but with Dean's face in shadow. She would try to capture the moment of nothingness like Manet, the light like Vermeer, the despair like Soutine. What a mess. No wonder she wasn't a painter.

"Goodnight, Dean." He didn't answer.

I'm an okay person, Didi thought to herself on the drive home, *an okay person. An okay person. Anyway, goddammit shit fuck, I'm doing the best I can. I'm a competent worker, an okay partner and a good aunt. Adrian is just a friend. I love him like a friend.*

19

Toward the end of his first week in Vermont, David drove his aunt's car to Grayson Pond, a mile off the main road—several hundred acres, more like a small lake, hidden in the deep woods. His aunt said no one swam here because it was full of snakes, but a breeze over the water stirred up tiny waves and the water looked clear and clean. Who knew what lurked beneath the surface of things?

The pond was big enough to accommodate boaters: its uneven shore obscured canoeists poking into tiny coves and offered some privacy for those wanting to fish alone. There were two other cars in the parking lot, or what passed for a parking lot in Vermont—a cleared place at the end of a dirt road where people could unload small boats—but their owners were nowhere in sight.

As Didi warned him, the piney trail from the boat launch led only a few hundred feet along the water's edge. The shore was rocky in places, but in some places the woods broke and a soft, grassy bank curled gently into the pond. At the end of the path David came upon a great pile of boulders protruding into the lake, left by retreating glaciers ten thousand years ago. He knew that much. In the sun, away from the black flies and mosquitoes, he observed the pond. What did he like about it? It was beautiful in a *National Geographic* sort of way, but where was its soul? Where its apple of mystery?

It had something to do with the trees—some tall and spiky, reaching upward unmindful of the water sucking at their roots, others soft and draped over the bank, embracing it, still others broad and expansive, as if their branches welcomed the water or maybe the opposite, maybe held back the woods. Collectively they lined the edge of the water, encircling, protecting, guarding. Therein lay the power of this scene, thought David, as he struggled for the words—in the dynamic of welcome and resistance. He liked this thought. He liked the word *dynamic*. His art teacher last year had taught him to look for the inner dynamic of a work. This intrigued him: what was his inner dynamic? He would like very much to know.

The water welcomed the trees, wanted them, pulled them toward itself, and the trees marched toward the water, inexorably. No, leaned toward the water, bent toward it as if with longing. They needed the water. But if they got too close they would drown. Better they stayed with their own kind. So they held back.

There was a secret, a tension, some power to be discovered, in the margins between things, the place where one thing became another—or wanted to. Or wanted not to. Maybe this next birdhouse would be less about a prison and more about this, the sense of things bumping up against each other, sucking and pulling at each other while desperately trying not to lose themselves—some tension between change and the limits to change. He didn't know how to do it yet, but he had a starting point; the materials would have to tell him. If—no, when—he got lost, he would remember that it had to do with where the pond met the shore—what was him and what was other.

David left his rock and made his way along the shore where there was no path, climbing over bushes and rocks, looking for what was odd or unfamiliar.

"What are you collecting?" a voice called.

A girl about his age perched on a rock above him not ten feet away. She hugged her knees, a baggy sweatshirt pushed up her arms.

"Just stuff."

"What for?"

"To make things with."

She nodded. She seemed friendly.

"You know. Art," he added.

"Art," she said. "Is that like prayer?"

David laughed. "Oh no, I don't think so. It's more active than that."

"Prayer can be active."

David nodded politely and looked around for a path to escape. She must have come the same way he did, bushwhacking. He started back.

"Sex can be prayer," the girl said, so softly he wasn't sure he'd heard right. He ignored her.

The next thing he knew, she landed a few feet behind him. He wheeled around to see a girl a few inches shorter than he, a little rumpled, hands jammed in her jeans pockets, chin thrust forward, challenging him, like someone used to having her way.

"You're gay, right?" she said.

David took a step away from her. "How can you tell? Are you some kind of witch?"

"Good guess. I can't always tell. Sometimes I guess wrong. Man, people can get really offended."

David laughed. He liked her twinkly eyes. "I bet."

"Do you live here?"

Quickly they discovered their mutual connection: each visiting for the summer, with a tie to the museum. Lucy's mother was on the board.

"Does your aunt know you're gay?" Lucy asked.

"Sure. She's a—she's very supportive."

"Have you ever had sex?"

"Jeez, you ask personal questions."

"Sorry. It's just that you seem like you might not have. You're a little skittish around the subject. Sweet, but skittish."

"Are you a nympho?"

"No, I'm a Christian. What have you found?"

David held out his hands.

Lucy touched the larger pine cone lightly. "It's a male flower shoot. And that's a female flower cone."

"How do you know that?"

"Sex is a gift from God, you know," Lucy said.

"Is that what you do when you pray—think about sex?"

Within a half-hour, David and Lucy had decided to spend the next day together, "—if you can stop talking about sex," David said. "You're fixated."

"It's a deal."

20

Saturday, June 19
Dear Cynthia,

All I want is to give something of myself to this museum. That's all anyone wants, any human being even dogs. Who made the supreme sacrifice, Abraham willing to kill his son, sacrificing his son's trust forever, or Isaac, willing to give up his life in order to keep that trust in his father? Or was it God, who sacrificed humanity at that moment forever, on a whim, to make a point, and to whom? The devil his secret challenger, his playmate from childhood who perhaps haunted his dreams: I love you, I hate you, nah nah nah nah nah. I can do anything. Was that the message? I can destroy souls that trust in me; what can you do?

21

Didi spent Saturday morning in the garden. Though the garden was Maude's province, Didi had offered to keep it watered and weeded during her absence. She had wanted to. It was their garden, for heaven's sake. How symbolic could you get? Then she did horrid errands and set out to make dinner. A perfect domestic day, dull and selfless. Maybe she could salvage something of the day with a creative dinner.

David came home in a good mood and offered to help. While he sliced onions, he told her about his day with Lucy.

"David, do you ever find friendships with girls . . . complicated?"

"What do you mean?"

"Never mind. Oh, hey." Taped to the back of a spatula in the rear of a drawer was another poem.

full mind rose / in the lusty dark / burned like wild sugar

Another one fell out of the placemats when she pulled out a fresh set.

some true place / not beautiful / not warm / but you are

"Oh Jesus!" she exclaimed "These damn things are all over the house. What was she thinking? You're not to read them if you stumble across one. It's lesbian erotica."

David rolled his eyes. "Not to worry, auntie." Then, "I still haven't met anyone."

"How so? You just told me about Lucy."

"Oh, well, sure. I meant a guy." He tasted the mixture in the pan. "Needs curry. What did you study in college, Aunt Didi?"

"It's not a curry, it's Italian. Mostly literature. Here—garlic. And art. But I didn't major in English because you had to study criticism then." She was glad for a change of subject. "Critics bore into the heart of a piece and suck the blood out of it. Writers hold up a piece and look at it carefully and admire and notice and try to understand, and when they're done, the work is still intact. That's it." She whacked his hand with her wooden spoon. "Out of my meal." She steered him to the kitchen table, and gave him some apples to slice. "Critics are like dogs that have to pee on everything; they like to make their mark, and so they ruin it for everyone else. Remember that when you're a famous artist."

"Architect."

"Same thing. I majored in anthropology, where you learn that cultural truth is relative. This is a useful thing, almost as useful as knowing how to fix cars or build houses. If truth matters to you. For example—"

"But you studied art, too."
"Yes."
"So?"
"So what?"
"So why didn't you ever do anything with it?"

Didi washed her hands and dried them. She dug around for the olive corer in the cluttered drawer next to the sink and began popping the pits from the kalamatas. David worked comfortably at the table. She added the olives to her mixture. It wasn't a curry; it was her own capellini putanesca, with broccoli instead of anchovies. How else could you disguise broccoli? She dropped a handful of angel hair into a pot.

Halfway through dinner, after they had talked about politics, gay architects, portabello mushrooms, and running—avoiding a gay murder in the midwest, a freak storm in the Caribbean, and anything to do with the museum—Didi said, "Did I ever tell you about a game your mother and I used to play when we were kids?"

David was slurping his pasta Italian-style, as he thought, and shook his head.

"We called it Playing Artist. One person was the Artist and the other was the Scribbler. Your mother had to be the Artist or she wouldn't play. The Artist went out of the room, and the Scribbler, me, sat on the floor and drew a picture. A real simple picture, really a caricature of a child's drawing—you know, a big sun, some stick-figure people by a house, that kind of thing. After a few minutes, the Artist came in—stomped in with her arms folded, looking stern—and basically trashed the picture. Grabbed it from the Scribbler and scrawled a fat, red X over it. Sometimes I'd grab it back from her and tear it up into a hundred pieces."

"How fun. No wonder she likes you."

"But you know what? She says she doesn't remember the game at all. We played it for years. She says she only remembers how nice I was to her and how I used to play with her when she was sick."

"I wish I had a brother," David said lightly.

"Yeah."

Maude called late that night. She was trying something new, and what did Didi think? There was a woman in a nearby studio working in fabric art, who had material left over from a piece she'd just finished, which she was going to throw away but gave to Maude instead. Maude had a vision: it was the same image she had planned for the next big painting, but suddenly she saw how it could come alive in fabric, and she was so excited she could hardly sleep. She had worked on it nonstop for two days. Yesterday she'd gone into town and bought eighty dollars' worth of silk and satin and netting and light cotton seconds from a fabric shop.

"It's about water—rain, and waves, voluptuous women, a huge wet celebration. Wait till you see it. I can't wait to show you what I've done. The material gives me exactly that shimmery consistency that's eluded me. You'll be able to see it from both sides: I want it to hang free, not against the wall. I can work with light differently—it's a whole new thing to learn, Didi. It's great to be here. It's really good that I came."

Didi went to bed feeling unsettled, wondering whether Maude would give up painting if she found fabric a more exciting medium. She felt cold inside; another blanket didn't help. What would the house be like without the strong, soothing scent of linseed oil that emanated from Maude's upstairs studio, clinging to clothes and walls the way the smell of sautéed onions clung to other houses?

She tossed and turned and finally got up. She let herself out of the house quietly and curled into a chair on the porch, wrapped in a robe. It was late, cool enough to slow the mosquitoes. In her neighborhood, the stars were not bright, but bright enough to give some comfort. What was it about the night that soothed her? Without a moon, there was a refreshing dimming of light and shadow, as if the world were made simpler, cooler, in order for the excitable eye to rest. Trees and houses were reduced to shapes and outlines, leaf canopies tried to block out streetlights, and beyond their meager, harsh pools, the night swallowed up the light. If Didi could paint, which of course she couldn't, she would paint in dark colors, the most subtle shades of blackest blues and purples and browns, dark dark dark, with only a hint of color, but full of life.

Didi had never used oils herself, though she had once longed for the day when she could. Back then, oils belonged to the grown-ups, the real artists. When she was very young, she had used crayons and chalk provided by her mother, and then long boxes of colored pencils, and tempera, and a black, oblong tin of watercolor squares. She had always worked with great concentration. Even as a two-year-old, she liked to fill the paper with color. She had no more control than any other very young child, but her desire was more intense. If her mother took away her paper before she was through, because it was dinnertime or bedtime, Didi screamed until her mother gave it back.

It was always her mother to whom Didi showed her work. Her mother smiled, exclaimed, did what mothers do when they love their children and consider their output worthy. Though Didi must have gone to her father's studio from a very young age—she couldn't have been more than two or three when she first discovered the rags, or so her mother would tell her later, her mother whose memories became less and less dependable for their truth but always startled with their vividness. Though she went to her father's studio from a very young age, Didi did not connect him with the act of drawing or painting. That came later. She never saw him at work. She knew that he painted—"Where's Daddy?" "He's painting." was the refrain of her childhood—but she knew this in the odd way one can know and not know something at the same time, in the same way one knows, say, that one's parents have sex. She did not see that what she did and what her father did had any connection.

The first time she understood that her father actually made the paintings in his studio was not as one might think during one of her infrequent visits, made with great solemnity with her mother. It was, instead, one winter afternoon—she was not of school age yet, Saskia wasn't yet born—when she was making a picture at the kitchen table, while her mother worked in the kitchen. She had nearly finished; she had drawn two elephants, a mother and baby—one of her favorite themes—in the Virginia woods, the only landscape she knew. It was winter, many of the trees were bare, and it was dark in the background because a storm was coming. It might be a snowstorm. Young Didi did not remember snow and she hoped it would snow that winter.

Her father came in unexpectedly. It was one of his days to work all afternoon in his studio and he kept to a rigid schedule. Didi looked up full of anticipation, pleased with her drawing. He stood over her, scowling at her work.

"If you're going to paint, learn to paint the truth. Elephants don't live in the woods."

Didi said nothing. She stared at her drawing and felt his eyes on it, too. She felt stupid. She had liked the drawing very much, liked the elephants, liked the way the bare trees looked against the dark sky.

Slowly she crumpled it up. "I know," she said. "I was just playing."

He left, and she went to her room where she shoved the crumpled drawing to the bottom of the trash can, and then stepped inside the can to make doubly sure it was gone for good. How could she have been so dumb? She had known of course that elephants live on the plains in Africa. Or in India. She even knew there were two kinds of elephants. She knew there weren't any elephants in Virginia, but she loved elephants and so she had thought, she had thought . . .

What had she thought? Didi wrapped her robe more tightly around her and pulled her cold feet closer beneath her. She did remember, now, that she understood at that moment that her father made pictures, too. That he felt the same way she did, or rather that there was something the same about what he did and what she did, though she wasn't sure exactly what it was and couldn't explain it, wouldn't be able to explain it for years. There was something the same, only he was a grown-up and knew how to do it right, and she didn't. She didn't know anything.

What did it mean to paint the truth? Didi didn't know. She had asked her mother.

"I don't know, darling. He certainly doesn't paint what you and I see, or what I see anyway, but it may be what he sees. You'll have to ask him what he means. But you might want to wait a few years."

A few years? Didi couldn't wait a few hours, for anything. But neither could she ask her father such a question, any more than she could speed up time when she was hungry, so she didn't.

Once she entered school, Didi brought home her drawings, but only to show her mother. "Tell me about this," her mother always said, and she did. She knew her mother liked her drawings. She never thought about it at the time, of course, but later she reflected that she could tell her mother liked *her*. Didi adored her mother, no less when her mother began going crazy a few years later.

One day—perhaps in second grade—Didi brought home a collage she had made. All the kids had made them. Didi had liked them all, had loved the freedom of the project. They had torn shapes out of colored construction paper, glued them together, and painted on top of the whole thing. Didi had made hills and trees—or the general idea of trees, she explained to her mother. "It's like when you come over Mason's Hill if you close your eyes part way and everything is blurry." Her mother laughed and hugged her. She hung the picture on a kitchen cabinet, a rare and extraordinary event, as Didi's father preferred bare, empty surfaces. He did not like clutter in his house, fretted that it distracted him. Only one of his paintings adorned the walls, one he had given to her mother early and that she had hung on her side of their bedroom—the one she later turned upside down when he wasn't present. He kept all the rest in his studio or sold them at shows. No work of hers or her sister's ever hung on the walls. It was only after years of living with Maude that Didi began to understand that others' hanging their work where they could see it, live with it, admire it, was not hubris, not a grotesque arrogance as her father seemed to think, but taking a simple pride in one's creation. For her father, such pleasures were sloppy indulgences.

That night, at dinner, which the four of them always ate together, her father had spoken to her with more than usual abruptness.

"Didi."

"Yes, Daddy?"

"If you're going to be a painter, you're going to have to learn how to see."

Didi said nothing.

"Do you understand what I mean?"

She thought hard. She understood he didn't like her collage. Why had her mother hung it up? She felt betrayed.

"Of course she doesn't understand," her mother said. "She's only a child."

"Children have eyes. Open your eyes, Didi, and look around you."

Didi looked around, obediently. Saskia, then three, opened her eyes wide.

Their mother laughed. "Such good children. You'll learn everything you need to know from your smart, talented father. Now finish your dinners."

Their father scowled. Something was wrong but Didi didn't know what it was, nor could she tell now, on the porch of her own little house wrapped in comforting dark. She remembered only her mother's laugh, her cheerful effort to keep the family happy, and her father's inability to be happy, his anger, which he had not yet turned on her, or so she had always thought.

But perhaps he was angry with her even then.

22

On Sunday morning, Didi called her sister.

"When did Mother start acting crazy?"

"I don't know. Why do you want to talk about that? David doesn't need to know about his crazy grandmother."

"This isn't for David. It's for me. I've been thinking about her lately."

"What for? It's not the anniversary of her death, is it? I always block that out."

"No. She died in December, don't you remember? The week before Christmas, we were going to drive up and get her and bring her down and she—"

"I don't actually."

Didi took a breath. "Saskia, know what I remembered this week? Some things I'd forgotten. Once I came in the kitchen—maybe in seventh grade—and Mom was standing at the window looking out, very peaceful. I walked up next to her and she put her arm around me, and she said, 'I'm glad we live here. It's a good place.' Something like that. Then she said, 'It's a very nice hotel.' It made me so furious, I wanted to kill her."

Saskia murmured politely, as if she were doing the dishes or reading at the same time. Didi forged ahead.

"The other thing I remembered was a couple of years later. I'd been out with friends and I came home and kissed her hello—she was sitting in the living room—and she said, 'Who are you?' Not mad or upset, just curious, like she'd never seen me before. I wanted to turn away and not answer. Remember that feeling of the floor dropping out from under you? But I didn't. I said real calmly, 'I'm your daughter.' And she said, 'Isn't it nice that I like you?'"

"Why don't you let it go, Didi? Look, how's David? Can I speak with him?"

"He's fine—still asleep. He's made a friend already. A girl. Young woman."

"Really?"

"Just a friend, Saskia. Why don't you let it go?"

"Didi, I didn't mean anything. Don't be offended. It's just that you don't know what it's like to be a mother."

"No, I don't. And you don't know what it's like to be gay."

"All right. I'm sorry. You've got me upset, talking about Mother."

"I'm sorry, Sas. I know it's different for you. You didn't have her for very long. I've been thinking about how much she gave me."

"I had you instead. No wonder I'm so neurotic."

"Bye, Saskia. I love you."

Didi hung up without telling her sister the other memory that had been haunting her lately—not one she had just remembered, one she had never lost.

Saskia had always said she'd never wanted to be an artist. What Didi knew, that Saskia herself seemed to have forgotten, was that Saskia, too, like most children, did like to draw when she was very young. But Didi remembered as if it were yesterday the time she responded to her little sister's scribbles by yelling, "Bad art, bad art!" Saskia's eyes grew large with the stunned expression of a two-year-old who has just been bitten by a playmate. Several seconds passed before she began to wail as desperately as if Didi had hit her. Didi had been horrified. She had never been mean to Saskia before—she had always adored Saskia, had climbed into her crib when Saskia was an infant to hold her and feed her, had played with her by the hour, had carried her around and taught her nursery rhymes and sung to her as if Saskia were her own baby.

Saskia stopped drawing early. They made up other games—Artist, Monsters, Prison Camp—but of the two sisters, only Didi kept drawing, for a while. Many years later, Didi would apologize for this agonizing betrayal, but Saskia would only tease her serious sister for having worried about it for so long.

Didi had never talked much about her father. But she told Maude about her mother soon after they became lovers. She wanted to make sure Maude knew she might end up the same way.

"This is my mother when she's off. This is how I think of her in my childhood. We're having dinner, the four of us, which she has made, maybe with my help. And all of sudden she says, 'Can we go to the movies yesterday?' Saskia and I freeze. We look at each other. I'm fifteen, say, and Saskia is ten. We hold our breath. What's going to happen next? Dad keeps eating, like nothing unusual has happened. Now everything depends on him. If he says,

'We're not going to the movies yesterday, or any other time,' her face falls, and she might even start to cry at his tone—or she might be fine, you never know. If he says, 'We'll see,' and keeps eating, doesn't even look at her or nod or anything, just takes it in stride, she's all smiles, and Saskia and I look at each other and I know she feels exactly like I do, and we relax for a second—*this* moment of crisis has passed, we're all okay again for now.

"Or my father ignores her, and then either she could say something else weird about a completely different subject, or she could start crying, or the moment would pass, again, and everything might be fine. Until the next crazy, loaded moment. It was exhausting. I never knew how exhausting it was, or how on edge I was all the time, until she was gone, and it was such a relief.

"But I can't tell you how much I miss her."

Didi stopped bringing home her art projects. Or if she did, she hid them in her room. But one day, in fifth grade, she had to. She was working on something with several others. She liked working with other kids. They thought she was good and wanted to work with her, and she always found something in others' work to admire. She was generous, if not by nature at least by training, as her mother's daughter. For whatever inexplicable reasons, Didi was kind to other children about their art—except her sister. She asked questions as her mother always did.

At home, Didi spread out the multiple-page project on the kitchen table. Her job was to prepare the background and do the first scene. It was to be a battle triptych of the Civil War. Didi sketched in the background shapes with a pencil; she would paint them with the thick school paints later. In the foreground, in her panel, she imagined a scene. The teacher had said they could draw anything they wanted. Didi wanted to draw a broken fence, a farmhouse, a wounded soldier leaning against the side of the farmhouse, or maybe it was a barn, and a little girl giving him water. She saw it perfectly in her head.

She drew the soldier sitting against the wall of the barn, with his head tilted back and one leg bent strangely under him. His leg was broken, he had crawled from the battle not far away. In fact, the battle was just on the other side of the barn where you couldn't see it. The little girl had come out to do her chores and found the soldier. She wasn't scared. She was afraid of the war—her father and her brothers had all been killed—but she wasn't afraid of this wounded soldier. He was kind and good. She ran and brought him water. She—

"What's that?" Her father appeared out of nowhere. He scowled at her drawing. She waited, held her breath. He shook his head. "Is that art?" He strode out of the room.

Didi proceeded with her project. That is, she colored in the parts she had already drawn. But she left the features of the soldier and the little girl blank. It was strange, but she couldn't remember what she had thought of, or what she thought anything looked like. It had gone out of her head. Of course she could see the drawing looked terrible. Flat and stupid. She wanted to tear it up, but it was homework and her friends were counting on her.

She gave up drawing for good. She didn't mean to make trouble at school, so she participated as she could. She tried to do her part. She would paint a background blue if someone else drew the outlines and gave her the color to use and told her what to do, but she wouldn't do it on her own. She was ashamed of her efforts. She didn't know how to draw. She was a terrible artist.

When David woke up, they went for a long run together—"You set the pace, Aunt Didi," David said graciously, stretching his long, lithe limbs, to her amusement—and after lunch Didi insisted on a field trip to the art supply store. David said he didn't need anything, but finally he allowed her to buy him a new drawing pad. She wanted to do more, and felt reluctant to leave, but after some lingering, she released him. He would walk home, relieved to be free of all hovering adults, no matter how well intentioned. Didi drove home, vaguely disappointed. What was she going to do this afternoon? With nobody around but the damn cats and a bunch of erotic poem fragments on sticky notes?

23

On Monday, David returned to the museum. He couldn't spend all his time in the woods, after all. There was the matter of preparation for his chosen career. Today he planned to sketch the round barn. Once there, however, he found himself drawn again into its interior. More comfortable now, he took his time examining the tools hanging on the walls, the photographs of old sites where the tools came from, the old wagons and odd things. Swing churn, paddle churn, ox yoke, grubbing hoe; he could not always connect the label with the artifact being described—which was the fiddle bow seeder? What was a gambrel stick?—but he loved the words. He was intrigued by an old wagon, small, barely big enough for a driver and a small load. It seemed more suited to medieval peasants than Vermont farmers; look how simply the wheels were attached to the chassis.

"You like chariots?"

David straightened up hastily, as if he'd been caught. Dean Allen hovered nearby with an impatient air.

"Looking for something? Full of idle curiosity, aren't you? You know Prometheus rode his chariot too close to the sun? That was when he tried to steal fire from the gods."

David looked puzzled. Was this guy putting him on? "Not Prometheus. He's—"

"No one in your generation knows the old myths. I will teach you, and that will be my gift, so that you will understand this exhibit. Zeus then chained him to a rock so his eyes would be pecked out by ravens. Quoth the raven, evermore. Prometheus was bound and unbound, bound and unbound. Never knew when the darkness would overtake him." David laughed, reached out involuntarily. Dean Allen regarded him sternly, but then he winked and continued. "His real name was Zuckerman. He was a Jew. But the point is, these tongs. They're blacksmith's tongs, not Jupiter's. And they give the wrong impression here, lying about on this pallet."

David was delighted and bit his lip to keep from laughing. This guy was like a weird version of Mr. Marcus. "What impression are they supposed to give?"

"Who was the great blacksmith, I ask you. What does a blacksmith's shop have to do with a barn? Nothing! A barn is not a circus!"

"Maybe they're not blacksmith's tongs at all," David offered. "Could they be those things you use for picking up blocks of ice?"

"Aha! Ice, cold, the frozen dark. You see? That brings us back to the underworld, doesn't it? Persephone seeking her mother in Hades, going deeper and deeper, finally catching a glimpse, finally embracing her and—nothing! She is but a shade! What's the matter, boy? Don't you know the story of Persephone who brought six months of winter to the earth?"

"Wait. Persephone—"

"You thought it was Pluto who punished her, who wanted her for his own and then banished her but kept her mother in Hades instead. Didn't you? Never mind, David, these myths are hard to keep straight. All the relationships."

"But it was Odysseus—"

"Relations between the sexes are much too complicated. Not like the bond between two men, is it? Not like Jekyll and Hyde. Or Scylla and Charybdis. Eh, David?"

By the time David broke free to meet his aunt for lunch, he felt a little drunk.

"What's the matter? You're all flushed." Didi led him to a picnic table behind the offices where they could eat the peanut butter sandwiches and cherry tomatoes that David had brought.

"I ran into Dean Allen in the round barn. I sort of followed him around all morning while he lectured. I didn't want to leave. He's, he's completely off his nut."

"Yeah, sometimes."

"But it was exciting! He goes off, and I can hardly follow what he's saying, and then he stops and looks at me like . . . like . . . I don't know. I can't explain it." Suddenly he no longer wanted to explain it.

"Did he say anything about fire?"

"I think he's lonely, Aunt Didi."

"A lot of people are lonely."

They sat quietly. Traffic from the nearby highway combined with the chittering of summer birds. David wished he hadn't said so much. Why was he so talkative when he got excited?

"Aunt Didi, do you believe in ghosts?

"No. Do you know of one?"

"In the round barn. Dean says."

"Really? What's he doing there?"

"How did you know it was a he?"

"I don't know. The glint in your eye."

"His name is Hoke."

"That's funny." Didi held up a tomato, considering. "I don't believe in ghosts, but I saw one once. Don't tell your mother, she hates this kind of stuff. It was my grandfather. Your great grandfather. I saw him ahead of me on the street one day, this was years ago, he'd been dead years already. He went into a bank. He was about a couple hundred yards ahead of me. I ran in after him, and he wasn't there. I was absolutely positive it was him. He looked just like a picture I have of him. Of course I could have been wrong; it could have been someone else, and not my grandfather. But that man, the one I saw, was nowhere to be seen."

"Cool."

Didi sighed. "Since you're an artist—like your grandfather—maybe you won't always know what's a ghost and what's real. But I'm not sure it matters."

David pondered this. He wouldn't, couldn't, be like his grandfather. But Aunt Didi had called him an artist all his life. He was used to it; it didn't mean anything. Still, when she left him to return to her office, he watched her with a great rush of love. When he was little, he used to wish she were his mother instead of the one he had.

He returned to the round barn and found no trace of Dean Allen. He wandered through the barn looking for a sign—of what, he wasn't sure.

David felt he had waited long enough. He had been patient, and now it was time to take action. He had been here ten days and hadn't met anyone who fit the bill. No lovers. The hell with it. It was time to stop mucking around and get started on his creation. He had plenty of material.

He set up a card table in the corner of his aunt's small living room. The breeze that blew through the open windows to his left and right rippled the curtains but passed over his treasures. It was still light out, the longest day of the year—a good omen for beginning. With care, David laid out what he had collected. Dozens of small sticks, two small, squashed pine cones of a kind he had never seen before, a small burl he'd painstakingly sliced off a tree, some oddly shaped seed pods. He had bits and pieces of nature from Grayson Pond, Red Rocks, East Woods, the museum grounds, his aunt's neighborhood. He had square stalks and round stalks, broad and narrow grasses, small round leaves and wide pointed leaves with holes chewed in them. Later he would learn that he had crenated, dentated, sinuated leaves, and stamens, sepals, and petals. For now it was enough that he had stuff: pieces of bark, slivers of root, seeds, grasses, and stalks.

He would not use everything, but the way he worked now, he needed to have most of the ingredients before he began. He used to build birdhouses by putting pieces together as he found them. There was a certain freedom in this, but he found that he often had to take walls apart and start over, or completely dismantle a roof, as he found other wood or grasses or leaves that worked better. As he became more confident, more sure he could carry through a vision he began with, he became less hasty—a more experienced lover. He smiled at himself. A good joke. But there was a certain truth to it: he often found himself aroused while working on his birdhouses. He supposed that the simple act of creating was exciting. He rode the feeling, put it off as long as he could, then relieved himself and returned to work. It was part of the joy. And the loneliness.

Now, with his materials piled before him, he felt the familiar pleasure and excitement mixed with uncertainty. He touched them, held them close to his face, rearranged them on the table. He loved this part, when the meaning of his materials revealed itself to him slowly. Each twig, each seedpod's significance was determined as much by its relation to others as by any inherent qualities, and this was right. This was as it should be. Connections everywhere. On the one hand he had a vision, but that was only the starting point. The real joy came from discovering how things fit together to make a whole. The joyous surprise. He could not quite explain it in words, but he knew when it worked, and the words would come in their time. And someday he would build something absolutely true.

In the meantime, he settled for true parts. He surveyed his collection with a radiant expectation, and began with the doorway.

24

June 22
Cynthia,

There is a young man lurking about lately. He belongs to a colleague of mine, if you can call her that. Ptui, ptui—I spit against the Evil Eye. This woman, with whom I try to have as little to do as possible, lives with—Lives in sin. It pains me to imagine. I hope that you—

The boy's name is David. He came upon me in the barn, stumbled against me, and being a tall fellow nearly knocked me over. He apologized so profusely I felt sorry for him. I knew who he was and introduced myself. I know everyone because I keep watch from my window.

He shadowed me the rest of the hour listening to my explanations of the artifacts like a young pup. I don't know the building yet, but of course I know the works. I'm not an idiot after all, though some people around here may think so. It was flattering, really, although I wonder what he really wants. Perhaps he is just a nice boy, but I doubt it. Few are. As you of all people know.

25

Tuesday Bailey carried a beeper when he was on call in case of emergencies at the museum—fire, flood, hurricane, death, any such disasters as might be created by man or nature. He was rarely called, unlike a man he knew who worked at a home for the elderly where someone died every month. No one had ever died at the museum; all emergency sufferers had survived fainting, a heart attack, attacks of appendicitis or gall stones. And the museum had never been vandalized or burglarized. As one of Tuesday's men joked, "Ain't nothing worth stealing." In any case, nothing an ordinary thief could dispose of easily.

Tuesday had left early on Wednesday and was only halfway home when his beeper went off. A half hour later, heart still racing unnaturally, he met the town police chief at the round barn, along with Sam Desautels, head of security. It was early evening; the last visitor had left an hour ago. The chief greeted Tuesday.

"I don't know, Bailey. No sign of forced entry, and no alarms went off."

"The system is working fine," Sam added, shaking his head. "I just checked."

Sam showed Tuesday the damage, which the chief called vandalism. It was as if a small whirlwind had passed through the second floor of the barn, but like a tornado had whipped across only a small and unpredictable space, leaving everything else untouched. In one section alone, several small displays were knocked from their pallets and scattered about. An apple peeler, an apple corer, and a wooden stirring paddle had been ripped from a hanging panel about harvesting. Stoneware preserve crocks lay on their sides—one was cracked; had it been cracked before? A brass kettle lay next to them. A few tools were upended. The wagon lay on its side. Wall labels hung crookedly.

Tuesday rubbed his tight chest without knowing he did so. That someone had purposely tried to harm the museum . . .

"It's like somebody threw a fit," Sam said.

Right. It would not do for Tuesday to throw a fit. He was known to be a calm man, a man of restraint. He didn't throw chairs or shoot people. He didn't even yell at his staff. He wanted to do all these things often. He wanted to do them now. Instead, he checked the windows again, and the two doors—the one bolted and padlocked from the inside, the other opened by Sam when he came in a half an hour or so ago.

There wasn't much to say. Sam had been on duty because one of his guards was sick. Sam had locked the doors after the museum closed, checking the building as required. A half hour later, the skinny woman who ran the gift shop, less than twenty feet away from the entrance to the barn, had heard a commotion as she was leaving. She called security. Sam arrived within minutes, having alerted police. The police arrived a few minutes later. The gift shop woman reported that no one had left the barn by either the main door or the one below. She assumed whoever it was had either slipped out the back door on the bottom level, or was still there.

But no one was there, and the back door was bolted from the inside.

Sam went off with the police chief to complete the paperwork. Tuesday remained in the barn.

In fact, nothing was actually damaged. Artifacts that had been knocked over could be righted. Labels knocked off could be reattached. Nothing was smashed or broken in two. He had to conclude that whoever had been here had not intended to cause real harm. But then what? Why?

Tuesday rubbed his chest and took a deep breath. Probably there was nothing to worry about. Probably a simple explanation existed—a localized earthquake or something. In any case, there was nothing he could do about it now. He went home.

The last time he had encountered something completely foreign was in Maine, where he had fled to learn about men and women, a subject that had defeated him back home. He'd left in the fall, after he graduated from high school and had nothing going for him but a custodial job at the museum an hour away.

After Grandpa Bailey died and he talked to Mary. After Jimmy in the woods.

He spent the first winter and spring in Maine at odd jobs—bartender, road crew, part-time companion to a teenaged boy in a wheelchair until the family moved away in July. When he'd answered the ad in the Lewiston paper, he'd had no idea what a Buddhist was, but he was feeling reckless. He expected to find a Chinese farmer, not a trio of vegetarian Jews from New York. But he'd never met a Jew before, either. In exchange for three meals a day taken with the family and a place to stay in a tiny cabin on their property, he'd help them with the farm. They needed someone to pick bugs off their vegetables because they couldn't kill the little critters themselves. His first task was to collect slugs every morning and drop them into a pail of soapy water, a disgusting but not difficult job. Harry and Esther, the parents, had come to this sad compromise only after other efforts—like collecting buckets of slugs and dumping them a few miles away—proved unworkable.

Liza was the long-legged daughter who watched him from a distance for nearly two months, sizing him up, it was obvious, but speaking to him directly very little, except about a task that needed doing.

When he thought she wasn't looking, Tuesday observed her in return: her black wavy hair that fell over her face when she stooped over the rows revealing her delicious, bare breasts beneath her loose tank top. She was tall and strong—almost as tall as he was—with a quiet presence and a soft laugh. She was two years older than he, taking a year off from college to get something out of her system, he didn't know what.

Tuesday began working for the Buddhists in July. One day in early September, after a warm morning during which he and Liza had picked blueberries for several hours—fat, cultivated blueberries, not the tiny kind that grew wild—and during which Liza had worked her way slowly through the rows until she picked from the same bush as he, she stood up and stretched. She untied the pail of berries from around her waist and set it down. Tuesday straightened up, and Liza untied the cord around his waist as well. He smelled her sun-warmed skin. She smiled her easy smile and pulled her tank top over her head. He kept his eyes on her face. She took his hand and led him down the row beyond the blueberry bushes to a place behind the sugar house at the edge of the woods, where the ground was cushioned with tall, soft grasses.

Wild mind. They were the first words she had spoken to him all day. He thought she said *Wild mine.* He still remembered her soft lips, bright eyes, the way her skin felt against his. It was not his first time with a woman, but the first time with someone he really liked. The first time he ever felt he was making love.

Her parents seemed to accept that the hired man was sleeping with their daughter. Nothing changed, except Liza spent most nights in his tiny cabin. Tuesday became one of the family. And he and Liza began to talk, revealing themselves slowly. They didn't expect overmuch from each other, except in their lovemaking, where they were tender and passionate. The intensity of their hunger for each other at night—or in the afternoon, or in the morning—and the absolute confidence they would satisfy and be satisfied—allowed them an easiness with each other while they worked, ate, talked about the farm. They harvested kale and Brussels sprouts, picked off Japanese beetles and slugs, and drove the chickens to the slaughterhouse before winter.

Liza's secret was that she didn't mind killing slugs. She was brought up Buddhist but she thought killing was all right if you weren't cruel about it. Pouring salt on slugs was cruel; she showed Tuesday once, so he'd know the difference. Tuesday didn't mind drowning them, but the slime you got on your hands from picking them up, slime that wouldn't come off even with soap, and their soft orange underbellies, and the buckets heavy with soapy water and oozing slop—small, brown baby slugs early in the season and long, fat granddaddies toward the fall . . . At first he was afraid he might throw up. And then, though he didn't mind killing slugs exactly, he worried about mass killing on purpose, even of slugs. Was that right? He never got used to it.

He'd told Mary once about the Buddhists, though not about Liza. Mary thought he said nudists.

Once, when they were working in the fields, he'd asked Liza what women wanted. What made girls happy?

"What makes guys happy? Everybody just wants to be loved, don't you think? To be known, and loved, in spite of all your quirks."

"I don't think I want anything."

"Oh, bullshit. That's only because you want so much."

Tuesday shook his head, sure she was wrong.

She laughed at him, draped herself around him and licked his ear and slid her hand down the front of his pants. He tried to ignore her, but—all right, there were some things he wanted.

Afterward, they lay together.

"But—" He tried again.

"Buddhists are supposed to live beyond desire, but I think that's crap. Or maybe I'm just a crappy Buddhist. I want things all the time. I want sex, I want to have a baby, I want to be happy. As far as I can tell, everybody wants, it's just how it is. What you want is who you are."

Tuesday rolled away from her. "No babies."

"I know. You don't want anyone to feel about you the way you feel about your parents. But maybe I want a baby more than you don't want to be a father."

Whatever happened to Liza? Tuesday hoped she had a whole pile of babies and a good man to stick around and love them and play with them and send them to college, too. Who knew, it might even have been him, except for Mary, and maybe even then, but for an extra windy lake and bad luck—and too much to drink. His parents must have had too much to drink, otherwise how would they go smashing into a cliff full tilt on a calm day and get thrown out and one crack his head and the other just drown?

Always remember, Liza said when he left. She gave him a book of Buddhist poetry. She showed him a poem about cicadas, and she wrote in the front, *Always remember, our love like cicadas' voices penetrates the rocks.* He still had it somewhere. It was the second book she'd given him. The first one was another book of poems by somebody Burns. He'd flipped through it, and caught the word

Mary. It was the only poem he'd read, but the lines stayed with him: *My Mary's asleep by thy murmuring stream—Flow gently, sweet Afton, disturb not her dream.* And something about wild, whistling blackbirds.

Wild mind, Liza had said. He never got it. Wild mind free of thoughts? His mind wasn't free of thoughts; when it was most empty, in rolled Mary. He didn't think about her exactly—at least not all the time. She was just there, in his mind—with her smiling face, laughing, or arguing with him, or singing.

When the lawyer contacted him about his parents' deaths, he had returned to Vermont. Were there ever simple explanations? He had asked too many questions for the lawyer's taste, a young lawyer who had handled too much death—or not enough. *Don't worry about it,* the exasperated lawyer said finally. *There's nothing you can do about it now.*

Some things would never make sense.

26

The next day, when Didi returned from a meeting, she found Adrian waiting in her office. He kissed her lightly.

"I'm all business," he said.

"Do you ever feel like a vulture descending on its prey?"

"Never. Vultures eat dead meat. I'm only concerned with the living. Soft, warm flesh, breathing and sighing."

Didi rolled her eyes.

In fact, Adrian had come to interview Charles Hopper again for a follow-up story about the paintings. It was sheer luck, he explained, that the barn had been vandalized the night before.

"Not exactly vandalized," Didi corrected him. She offered to walk him to the barn, though there was nothing to see. Curators had reestablished the exhibit quickly that morning, and the barn opened only a few minutes late. She tried not to touch him as they walked, though she wanted to lean into him.

He quizzed her about the impending sale. "Are you sad about it? Does it feel like a big sacrifice?"

"No, it doesn't." She stopped, to look at him directly. "We can raise thirty million dollars by de-accessioning five major pieces. The endowment that creates will allow us to improve care of the remaining work."

They stood too close together. Here she was at work! He watched her intently as she spoke. He wore a short-sleeved polo shirt and slacks, and the sun behind him lit the light hair on his arms. They were both sweating lightly; she could smell him, a pleasant, earthy smell.

"Some of the paintings now don't even get dusted."

He nodded. She touched his arm with her fingers. They gazed at each other without speaking.

"Adrian!" Didi exclaimed, turning away. "What do you want?"

"I want to know everything. I'm a reporter. I'm hungry for knowledge."

They resumed walking. Didi shook her head. "The remaining art includes other Degas and Manets, as you know." She wouldn't look at him anymore. "We'll improve lighting—the old wiring in some of the buildings is a fire hazard. And increase security."

"That's what the American Association of Museum Directors doesn't like, isn't it? You're supposed to use money from selling art to buy more art, not for what you people call 'collections care'."

"You know the issues. Why are you asking me about it?"

"I like to hear you talk." He grinned. How could he be so free of guile, so open? If they were cave people, they would simply grab each other and move off behind the bushes—or maybe not bother with bushes.

"We have a hundred and twenty weathervanes, twelve hundred waterfowl decoys, six hundred historic circus posters, seven hundred quilts, a two-hundred-twenty-foot steamboat—"

"Didi, who's that?"

Dean Allen loped past, scowling and mumbling.

What a relief. "The Lurker. He works here."

"I'd like to do a story on him sometime. Looks like quite a character. People are interested in this place now."

"Please don't." She left him at the barn to do his own investigating. When would it end?

That evening, David began again. He knew there was something missing but had decided to keep working, to have faith that whatever it was would come eventually. It felt very close. Perhaps the answer was within him already, maybe would reveal itself in the birdhouse as he built it.

He had decided on an irregular form; the walls curled and waved rather than turned at corners. The windows were rounded and asymmetrical. The doorway leaned sideways as if it had melted into softer lines. The walls had acquired a rich texture of woven grasses, embroidered by seedpods of various shapes and sizes, singly and in clusters. Tonight he would begin the roof, while Didi ironed some shirts to keep him company.

He measured twigs against each other to make a skeletal framework. With a Swiss army knife, he cut them into unequal lengths. He wanted them close but not identical. Harmony, he explained to his aunt, came from allowing each element to find its own wild way.

Maude phoned from Virginia. She and Didi talked for half an hour. A few minutes later, Lucy called for David, to confirm their plans for the next day. Didi finished her ironing and sat opposite David, observing him while he spoke. He waved her away. She ignored him. When he hung up, she leaned back in her chair with her fingertips together.

"Who is this person you're spending all your time with, hmm? What's she like? What is she going to do with herself?"

"You mean after she kills her mother this summer?"

"I mean after college. What is she interested in?"

"She thinks she's dumb, so who knows. She's kind of religious."

"Dumb, religious older woman. Murderous. Are you collecting stray dogs? It's not a good idea, you know."

"Oh no, Aunt Didi. Not at all. She's not dumb, it's just that her mother has told her she was all her life. She's tough and, I don't know, innocent at the same time. She has some strange ideas . . . her mother is awful and her grandparents might have been Nazis. But then so could mine."

"Oh, David."

"Aunt Didi, you know what? I hate my grandfather. I've just realized it this summer. If he's supposed to be a sort of substitute father, he's a miserable failure. And if you don't stop telling me I'm an artist like him, I'm going to kill myself."

"David. I understand how you feel about your grandfather. Believe me. But he's not . . . Listen, I never knew your father, he sort of came and went, if you know what I mean. But your grandfather. He's, he has a small heart, but he, in his strange way he has a generous spirit. Look, who do you think paid for your private school all these years?"

"I don't know. I guess I thought Mom did."

"On her salary? Our father helps her. He doesn't want you to know. He doesn't want you to feel obligated."

David stared at his half-finished birdhouse. "Is he paying for my college, too? Mom always says not to worry about it."

"He believes in you. Maybe he sees himself in you."

David bent over his birdhouse so his aunt couldn't see his face.

part two

27

I do not ask forgiveness; I do not believe in God. I ask only to tell my story to the universe, as I sit in this empty parking lot of St. Joseph's. It is Sunday after all.

My husband died a year and a half ago, leaving me with the care of my daughter, Lucy. She is twenty, and I have never liked her. I love her of course, she is my daughter, but she is slow, perhaps. I collect art.

I am not accustomed to talking about myself and feel awkward in the attempt, but I expect to warm to it as I go along. I live, after all, a good life.

I loved George.

I am American. I was born in Germany, to German parents. My mother, for some reason still and forever unknown to me, was at first Catholic. I was raised by my mother and my uncle, not my father. My father left when I was five. My mother loved me though I did not understand it. Her life was very narrow, as mine would have been had I not left, perhaps, constricted on all sides by the dying man with the upward gazing eyes. Whom my mother loved and I hated. I believed he had stolen my father.

My uncle who raised me used to say, "Find something you love enough to die for."

At fifteen, I wanted nothing more than to do exactly that. But what could it be? I did not believe I could find it in Germany. Then I came to the United States, to the home of my uncle's friend, and the next year I went to American college—and stayed.

Two years ago when my mother was dying, I went back to Germany. Naturally, collecting art takes me to Europe often—though rarely to Germany—and I always take the daytime flight, since I cannot sleep on a plane. I pull the shades, and while others watch silly movies, I think. On this trip I thought of my mother; one image returned to me again and again, of my mother in the garden.

My mother loved to garden. I did not. She often asked me to help, and I tried, but I did not know what to do, and she would not tell me. She disliked giving orders or even making suggestions. She seemed to expect me to know what to do as if by some instinct, which I lacked. I resented it deeply.

Or perhaps she didn't expect me to do anything, I thought now. Perhaps she simply enjoyed my company—but how could that be? I remembered her kneeling in a boxy summer dress, digging cheerfully in the dirt, patting the soil, transplanting perennials, thinning, weeding, while I looked on through a haze of barely suppressed rage. Sometimes she asked me questions. I loathed being questioned by my mother. Gardening was so ordinary, so bourgeois. I wanted to see the world, to learn new things. In the United States I would have a life full of sophistication and worldliness, thousands of miles from my mother gardening on her knees, asking me stupid questions while I plucked fitfully at stray grass.

Why was she so contented, with such a sullen, miserable child? Did she worry about me? Why did she not know what I wanted? How could she be so satisfied with her life, when fear of that same life drove me away?

I wiped my eyes. How unlike me to become emotional. My mother, cheerful but otherwise unexpressive, would not approve. I wondered whether my mother's illness had changed her. I myself would not like to be changed by illness. I would not like to be changed at all.

The room in the hospital was bare except for a small wooden cross on the wall. A clean Lutheran hospital, run by nurses, not nuns, but there was the cross. Perhaps my uncle put it there for her. My uncle was wealthy; my mother had her own room. I think she would have preferred company, but I did not know her and cannot be sure.

I asked her what she had loved. I asked her this because you may ask a dying person anything, even when she is your mother. They may have wisdom in their last days, perhaps.

My mother, who could barely talk, spoke clearly. She said, "Why Frieda, I love you."

Why Frieda, I love you.

And then George. George had a heart attack, Mother not yet dead a year. I had gone to a gallery opening. I found him on the floor of his study when I came home. That is all I can say. It was too much death.

Lucy was conceived under circumstances that were unpleasant. That is not a problem, or the cause of our distance. It is simply a fact. Life is much more complex than that, a Cubist painting; the parts make sense—such sense as they will ever make—only when seen together, layered one on top of another, shifted, turned, distortion and truth intermingling, changing places.

My Uncle Hans was a good father to me. He was kind. Is kind. He lives in Germany, alone, sees his friends. He owned a factory. He complained about the workers, that it was always a fight. I took him literally and feared for him. But he never came home hurt, so I concluded he won. This did not comfort me. Every small child knows that the strongest, fiercest person usually wins, not necessarily the one who is right. For a German child winning and losing are perhaps more complicated than for others.

I don't know why the workers struck. I thought I knew a secret about my uncle's hidden violence. Looking back, I doubt any bloody clashes ever took place, but how could I know? Was my uncle the factory owner cruel and unreasonable, or kind? It is impossible to look back at one's past and know the truth. He is German and Germans are freighted with a shadow of duplicity that weighs as heavily as if it were made of iron.

I feared many things. I believed the man on the cross ate my father, the way that we ate bits of him, the man on the cross, every week when I was a child. If I swallowed enough of him, I might get my father back. This eating of flesh was a complicated matter; I did not know what was possible and what impossible. All transformation is difficult.

When Lucy offered to come with me to Vermont this summer, I was afraid. I did not want to spend a summer alone with my daughter in a strange place. I could not tell her this. I decided finally that perhaps it would be good for her. It might change her. Or me. I might become a loving mother. I say this in jest.

It was all the deaths, you see.

The truth is, I gave up on hope when I knew the man on the cross would not give me back my father. From that point, I focused on desire.

After George died, I was looking for something to do. I joined the board of the museum because I thought—I suppose I thought the paintings would save me.

I have a lot of money. For better or worse, a simple fact. George took pride in his financial success, at the same time that he took it for granted. And I invested well. When we met, George asked me what I wanted. I said I wanted to be rich.

"What will you do with your money?"

"I will buy art."

My answer pleased him.

I told George over breakfast one day, before we were married, that I was pregnant. I did not say "expecting a child" or use other language he might have preferred. I was not expecting a child, after all. We met downtown in a fancy hotel. I don't remember which. I remember the white damask tablecloths and gold-rimmed plates, the crystal glasses. It was the kind of place George felt comfortable in. Gold-handled forks and spoons, for breakfast.

George and I had not slept together during our engagement, though we had before. It wasn't my idea. I went to a party. I danced with a man, a boy I suppose I'd call him now, we were so young, a young man who pressed himself against me so that I could feel his body change. I don't remember the party or why I was there or who I went with. I suppose we drank wine, smoked. I remember the music was the kind that is so loud your ears ring in the morning. It wasn't a party for talking. I went into one of the bedrooms with this man. I don't think we exchanged names. The room was dark, dimly lit by a small bedside lamp with a dark shade, with deep red, flocked wallpaper and heavy velvet curtains to keep out the city noises below. We had sex on the bed. I kept my dress on; I don't think he took his trousers off. He lay on top of me, I held onto him with one hand and with the other, I unraveled the bedspread.

The bedspread was quilted, a wine-colored background with oversized flowers in lighter shades, peonies and dahlias, and imaginary, indescribably lush flowers in crimson, carnelian, faded maroon. The flowers were outlined, quilted, with plastic thread. The bedspread itself felt slippery to me, as if I could slide off at any minute, as if I wasn't quite touching it but floating on a skim of water, wasn't quite touching the man on top of me either, but floating under him. And he floated inside me.

I had never seen plastic thread before. Nylon I suppose. A piece of the thread stuck up from the quilt and I tugged on it, while this man lay on top of me. I pulled at it and watched it unravel around a plump, purplish peony, with my legs wrapped around this man's waist, this man whose name I didn't know. Still I enjoyed it.

I did not feel remorse afterward. It was the time, you understand. I liked sex. I knew I would be faithful to George once we married, and I was. But I was not married yet, and I felt free and took delight in my body and its power to arouse. And there was the wine and the smoke—it was the time, after all. And I had never seen plastic thread.

But I was sickened at the idea of being pregnant—and particularly being impregnated by someone I didn't know. I wished to be rid of it.

Why did I tell George? Why did I not simply act on my own? How different things would have been. But . . . I cannot look at Lucy and wish she had never been. She exists, she is a real person. I am sorry, rather, that . . . I should not have been a mother.

I fear I will be judged harshly. But I have never been cruel to Lucy. I am capable of love. I loved George, in my way. And there was the man who taught me about art—did I love him? I can't remember. I love art. I love the German Expressionists, oddly, perhaps. You might think I would be drawn more to the peculiarly unemotional wildness of Jackson Pollack than to the blatant sensuality of Nolde and his poppies. It may be that people find me cold. But that is not it, not the whole of it. Even Corot had a spot of red in his paintings.

I learned early that feelings color your judgment. The reason I am an extraordinary art collector—I do not brag, it is a fact—is that I make decisions with a cool head. If a work moves me, I dismiss it. I have found this method entirely trustworthy. I do not claim to have a perfect eye. I have never claimed so. There are works that touch me, and which I therefore reject, which others believe to be good, even excellent. But I do not work that way. How could one not be moved by Nolde? But I am not. I am filled, rather, with a clean, clear-sighted, sharp sensation, as if I am being run through with a knife between my breasts, like a sudden stab of loss, but I think of it as no-feeling, and I know then that I can judge properly.

I do not trust my feelings, I trust my brain. It is because of religion, you see. I hate religious art. I realize this colors my judgment, and this angers me. You see how it is.

Lucy involved herself with a group of religious fanatics at the little community college she went to. My slow daughter named for the light by her father. I mean George, of course. Not the man whose seed carried the germ of her into me. George wished to name a child of his own for his mother, but we never had another.

After I told him, he wouldn't look at me. He ran his finger around and around the edge of his water glass. Crystal, with tiny beads of condensation up to the water line. It was summer in New York City, hot and muggy though it was cold in that hotel dining room with the gold-rimmed plates. I looked at the plates, but watched George out of the corner of my eye. Finally he figured out what he thought—he was always very deliberate—and he spoke to me, but he still wouldn't look at me. George never raised his voice when he was angry. He spoke more and more softly.

Our wedding was scheduled to take place in another month. We had agreed on details easily, which made us think we'd have an easy marriage. Perhaps a marriage is easier without a child, or perhaps not.

He said, in his softest voice, "You will have the child, and it will be our child." He wiped his mouth with his napkin, though he hadn't eaten anything yet. But he had been working hard, and beads of sweat had broken out over his lip. Then he looked at me for the first time and asked me not to do anything like that again. He asked me, in a way that let me know how he felt.

He could have said, If you ever do anything like that again, I'll divorce you on the spot. That's what he meant, of course. But that's George. He never made a scene, and he never overstated a case. He took a sip of coffee, and then he left.

I was not surprised by what he said. But I was shocked that he left me alone at the table in this fancy hotel. What if I didn't have any money? I was twenty-two. He left, knowing I would take care of it. Knowing I could. That is why I married George. Because it didn't occur to him to worry about my ability to handle the situation—to call the waiter, to pay the bill, to make a graceful exit on my own.

I couldn't make myself like the child.

George loved Lucy, however, and that seemed to be enough. People said she was pretty and sweet. She didn't excel in school, but she did make it to a little college where, as I said, she fell in with a religious crowd. I believe she fell in love with the leader. He likely had ten girlfriends and slept with all of them.

The first fall, Lucy came home quite a bit on weekends, bringing with her religious "art," to which I objected. Nothing I said made much difference. At her father's suggestion, she kept it in her room. Postcard paintings of Jesus with clasped hands and that pitiful heavenward gaze. The dark, sad eyes with long lashes. Occasional, if poor, reproductions of famous paintings—Michelangelo's God reaching out to Adam, other scenes from the Sistine Chapel, an El Greco, even, once, a Chagall. I doubt she knew where they were from or who the artists were. Just as often she would bring home a crucifixion painted on black velvet, bought from a street vendor. How could she buy something so atrocious, I asked impatiently. Was she perhaps moved by compassion for the artist producing such horrendous work, or did she merely want to annoy me? She could not possibly like it.

"On the contrary, Mother. It is an expression of a particular religious sensibility—and it moves me."

"It's trash, Lucy, not art. Do what you want, but please keep it out of my sight."

"I plan to. Anyway, Henry gave it to me, not you."

It pains me that this is what she learned in college. From Henry. I learned about men, too, I suppose, but my lover taught me about art, and how not to be a fool, though that was not his intention. Lucy is still a fool.

It is not true that I cannot remember the man who taught me about art. It is painful for me to remember. But I have been remembering it lately, thinking about Lucy, trying to understand.

He taught art history. He introduced me to the German Expressionists, but what he liked best was contemporary art. He kept a fresh bottle of Bordeaux in the bottom drawer of his desk in his office.

I was a student at a large university in New Jersey. He took me with him to New York on the bus one Saturday, and we spent the afternoon visiting galleries. Afterward we went to his office and talked about what we had seen while he undressed me. He took off all my clothes, slowly, all the while talking to me about light and shadow, form and substance. He ran his finger across my nipple murmuring about an artist's firmness of line, brushed his lips against my neck whispering about elements of design.

He never undressed. He unbuttoned his jeans; I'd never seen jeans with buttons. He sat on the edge of his desk, lifted me on top of him and rocked me back and forth, teasing me with talk about the repetitive motion of Kandinsky, the whimsical passion of Klee. He kissed me and stroked me, his art talk finally dissolving into wordless sounds until his release. I had wanted to come to America a virgin, and I had, a year before. But my teacher was not my first man. Still I did not yet know how to ask for satisfaction for myself. I did not yet know what I was missing.

I was still so new in this country. I liked being naked because I felt confident in my body. Clothed, I feared doing the wrong thing or saying the wrong thing. It seemed right to me that he, my teacher, should remain dressed. He knew things. He had things to hide and knew what to hide and what to keep visible. I had nothing to hide, or perhaps everything. He had style, in the painters he knew, the clothes he wore, the wine he drank. I longed to have style. Only naked, exerting the only power I had, did I feel equal.

If life were a story, the story of my first love would stop here. But it isn't. I was young and hungry, I wanted more. We went to New York every Saturday for a month, followed by lovemaking in his office, surrounded by books and piles of papers. It was spring, he wore jeans and a white T-shirt on the bus, I stroked his arm. He touched my breast under my shirt. During the week, I studied hard, with my hand between my legs. I thought I had found something to die for. I lingered after class to talk with him. One Friday, I walked him back to his office.

I closed the door behind me and waited. He said nothing. I willed him to come to me.

"It's the middle of the day, Frieda."

Come to me, I thought. *I'll love you to death. I will die for you.* I closed my eyes.

"I'm afraid I must do some work, Frieda. I'm meeting a student in an hour."

He sat behind his desk, the very desk upon which he had made love to me a few days before. It was a heavy wooden desk, with a leather top, strewn with papers. I knew the feel of it on the bottom of my feet, as I pushed against it while he clasped me to him, me arching back, grasping his shoulders, he kissing my breasts.

His hands now moved restlessly over his desk; one held a pen as if waiting for me to leave.

Could I cross the room, put my arms around his neck, lean my breast against his shoulder, kiss his ear? Would he reach for me then?

He flicked his head impatiently as if he read my mind. I fled.

That night I had desperate thoughts. I thought of calling him, which I had never done before. But the phone in the dormitory hallway was much too public, and what if his wife answered? Yes, he had a wife, but I did not care. I cared then only that she probably spoke perfect English and knew how to wear the right American clothes, and I did not want to hear her voice.

When George died, it was not the typical things that were hard for me—shopping for one instead of two, for example, having no reason to buy the mate's favorite foods, buying them accidentally and then not knowing what to do with them because both eating them when you never really liked them in the first place and throwing them out feel like equal betrayals. I have a maid that does the shopping, what little I need; I have always preferred to go out. I did not miss eating with him every night because we had led such busy, separate lives; I often ate out with some gallery owner or another. It is important to keep up those connections.

I missed him when I knew I would—at night, in bed—but at unexpected moments, too, when I saw someone on the street whose curved back in a tweed jacket reminded me of him. I missed his clothes.

I could not give away his clothes for a long time.

George's smell lingered in our bed. How can you describe the smell of another person? The sweet smell of the flesh of the person you love.

After a few weeks I could not smell him anymore. I went into his closet where his clothes still hung, and I carried his shoes, one pair at a time, into my closet. I shoved my own shoes against the back of the closet; I did not care about them. George had loved good Italian shoes; it was one of his few indulgences. I lined up his expensive leather shoes neatly under my dresses.

On a hook in his closet hung his pajamas. I hesitated, afraid to be disappointed, then pressed my face into them. Yes. They smelled of George. Oh it was faint, unnoticeable perhaps to anyone else, but I knew it. I did not know it was possible to feel such grief as I felt then.

I held his pajamas as if holding a lost child and wept. Later, I put them under my pillow. I thought I would sleep with them for years, or until I slept with another man. If I never slept with another man, I would sleep with George's pajamas for the rest of my life.

The next day, I went through his clothes. I kept a gray jacket he had liked—he called it classy, but it wasn't particularly classy, and George had exquisite taste. I think perhaps he simply liked it. The rest of his clothes I piled onto chairs in the living room and had the maid take away.

George died in April. Lucy had gone back to school after the funeral to finish her classes. Six weeks later, she came home for the summer. She expressed surprise at finding so little of her father. I didn't know what she meant. Was it George's presence itself that had seemed to fill up the corners of the apartment?

"What did you do with all his stuff?"

"What stuff, Lucy? I gave away most of his clothes last week, if that's what you mean."

"Why didn't you ask me if I wanted anything?"

She made me tired. "I'm sorry, Lucy. It didn't occur to me. I didn't mean—"

"It didn't occur to you I might want a picture, or a keepsake, or something of my own father? What did you do with it all?"

Lucy had never spoken to me in this way before, challenging me so directly. It occurred to me then, for the first time, that Lucy might have a lover. While I did not. I felt something shift between us.

"Lucy, look in your father's study. It is full of his books. Any pictures we have are still there. The drawers to his desk are full of papers. If you can find a 'keepsake' as you call it, it's yours. I can't imagine George ever going in for that sort of thing."

"Ach. Books. Papers. Who wants those?"

"What do you want?"

Either she didn't know, or she found the question too stupid to consider. She left the apartment without answering.

We had an uneventful summer. If Lucy's Henry was around, I didn't know about it. Nor did I ask. I suppose we were both, Lucy and I, immersed in our own grief. We didn't talk about it. I did not think about Lucy then, what it must have been like for her. I have never had an easy time imagining life through her eyes. Only now for some reason, a year later, can I think of her, as my own memories come back to me. As things shift. As I learn about a different kind of art, the art of the folk, people who had little.

That night, the Friday night after my college lover rejected me so cruelly, as I thought, I barely slept. What should I do? The next day was Saturday. Should I meet him at the bus stop at the usual time, discreetly, a student and teacher riding the same bus to New York? Should I sit next to him, and run my fingers lightly over the hair on his arm as I liked to do? Should I wear a light, loose dress that he could slide his hand beneath to stroke my thigh, or even, if the seats were empty, slip his hand inside my underwear?

The next morning I was exhausted, a starved wreck of an animal feverish from chasing its prey all night unsuccessfully. I knew I shouldn't go to New York. Shouldn't walk the long blocks from my dormitory to the bus station on the main street, shouldn't pull open the heavy glass door to the station, its bottom half covered over with cardboard, its top half smudged and cracked, the crack taped over with gray duct tape. Shouldn't lean into the counter, bend down toward the half-moon cut out of the bottom of the glass so I wouldn't have to yell in order to make myself heard, so the whole world would not know where I was going, I and my lover, my lover who was my teacher, who opened me with his words before he undressed me with his hands, whose soft skin and light hair made him seem innocent and pure of heart when he really was not, not, not, he had a wife and he had tricked me, me Frieda.

Shouldn't give the man behind the counter my precious money, the carefully folded American dollar bills I still hadn't quite got used to in nearly two years, shouldn't take the round trip ticket from his thick hand with the fat pinky ring, shouldn't wait on the long, smooth wooden bench as if I expected someone, shouldn't scan the sidewalk outside the station windows continuously, glancing past every new face at the door to see whether my lover was right behind rushing a bit perhaps, anxious not to miss the bus, *So sorry I'm late, I hope you weren't worried.* Shouldn't get on the bus when it came, just in case I'd missed him, and find a seat of my own, alone, feeling increasingly reckless and furious. Determined not to be bested.

Shouldn't go to New York by myself, when I didn't know the city at all and was too weary to think straight. Shouldn't walk the streets for hours, downtown and up. Shouldn't sit in a doorway sobbing, waving away a motherly woman who stopped to ask if I were all right. Shouldn't spend another minute, not another second, thinking about this man, this jerk, this louse who had made me feel special, as if I mattered, as if what I had to give mattered. Who probably fucked a different student every month.

I spent my last change on a hot pretzel, dribbled with mustard. I stood on a street corner at the edge of Central Park and ate it. And that is when I learned something. An old man on a bicycle rode by, turned in to the park. It may have been that the two events were unrelated—my rejection and the appearance of the old man—but they came together in my mind. I looked up from the pretzel, which was soft and warm, half wrapped in tissue paper, and from which I took the first comfort of the day, and I saw a scowling old man with wild white hair and fierce eyebrows, riding a rickety red bicycle. He—he was out of context, from a different world, and I slipped into it.

Looking back from where I sit now, I can say it is like viewing a nineteenth-century narrative painting in which an entire world opens up before you, with a history and a set of relationships and social conditions, all of which will come to life as vividly as the images and memories of your own life if you let them. If you simply stand before the painting and allow . . . allow yourself to be drawn into it, perhaps, but it is more than that. There is an exchange. You move toward the painting and the painting moves toward you. This, in any case, is how I understand art, and, without yet knowing how to explain it, this is how I experienced that moment at the edge of Central Park, in my desolation.

He looked German, or Austrian perhaps. Or perhaps it was the scratched, old bicycle that reminded me of the blue-smocked workmen I used to see riding to work when I was a child. It was a different world, one I had rejected but . . . here was this old man, disheveled and uncared for, pathetic in many respects, but still undeniably fierce, still unvanquished. Wild and angry, someone who scared children and kicked dogs—*Out of my way, miserable mutt!* Someone who kicked back at life.

That was how I wanted to be. Not like my lover, toying with a heart and casting it off, not like myself, a stupid child. Like that old man.

I found words for all this later, as I tried to make sense of it. At the time, I simply fell into the wash of another life. It was afterward that I vowed not to be made a fool of in love, again. I would not allow myself to fall into such a weak position. I was unused to thinking about power, but I thought about it then, though in different words: I understood that it would take more than leaving Germany for me to become a woman undefeated.

I thought about who I wanted to be, what kind of a life I wanted. An image came to me with astonishing clarity. I decided I would collect art.

I come now to what happened this summer.

28

The next Monday, David met Lucy in the museum office parking lot. He had brought lunches, and she had directions to Connor Point from someone she'd met in town. They drove Didi's car.

"What's that short for—Didi?" Lucy asked.

"Davita. She hates it. I'm named for her, actually. Where do you go to school?"

"A community college in New Jersey. You wouldn't have heard of it. It's a dinky school, the only kind I could get in. My parents think I'm stupid. I mean, my mother thinks I'm stupid. My dad died of a heart attack last year."

"Jeez, I'm sorry."

"Yeah. I'm a half-orphan. I wish it had been my mom who died and my dad was still living."

"What's your college like?"

"Well, the first people I met were these Christians. My mother and I had some rip-roaring arguments about it. She thought, she assumed, they were narrow-minded and shallow, when really they just had clear opinions. Like her. I used to not know anything about religion. Talk about ignorant. So I went with them to Bible study groups and prayer meetings, things like that, and they were fun. I felt gypped that my parents never taught me anything about religion."

"I was always glad not to have to go to church."

Lucy shrugged. "I'll tell you what I liked best about these guys. Don't laugh. They were really warm. You know, touch-y. In my family, people don't touch. We don't hug and we don't kiss except on special occasions. Didn't, I guess I should say. My friends, these Christians, hug all the time. This is how it works in my family. Worked, I mean. Like for a holiday, like Thanksgiving or Christmas, when they'd have another couple over—never anyone with children. It was like a ceremony. First my parents kissed. Then my parents kissed the guests. Then I was supposed to kiss the guests. Ecchhh! It was awful."

David laughed at the way she told it, but it made him feel depressed.

"It was so stiff and uptight, and it makes it seem like everyone is equal. Everyone gets treated the same. Me and the guests. No one is special. And you know what? That's wrong. People are not equal."

David considered this.

"So these kids at school, they hug and kiss each other all the time. I was really shy at first, but of course I liked it, they were so friendly, and they meant it. And there was this one guy. Well, anyway."

"You had sex with him," David said gloomily. Everyone had sex but him.

"You said it, I didn't."

"What was his name?" he asked sadly.

"Henry. He was a senior. Before I knew him, he used to do drugs and steal things and fuck everything in sight—that's what he said—until he found God. And then he found me. He was very sweet. I learned a lot. He taught me about religion and politics, too. He told me the Holocaust was a hoax, and he believed in the coming war between the races—"

"Lucy!" David sat forward in alarm. He looked at her too long and swerved to get the car back in the lane. "You don't actually believe that shit? People who put that out are really wacko. That's like the KKK and the neo-Nazis and people who want to set up their own government!"

Lucy smoothed her jeans complacently. "Well, I don't know. Henry was very persuasive. My mother said he was dangerous, and maybe he was. He might be out there somewhere making bombs right now. But he loved me."

"The Holocaust really happened, Lucy."

"Okay. If you say so. My mother is German, did I tell you that? My grandparents were in the war. If they killed Jews, I'd know about it, don't you think?"

"I don't know. How well do you know your grandparents?"

At Connor Point, David parked the car under a No Parking sign, between other cars parked in front of other such signs. But doing so made him nervous.

Lucy scoffed. "What are they going to do, tow us? Way out here in never-never land?"

"What if we all get tickets?"

"So you pay it," Lucy said, "or tear it up." That settled it. There was nowhere else to park, anyway.

The rutted road to the point itself, grown over with grass and weeds, was barred by a gate and two signs that said No Trespassing. But Lucy's directions told her to ignore the signs. Sure enough, a hundred yards beyond the gate they saw another sign, hand painted, that said, "If you are going to use this land, please observe the following: No fires. No hunting. No dogs without leashes. No nude bathing. Pick up your trash. Thank you."

“I hope we don’t see any naked swimming,” David said.

When he was fourteen, he and his mother had spent a week at the shore. He took long walks alone every morning. One day, as he climbed through the dunes he saw a naked man walking toward the water, his towel and swimsuit left in a pile on the beach. David lay in the dunes and watched. The man swam, beautifully, with powerful strokes, then walked slowly out of the water, glistening like an actor in a movie. The man looked around, stretched, seemed reluctant to put his clothes back on. David pressed himself into the sand. After the man left, David held himself until he came. What would have happened if he had taken off his own clothes and approached the man? It was a question he’d thought about for years.

Lucy and David strolled through the field toward the lake. David stopped to break off some weed stems with furry tops. At the edge of the lake, Lucy sat on a log on the stony beach while David poked through the underbrush. He might have everything he needed already, but it was better to have more than you needed.

Lucy said, “My mother hates God. I don’t think my father did, though.”

“Why?”

“Why what?”

“Why does she—what does she do that makes you think she hates God?”

“Well for one thing she never goes to church. I know, you don’t either. But she also hates religious art. I told you she lives for art. She loves art way more than she loves me. Anyway, when I came home last summer after freshman year and wanted to put pictures of Jesus up in my room, she had a complete fit. They weren’t all tacky pictures, either, though I had some of those, too, because I knew they’d get her goat. You know, the kind they give you in subway stops. Maybe it was even mostly those. But I also had some that were beautiful. Greek icons. Rembrandt’s portrait of Moses. God and Adam from the Sistine Chapel—you know, reaching out to each other, that’s a famous picture, I’m sure you’ve seen it—and photos of Renaissance sculpture. The Pieta, for God’s sake. You can't have grown up in our house without knowing the difference between shlock and art, you know. I'd have to be a total idiot. Which my mother thinks I am."

David joined her on the beach and showed her what he had. A tiny wisp of green smoke drifted from a puffball.

"Gasteromycetes," said Lucy.

"Apple of mystery. Something a friend used to say. Look at these." He turned over in his hands a group of flat, round, black stones with white lines running through them.

"Granite," said Lucy. "Perfect for skipping." She showed him her own handful. Her next throw bounced over the lake six times. David watched her intently, held a stone against his cheek, then tried to imitate her.

"But why doesn't she like it?" David asked. It was one of the things he liked about Lucy; they each seemed to know what the other was talking about. Most of the time.

"Well, she doesn't like shlock because it's shlock. But why the rest of it, I'm not sure. I think it's because deep down she responds to it. I think deep down she's a religious person, and she's afraid of her feelings. She's more like me than she thinks. I've noticed other parents who don't like their children, who are the same way. It means an incredible amount to my mother to be the perfect judge about art. She's always right. She has to be absolutely cool-headed, no emotion. Completely rational. I don't know why, but I think religious art makes her feel things, and that scares her."

"So what happened?"

"So I put up all this art, and she stayed out of my room."

"What happened to Henry?"

"Oh. He left. He told me all along when he graduated he was going to say goodbye. And he did. He has very firm principles."

In the late afternoon, David returned to the round barn. Since the vandalism he had avoided it, feeling vaguely guilty. What if he had sneaked in and thrown the artifacts every which way? Half the staff probably thought he had. What if he'd gotten drunk and didn't remember? But he didn't drink.

At first it was Dean Allen he'd hoped to see. Now he wanted to know something else. Was it true a man named Hoke Smith had died here? How? If he was haunting the barn, what did he want? Did he own the round barn, was it "his," did his spirit inhabit it the same way that John Barenholz inhabited Apple of Mystery, the birdhouse David built for him years ago? The same way Mr. Marcus lived in the Poetry House? David roamed the barn looking for clues, listening for a message. There was no sign of any vandalism; everything had been replaced, made to appear random as in real life; that was a relief.

What if Hoke Smith died of love? What if David could discover Hoke's story from the air in the round barn, or from inside himself, the same way he heard urgings that told him to choose one weed over another, or what sized twig to use? Would that be making it up, or would it be real? What if he'd been meant to come to Vermont in order to rescue Hoke—maybe build another home for him, even a tiny, symbolic one—so he could rest?

David didn't ask himself why he cared so much about something that might not even be real. He only knew it mattered. The birdhouses mattered and it mattered that they be true. His first birdhouse, his awkward clumsy structure in honor of his first friend, had been an experiment. That was perfect, how John would have wanted it—exploring the properties of pine cones and twigs. Poetry House had been his richest, most complicated construction to date, with the most varied materials and textures. Each of these, and others, had its own flavor and though they might be clumsy or flimsy or even ugly, each one was right in some small way. David knew this was true, because he did not let them go until he captured something right, and he knew when he had.

But something wasn't right in the barn, and he didn't know what it was.

On the bottom floor, David came upon Dean Allen, who seemed to be intensely involved in some kind of project although David couldn't tell what it was. The older man peered at the artifacts, and made notes on a clipboard now and then, and sometimes stared off at nothing.

"Have you seen the ghost lately?" David asked politely.

"The museum is full of ghosts. Life is full of ghosts, competing for attention with the living every minute. Sometimes one wins over the other, sometimes the other wins."

"But the particular ghost who lives here in the round barn?"

"Of course. That is the world I live in." He went on to tell David in extraordinary detail about the dismantling of the barn in its original location and its removal to the museum. When Dean Allen left a few minutes later, David felt, as he had before, both exhilarated and exhausted, as though he needed a nap. The museum would close soon; he still had time to draw for half an hour. He propped himself against the wall on the second floor, in order to sketch the sunburst construction of the beams. Instead, he closed his eyes.

"To whom are you speaking?"

David jerked awake. Had he been dreaming? Dean Allen stood over him. The man never said a plain hello.

"The ghost." He smiled uncomfortably and scrambled to his feet.

"Which ghost? The ghost of pure reason, the ghost of Christmas past, the ghost of an idea? What is it, boy? What have we today, Kant or Dickens, Schopenhauer or Shakespeare, Heidegger or Hamlet? Being and time, or not being, in no time, time that circles back on itself, foretold by witches? What's his name, eh?"

"Hoke Smith. Remember?"

"Ah, Hoke. What does he say?"

"Nothing. I can't even tell if he's there."

"You will. Listen hard. Listen to me, then. I'll tell you a story."

29

Cynthia—

The relation of the whore of Babylon, the boy whose name is David, continues to cling to me, but I have found a certain charm in the experience. He is hungry for something. It reminds me of my younger self. I wonder if anyone besides you has ever known that part of me, the part that longed. It is good that I grew out of it, or I should die.

This boy makes birdhouses. He wants to create. I on the other hand can only imagine fire. A brilliant blaze of glory. Glory is an interesting concept, don't you think? Military glory, heroic glory, glory in the flower? What kind of glory is there for a person like me?

30

Dean Allen had forgotten how to be a gentle lover, but he knew once. His sister taught him. He didn't remember much of it now, but there was a time when his sister's tenderness and his own desperate craving filled him completely.

His sister, whom he hadn't seen in almost thirty years, loved him. He knew this was so. When he was small, she'd carried him around and held him in her lap. He had a black and white photograph of this which he'd brought with him when he left home and had carried in his wallet ever since. He was only two years younger than she and in the picture, almost as big. As soon as he could walk, he scrambled away from her, unless she had something to offer him—a bottle, or a sweet doughnut. She liked to hold him, to feed him his bottle, and sing to him, and when they were both very small, their mother was glad for the help. If he fell and cried, his sister held him and let him suck her fingers; he gazed up at her, all but entranced by that solemn, pleased look in her eyes that made him take special care not to bite her though he wanted to.

From his desk at the museum, Dean could see in the entry Ella Lee Domenico, the receptionist. Today, at lunch, Ella Lee was painting her fingernails. Again. She laid out the tools before her on the desk, carefully—a small jar of fingernail polish of such a dark red it was almost black, a soft rag (a small square of an old red-checked flannel shirt she must have brought from home), and polish remover. She looked around, but if she saw Dean, she did not acknowledge him.

When he was four and she six, his sister liked him to lie on top of her, and he liked it too. She was at once solid and soft, and the combination comforted him. She tickled him and tried to push him off, and he clung to her. She didn't smile. Their struggle took place in silence, dead earnest, with their eyes locked upon each other's faces.

Most of the time they went their separate ways. Two other children came along—a boy and then a girl three years apart—and their mother concerned herself with them. Dean felt sometimes as though they were two families. He and his sister, as he referred to her, were one family, and everyone else—his parents and younger siblings—made up another family.

For several years, until the year Dean turned twelve, his sister seemed involved with other things. He remembered very little from back then. There was the time when he was about ten, when she walked by his room as he was getting dressed, and he called her in.

"Look."

"What."

He stood naked from the waist down. He stroked himself. "Feel how soft it is. Feel."

She slid one finger up and down his flesh.

"Isn't it soft?"

"Yeah."

"Smell." He smelled his own fingers.

"You're nasty," she said. He laughed, knowing she didn't mean it.

Ella Lee unscrewed the cap of the small, clear bottle of polish remover, dabbed it on the cloth, and rubbed vigorously at her thumbnail as if scouring a stubborn spot on a frying pan. She repeated this motion systematically, moving finger to finger.

He remembered several things from the year he was twelve. He believed things changed that year, and yet it was as if they had always been that way. She came into his room to kiss him goodnight. He asked her to scratch his back. She did it just the way he liked, lightly-lightly with the tips of her fingernails, so that it gave him goosebumps.

"Softer. Softer. Ah."

She sat on the edge of his bed, where he slept naked with only the sheet covering him.

"Scratch my arm." He held it out for her. "Ah. Ah." He held out his other arm. She ran her fingers lightly over his skin as he turned his arm this way and that. He turned over onto his back. "Do my front."

She did, drawing her fingers across his smooth, hairless chest in slow circles. The sheet was pushed down to his waist; she slid her hand under the sheet and her fingers brushed his hair. He wondered if she'd known he had hair there. The back of her hand touched him where the uncontrollable part of him pushed up the sheet. He kept his eyes closed, couldn't help the soft sounds he made. She continued her slow, easy circles back up his chest. She did not touch him there again that night.

But he did not have to wait long. A few nights later she came into his room again and scratched his back again, and then his chest. This time she ran her fingers through the curls of the new hair between his legs.

The next time, she touched him there, touched the part of him that once again pushed up the sheet like a tiny man in a tent, touched him purposefully, with the backs of two fingers, then held him for a moment as if curious. When she bent to kiss him on the cheek, he held her to him with both arms. Neither one of them made a sound. After a long moment, she pushed him away.

Having masterfully but matter-of-factly prepared the way, Ella Lee now took a deep breath. She spread the damp cloth on her desk and replaced the top of the polish remover. She drew the small bottle of polish to her, regarded it skeptically, unscrewed its top, and lifted to her nose the tiny brush dripping with thick, near-black liquid. She inhaled slowly and smiled. With her free hand she brushed something from her cheek. She wiped her hand on her skirt, and then rested it on the table before her. Carefully and slowly she brought the small brush upward over her left thumbnail. She started with the center of the nail and then pulled the brush up each side. Stroke, stroke, stroke. Start at the cuticle, rest the brush for a second to allow the polish to fill the curve, then bring the brush slowly toward the tip of the finger. She leaned back and blew, holding her lips steady and shaking her thumb ever so slightly before her.

The Friday in December that he aced the statewide history test, he came into her room in the evening. The curtains were not pulled over her window; the room's lights reflected back at him in the glass. He could hear bare branches clicking in the wind outside. Their parents were downstairs, the other children elsewhere.

"What're you doing?" he asked.

"Homework." She didn't look up.

He draped himself over the back of her chair.

"What do you want?"

"Nothing." He hung over her. He was twelve and she fourteen, he as tall as she. The hair on his arms was still blond, his skin baby-soft, but his forearms were broader than hers. He put his hand next to her hand on the desk. "Look how similar."

Then, almost in slow motion, as if she had been thinking about it for a long time, or perhaps she had never thought of it till that moment, he would never know, she covered his hand with hers, lifted it up, and almost in slow motion guided it down the top of her shirt, unbuttoning the top button to make it easier, and inside her bra. He listened to the sound of her breathing, soft and steady.

They stayed that way, and it was very quiet in the house, and he touched her nipple with his fingertips, circled it, felt the tingling in his own body as a result. Maybe they were meant to be twins. Maybe they were meant to be one.

She removed his hand slowly. "I've got to study," she said.

"You've always got to study."

"You should study, too."

"Oh, fuck off."

Three fingernails down—three shiny, wet, red-black fingernails. She waved them in the air as she might have done as a teenager. Why was it taking her so long? Didn't she have to go to lunch? Dean Allen was hungry, but how could he pass by her desk while she was painting her fingernails?

It was soon after that when, late at night, after their parents were asleep, she slipped into his room. He had been asleep. He woke up to her stroking his skin. He lay on his side, and he awoke to a tingling sensation throughout his body. She touched his hips, his groin. His body responded immediately. He opened his eyes as he rolled onto his back.

"Move over," she whispered. She slid in next to him. He wanted to climb on top of her at once, as he had when they were children, but she held him back. He put his hand on her breast. She guided his hand between her legs.

"You're all wet."

"That's what happens. Lie on top of me. Be quiet." She did not have to show him what to do. He felt as though he had always known. He felt as though he were doing the most natural thing in the world, the thing he was born to do, the thing that was completely right in a way nothing else would ever be.

That was the beginning.

The next morning he waited for her in the kitchen. Their father had left for work and their mother was asleep. Finally his sister sauntered in.

"Aren't you going to school today?" he asked.

She didn't answer, poured orange juice over her cereal. This was her usual routine. He didn't know why she didn't use milk; he had never asked. They did not ordinarily speak to each other in the morning.

"You're going to be late," he said. She waved at him absently, as if waving off a fly, and concentrated on the back of the cereal box.

"Bitch." It was all he could think to say. He grabbed his

schoolbooks and slammed the door. He didn't want to be late. He had more important things to do than talk to her.

She continued to ignore him in the next days as if it had never happened. Dean longed for the experience again—it wasn't the same doing it alone—but he didn't know how to go about it. When his sister came to him again several months later, after a basketball game at school, he was happy. It was a simple feeling—gladness, relief, comfort, as pure a joy as he had ever felt.

Ella Lee finished her left hand and started on the right. This required even greater concentration, but she had warmed up on the left, and that was how she was, orderly and methodical. Warmed up now and ready to tackle a more difficult task. She began with the middle finger of the right hand, at the side of the broad fingernail. Stroke, stroke, stroke. Then her index finger. After each finger, she fanned the air in front of her face and blew with gently pursed lips.

Their times together were not regular but became more frequent. Within a year, it was Dean who went to his sister's room. They did not kiss. He liked it when they rolled around on the floor of his room, liked his power to arouse her. She liked his finger inside her, and he liked her fingers pulling at him harder and harder until he found his way into her. He liked the feeling of going deeper and deeper into her, the feeling of tightness about to burst. They were gentler with each other in sex than they could be at any other time, arguing fiercely the next day over whose turn it was to do the dishes or take out the trash, as if the night before had never happened.

Sometimes they came together every night for a month and then not again for weeks. Dean turned thirteen, fourteen, fifteen. He did not wonder about pregnancy. If it had occurred to him, he would have dismissed the thought: she was the oldest, she would take care of it. He did not wonder whether he loved her. He didn't love or not love her; she was his sister, a part of him, a person he knew as he knew himself, a person he felt in some way that he owned, and who owned him, a person without whom he would be lost.

Ella Lee touched the nail of her thumb with her other thumbnail. Apparently satisfied, she held both hands out in front of her and sighed. She packed up the cloth, tightened the top to the polish, and put everything away in her large, cloth bag. With a quick glance at the clock in the entry, she drew a pack of cigarettes from her drawer and left her desk. She reappeared outside in the parking lot. He watched her light a match and drop it onto the gravel.

When he was fifteen and she seventeen, his sister left home for college. She never came back. California was too far away for her to return for short vacations, and the first summer she stayed and worked in a doughnut shop, setting a pattern that remained in place until she graduated, at which point she fled California for New Zealand with a friend—just that, "a friend." He received several postcards from her over the years, and then nothing. His mother had cried a lot, but he could not comfort her. He felt no one deserved comfort.

31

Lucy agreed to walk up Mt. Philo with David because it was only a walk; Mt. Philo was more of a hill than a mountain, a little bump in the surrounding farmland, and a paved road to the top made it easier for cars and families. It was idiotic to climb a mountain for the fun of it, said Lucy. Exercise should have a point; it made no sense to strain one's body for the sake of strain; physical effort should result in valuable work, not merely in a raised heartbeat and lots of sweat. Such ideas were a natural production of the idle rich.

"Did Henry tell you that?"

"Yes he did and he's right."

David smiled. He admitted that Lucy knew things he didn't—about sex for example—but sometimes, admittedly on rare occasions, he felt himself the older of the two. As if he were the one from New York and she the protected girl from Connecticut.

"Lucy, do you believe in ghosts?"

"Sure. The Holy Ghost was a ghost."

"What if there was a ghost at the museum?"

"Is there?"

"First I have to tell you there is a really weird guy at the museum. His name is Dean Allen."

"My mother's told me about him. I don't know if she's met him, but Charles is a little worried about him."

"Charles?"

"Charles Hopper. My mother's new boyfriend."

David felt as though he'd been kicked in the stomach.

"So? Go on," Lucy urged.

"Wait a minute. Is your mother going out with Charles Hopper?"

"Look, I don't know if it's supposed to be a secret or anything. She barely tells me anything, I have to ferret it out of her. But maybe you shouldn't tell anyone."

"I mean, are they sleeping together? And all that?"

"I guess. Probably. What's 'all that'?"

"But what about your father? I mean, Jeez, your own mother!"

"What's with you? Are you really that much of a prude?"

"Forget it." David scuffed along, scowling, feeling now like a child half Lucy's age. *What's wrong with me,* he thought. *Why am I so emotional? I must have PMS.* He laughed out loud.

"I was telling you about Hoke," he resumed, equanimity restored for now. He did not want to talk about Dean Allen anymore, or Lucy's mother, or Charles Hopper. What did he care about Charles Hopper? He was just a skinny old straight man. Warm and charming, but vacant. Lacking an inner dynamic.

"Who's that?" Lucy demanded.

"The ghost. Dean Allen told me this weird story about Hoke and some woman that might have been Hoke's sister. It was hard to tell. That he killed himself over. Hung himself in the round barn. 'Hanged,' he said; is that right? But it's weird: not that a guy couldn't be in love with his sister—I mean, none of the guys I know ever want to hang out with their sisters, but how would I know, I'm an only child. It's just that it seemed like, I don't know, like he was making it up as he went along."

"Well."

"Do you want to come to the round barn tomorrow and see for yourself?"

"No. I don't want anything to do with the museum."

"Because of your mother."

"That's right. Besides, she wouldn't want me to."

They reached the top, where the small ranger's hut was unmanned. An envelope was tacked to the wall for visitors to leave the entrance fee. Lucy argued against it; who would know? But David put in two dollars for each of them, chiding her for being so cheap. Lucy only shrugged.

At the end of the parking lot they followed a trail down an incline to a lookout, from which they viewed the irregular criss-crossing of farms and roads below, and beyond the farms, the lake and the Adirondack Mountains, bathed in haze.

"If I were God," David said. "I would build a building for each person that exactly expressed their inner dynamic. Each one would be unique. I would be God the Great Architect."

"People would be lonely in their own houses. Why can't they share?"

Share? David surveyed the landscape. He'd never thought of it. Was there something wrong with him? His birdhouses were for individuals, not couples or families. Was that why he was alone? Was that why he had no lover? Was he fundamentally—was he doomed to be forever solitary? But his houses were houses of the spirit! Yes. But now he doubted himself. He scowled at Lucy and could not tell her why he was upset.

32

Dear Cynthia,

They would like me to go away. I make them uncomfortable. That woman is at the head of the phalanx, a fifth column, a wooden horse, a poisoned spear-head. I think she is evil. I am afraid.

She treats me badly. How did this happen? I want what is best for the museum. It's all I've ever wanted since I've been here. Why—

Do not worry about me wherever you are, whatever hell you're in. No one takes advantage of this character for long. I have shined my helmet and polished my armor. Sharpened my sword and readied my steed. I am prepared to do battle with the blackest of Black Knights if need be. I—

33

David tried to interest Lucy in helping him find materials, but she was unimpressed by his delight in grasses, seedpods, and mushrooms. Lucy was interested in people, and especially, right now, in her mother. On Friday, July 2, they walked up to the overlook at Morgan Farms. It was a floating holiday at the museum, and Lucy's mother had been out all night, and still had not come home when Lucy left for the afternoon.

"They'll probably spend the whole day in bed!" Lucy said.

David said nothing, could think of nothing to say besides *Fuck 'em,* which he refrained from saying because such inarticulate utterances did not express the sensitive, judicious person he aspired to be. However, he could think of nothing else at the moment that expressed his feelings properly. Maybe he was a Real Man after all.

"My mother doesn't believe in ghosts," Lucy said. "I asked her. When I told her I knew someone who'd seen one, you know what she said? She said everyone has seen ghosts, that doesn't mean such a thing exists."

David shrugged. He did not think much of Lucy's mother.

"My mother is concocting something about the museum."

"How do you know?"

"She makes all these surreptitious phone calls that she cuts off when I come in. I ask who she's talking to and she waves her hand in the air, *Oh, you know, museum business*. I think she's lobbying about these paintings. She's gotten all excited about whether or not they should be sold. She won't tell me, of course. I overhear her talking with Charles. She stayed out all night the last two nights. With Charles, I assume. My mother hates me. What about your mother? When are you going to come out?"

"I am out—sort of." David felt unaccountably irritable. What a roller coaster it was being with Lucy sometimes. He tried to be reasonable. "My aunt knows. You know. Some teachers know. My best friend from high school knows. Not that there's anything to know. And I'm sure your mother doesn't hate you."

"You don't know thc first thing about it, actually."

"Well if you know so goddamn much about everything, why don't you go fix your life? And stop whining about it."

"Fuck you."

"You wish," he said automatically. Lucy laughed. She took his hand and simultaneously elbowed him gently in the gut. David laughed, grudgingly. "You're a nut," he said.

"Yeah. And you're neurotic. Unlike me. I know exactly who I am. More or less."

"Someday I'll build something huge and magnificent. A massive, stunning city that people will come from other *planets* to see. Just watch me." But David had begun to wonder recently just what he did want to build, after all.

Lucy held his hand until they reached the clearing with the stone bench on top of the hill, from which they could see the lake, sparkling in the sun and dotted with sails, and the dark, jagged Adirondacks, as steadily comforting and they were unremittingly fierce. Mountains and lake, thought David. Soil and water. Everything came in pairs.

"Dean Allen knows all these strange facts about the museum,

important and trivial all mixed up," David said. "He's a walking encyclopedia, if you can follow him. He explains where things come from, and he goes off on these wild riffs on things you've never heard of. He has this amazing energy. He makes me a little nervous—well, not nervous exactly, more like electric, like anything could happen."

"David Michaels, are you attracted to this creep?"

"Don't call him a creep, he's not a creep, he's a major oddball. He's smart and he makes he laugh . . . and I think he likes me."

"Whoa! David's got a crush!"

"No, no. Not a crush."

"Don't be so terrified. It's all right. Just because he's a total loony tune."

"Wait, Lucy. It's not a crush, exactly. It's more like being caught. Captured, sort of."

"Drawn like a moth to fire? No, I know: frozen like a deer about to be shot."

34

Dean Allen had kept his secret life with his sister to himself not because he was ashamed of it—he knew other people wouldn't understand but felt it was their failure, not his—but rather because the memory of it was his alone. His memories belonged to him and no one else; sharing them would have been like sharing a part of himself, which he was not prepared to do. After a point, growing up, he had felt the memory of his experience had not even belonged to his sister. When it became clear that her departure from his life was in fact permanent, he was confirmed, finally, in the knowledge that he was on his own, and what had happened between them was therefore his experience alone. His dream. His life. He would never feel for anyone else, and certainly not for himself, the tenderness he once felt for his sister.

After his sister left, Dean might have sought out certain girls and perhaps earned a reputation as a lover, but he was not interested. He wanted sex, and he relieved himself every day, but he did not want any of the girls he knew. He thought about some of them as he leaned against the bathroom wall or rubbed against the sheets, but when it came to talking with them or *putting the moves on* as the other boys did, he couldn't bring himself to do it. He felt silly, false, young. He felt outraged at having to perform this social dance when what he wanted was to say, "Let's fuck," and lead the girl without fanfare into the bushes.

It wasn't until he was in college that a woman approached him in this way. And he went.

The girl who propositioned him and led him to the shadows outside the big party had to tell him to slow down, slow down. "It's not your first time, is it?"

He kept from bursting into tears by biting her. No biting, she told him. He wanted to hurt her, but he held back. He held on. When finally he exploded inside her, he wanted to die. He rolled off her and lay looking up at the stars, with the grass prickling his butt, and thought there was nothing as pitiful as sex and wasn't life a joke that children were made this way.

The young woman quietly pulled on her pants and left him there without a word. The few times he saw her on campus she ignored him and he was glad. A year later he met Clarisse. She asked him as they sat in the car after dinner in a cheap diner whether he was lonely.

"Sure," he said. "Isn't everyone?" He wanted to lean his head against her breast.

"I don't think I am."

They were married six weeks later by a justice of the peace. Dean sent his family an announcement after the fact. His parents sent him a food processor as a wedding present and said they hoped he would be happy because someone in their family deserved to be. His mother's congratulations card, a drawing of two white wedding bells with silver glitter sprinkled over it, was unsigned, as were all her cards, so he could use it again if he wanted. He threw it away.

Dean Allen and Clarisse operated separately within the same household. Dean wished vaguely for something else, but he didn't know what. He felt consciously lonely only when his wife spoke with her sister on the phone. Her sister in Chicago, the one she called "the good one" in contrast to the difficult one in Iowa, made her laugh. Brought out a warmth in her he didn't hear at any other time. She sat in the darkened living room in the red vinyl chair and talked and laughed easily, soft and low, girls exchanging confidences. Or from the hall he glimpsed her in the brightly lit kitchen, leaning back in a chair talking and laughing in an animated way that reminded him of children playing and made the hollow place in his chest ache.

If he entered the house and heard his wife on the phone anywhere—in the living room, in the kitchen, in her bedroom—he could tell immediately whether she was talking to the good sister. The air was different. The light was different. He knew that her face was shining as it did during the few weeks of their courtship, shining like the inside of the big ceramic bowl on the kitchen table that Clarisse never wanted to put anything in. She liked it empty. He didn't. Its emptiness upset him, it was such a waste. Every time he passed the table, he ran his finger over the bowl's hard, cold surface: at least it would have the residue of his finger grease, his spit, over the years.

He hated not knowing what they talked about, but he knew that if he so much as passed through her room, or lingered in the hallway, while she was on the phone, she would hang up. "Oh. Dean's here. Bye."

Dean did not want to divorce his wife. He never expected to be happy and accepted that this was what marriage was. It was true that other couples seemed to get along better, but did they really? He wondered. He did not trust appearances. He did not trust anyone else he knew well enough to ask. The only person he trusted, oddly enough, was Clarisse. She was his wife. He knew her. He thought he understood her. They had systems. They watched television in the evening together and never argued about what to watch. Whoever turned on the television picked the program. For one of them to ask for a station change would have shocked the other as much as if either proposed eating raw meat. It was the little routines that kept them going.

On Friday morning, Dean awoke from a recurring bad dream about an enormously high skyscraper, ten times higher than any real building, that swayed in the wind in a terrifying, ominous way. He was on the top floor, desperately afraid it would fall over. He awoke and turned to his wife. She murmured in her sleep. He curled around her, slipped his hand under her nightgown to hold her breast. He was only seeking comfort but suddenly found himself intensely aroused. His hand tightened on her breast, his fingers squeezed her nipple. He pressed against her. She tried to push his hand aside. Something akin to rage flowed into him and he rolled on top of her and began kissing and biting her neck. Clarisse made sleepy sounds of protest, soft, indignant whines like an animal, which grew fiercer as she woke up. She pushed at him and turned away from him, but he nudged apart her legs with his own. He found her dry inside, which infuriated him. She fought him and he thrust into her, harder and harder, punishing her and seeking comfort from her body, a comfort he knew was there, deep inside, deeper, deeper, if only he could reach it.

When he finished, panting in silence, she hesitated only a moment, perhaps gathering strength, before shoving him off with a violent grunt. She didn't speak to him. She stood next to the bed, her face flushed, her nightgown draped back into place as if it had never been disturbed, and regarded him from the greatest possible distance between two people. Dean closed his eyes, felt her despising him and didn't care. He heard the bathroom door shut and the shower door open and close and then he wept. He wasn't sorry, he would do it again. He would do it again now. He wept because he hadn't found comfort and he was afraid he never would. He would always live in a mile-high tower tipping dangerously and he would always be terrified, and no one would be able to help him.

That night, Clarisse moved her things into the guest bedroom. She cooked his dinner in silence. After they ate—she had not spoken all day—she said, "You forced me."

"That's ridiculous. You can't force your own wife." He never understood how she could so successfully change things around so that instead of her being wrong, it was he. He was the one after all who needed comfort and couldn't find it.

Clarisse wouldn't argue. But that night she left him and retreated to her own room and her own life. But she would go no further. It would suit her to have a husband, even one who had betrayed her.

"I know you didn't mean it, exactly," she would say the next morning. "But that is almost worse. I won't leave you, you're not the enemy, but you are not my friend, either."

"What am I then?"

"You are a husband. If you don't know what that is, I can't tell you. But I have my limits."

35

It was a pleasant, breezy afternoon, in the high seventies. Frieda Maxwell drove with the rear windows open so as to feel the lovely air without disturbing her hair. Never mind that she had felt deliciously disheveled and wanton only a few hours earlier. Now she was dressed.

She parked in the shady lot behind St. Joseph's and continued her confession.

I come now to what happened this summer.

First, I met a man. This is not the most important thing, and yet I do not think the rest would have happened had I not.

How does one describe that moment when someone you know becomes someone you desire? It is not a moment but a series of moments, perhaps. A dance of looks, laughs, words, suggestion, touch, all taking place within one kind of frame, while the possibility of another shimmers in the background. There is the delicate restraint of figures in a Japanese painting, tightly bound in their proper garments, hauling water, building a fire next to a bridge, before a misty mountain. But within it, or beneath it, lightly painted over perhaps, lies an erotic scene drawn just as carefully but with humor, the wildness in evidence in the oversized erections, the women's naked buttocks. The delicacy of the dance, the lovely mating dance of cranes, is missing in the erotica. I've hung a Hokusai print in the bedroom of the house I've rented here, to remind me of restraint.

What has come to me this summer is not hope, I do not hope, but the possibility of something else, some kind of life again, no, more than that, dare I say it? Redemption, perhaps, because of the paintings. There is the question at the museum of what to do with the paintings, and it interests me. That was enough, at first. And then entered this man.

I am too shy to say his name. It is a silly, stiff name. It appears I am drawn to formal men with stuffy names like Charles. Hopper. Like the painter. American and stark.

In January, when I was invited to join the board of a folk art museum in Vermont, I had no idea what my role would be. The truth is I didn't think much about it. I said I would consider it. I was elected at their February board meeting; the next meeting was in April. By then George had been dead a year.

Charles Hopper runs the museum. Now, I am cultivated, wooed in a sense, by gallery owners nearly every day, and I in turn cultivate them. There is a pleasantly mutual give and take; they teach you and you them. I published a small book about it a few years ago, a handbook for beginning collectors.

Charles Hopper took me out to dinner after the April meeting, let me know he was divorced, and held my hand longer than necessary when he said goodbye. I didn't know what to make of it. I didn't trust him. Still, I left Vermont invigorated.

During the next month, he sent me little notes. Short notes about the museum at first, but quickly more personal.

Dear Frieda, spring has finally come and I am giddy at the thought of it, glad to have survived another winter up here as a tough old bachelor. I look forward to seeing you in June.

Dear Frieda, I took a walk today worrying about this de-accessioning question and remembered our walk on the muddy paths in April. I think of your clearheaded concern and look forward to talking with you more about this.

He called me in late April and then began calling every few days.

"Why do you call me so often?" I asked after the fourth or fifth phone call.

He hesitated only a moment. "Would you prefer me not to?"

"Oh no. I enjoy talking with you very much. But I wonder about your intentions."

"Ah. I am . . . interested in you." He paused. "Is that all right?" There was a tiny note of anxiety in his voice, which charmed me. I invited him to have dinner with me when I came up next.

I made plans to come back to Vermont in May for a meeting of the development committee, to which I had been immediately assigned. I was not interested in fundraising, had already done my part with a large, initial gift, but I did care about what was being called an "alternative fundraising strategy"—selling off some of the museum's fine art. I had not known about the museum's small collection of fine art when I joined. Or perhaps I had known and not paid much attention. During the year after George's death I was not as . . . *precise* as usual.

It is common for a museum to sell its holdings. After all, no museum can afford to continually expand its collection. But this is often a controversial process; committee members and consultants involved in such a decision do not tend to agree on which paintings to sell and which to keep. This is natural; those involved with museums often take a proprietary interest in the museum's art, as if it matters which museum houses a particular work.

In the case of the museum whose board I had newly joined, the issue was intensified by the fact that the museum owned so little fine art. One could sell off several dozen duck decoys, perhaps even several hundred, without most people noticing, but sell a beloved Mary Cassatt, or a Degas? A Monet, Manet, or even a Berthe Morrisot? I understood this perfectly. A painting you love becomes a friend. One does not sell a friend.

Charles Hopper asked me to come a day early, to witness a dramatic event, the arrival of the crowning jewel of the museum's collection.

I was fascinated, eager. What could it be? A Renoir? A small Van Gogh? Perhaps a Degas horse, which would be in keeping with the rural setting. But surely I would have read about such a purchase in the press. I enjoyed the speculation.

He picked me up at my hotel in the morning. I had declined his invitation for breakfast. At the museum, I was surprised to see a sizeable group of people gathered outside a large, round building. Charles smiled at my perplexed expression.

"You'll see." He was boyishly excited, like a child awaiting Christmas.

Guiding me by the elbow, he introduced me to staff and local functionaries. Whatever we had come to see apparently had aroused enormous interest. There were at least two television stations represented, and no doubt several area newspapers. Charles pointed out his public relations director with obvious pride. She was quite lovely; I wondered whether he had slept with her.

And then, with a great deal of commotion and fanfare, not to mention a disastrous wind, a helicopter flew in like a giant bug, dangling a large, cylindrical object and a small, upside-down tree.

Charles practically hopped from foot to foot.

What was it, I asked politely, masking my amusement.

A silo, of course. A silo that was to slide easily inside the round barn. The imagery was not lost upon me. I laughed, and then suddenly my amusement turned to disbelief. This? This was the exciting new acquisition, this flying missile, this ridiculous boy toy?

Disbelief and then, inexplicably, fury. I turned away as the museum's purpose became clear. They would sell off an Impressionist, one of the great works of the century, in order to acquire such . . . silliness as a round barn and its silo—nothing more than phallic, military imagery, a flying bullet. I am not afraid of bullets—my husband was not murdered, he had a heart attack—but I trembled. I am not, in fact, afraid of anything, but I abhor bad art. Military imagery and religion, especially testaments to a sentimental way of life—farming, gardening, living off the earth—made me weak with rage.

I had made a dreadful mistake.

I went to the committee meeting the next day as scheduled, simply to listen, and perhaps I was unsure of my own purposes still. And then Charles took me to dinner, expressly romantic, in a dark, Italian place below street level with low ceilings and expensive wine. And after dinner, in his little sports car, outside my hotel, he kissed me. I kissed him back. He wanted to sleep with me. I said no, I had an early flight the next morning.

Perhaps I hadn't made a mistake after all. Perhaps I could be useful. The truth is I had nothing better to do.

On the short plane ride home, I thought of Lucy. As far as I knew, Lucy had no plans for the summer. Might the two of us spend the summer in Vermont, mother and daughter reestablishing a bond after the death of the husband-father? A ludicrous idea, with a certain pathos and humor. I own a Romare Bearden print of a woman standing at an open door, gazing longingly after a man on the street who appears to have just left: his back is turned to her. He is naked from the waist down, his bare buttocks offering a particularly intimate reproach.

But I find New York in the summer barely tolerable, and I couldn't very well leave my simple-minded daughter to fend for herself. If I went to Vermont, she would have to come with me. I missed George, and I wept the rest of the way home.

When I mentioned to Lucy I was considering spending the summer in Vermont, she said, "Why, Mother? You just got on the board. Are you trying to take over the museum already? It's only been two months. Don't you think that's a little obvious?"

"You'll have to figure out something to do with yourself,

then. You can't stay in New York alone. Find an internship somewhere where they can look after you. Get a job or something. Get a roommate."

Lucy laughed at that, and it came to me that Lucy had secrets, too. Perhaps she even thought of me with the same disdain with which I had thought of my own mother. This made me inexpressibly sad.

When I told Charles Hopper my intention, he offered to find something suitable. He asked me what kind of place I preferred—a condominium by the lake, a rustic little house in the woods a half-hour away, an eighteenth-century cape close to the museum? I chose the latter. A real estate agent sent me photos for my approval and I signed a three-month lease. It was a charming little house with two rooms upstairs for me, and a bedroom downstairs for Lucy, should she want to visit. There was a basement with a washing machine and dryer that I would never use. I have a horror of dark dank places with creepy crawly things in them and I especially hate basements.

At the last minute, Lucy surprised me. She had finished her sophomore year and apparently passed all her courses without running off to a cult.

"Mother, I've decided to come with you."

"Well, Lucy. How lovely."

"Don't you want me to come? You invited me! Jeez, I don't have to."

"Of course I want you to come. Your presence will be a moderating influence."

"What do you mean?"

"I mean, you might keep me from having a wild affair."

"Oh, Mother. Please."

"At any rate, I can keep an eye on your devotions and make sure you don't go overboard."

Lucy looked at me suspiciously; she has no sense of humor. I felt surprisingly cheerful. It is true that there is something about a year of mourning. I would have to tell Lucy in all seriousness that I expected to see a man this summer, but it would wait.

As it turns out, Lucy met a young man herself. I felt an immediate sense of relief to think of someone else offering her some kind of supervision, even a peer, and only secondarily did I feel any anxiety about the man. In any case, when I met him I could see that he was homosexual.

What is the difference between a cigar-store Indian and a life-sized sculpture of Jesus? Why does the one evoke mild pleasure in its primitive craft and the other a profound horror, even revulsion?

When I was little, I went with my mother to church. The Catholic church. The mother who loved me. *Why Frieda, I love you.* The church smelled of pine and plaster and wool most seasons. I liked the whitewashed walls and dark wooden pews and the soft droning voice of the priest. Everything about it was comforting, my mother in her black dress next to me, the singsong cadences of the chants, everything but the terrible man on the cross I tried not to look at. Of course I did look at him, the way one can't tear one's eyes away from a dead animal swarming with maggots.

He fascinated and disturbed me. I thought his wounds bled a little more each week. The holes in his hands and feet were a little fresher, the gash in his side a little darker, and surely those were new drops of blood on his forehead from the thorns that must have forced their way into his skin a little more deeply in the intervening days. Why did his wounds never heal, the way my own scrapes did? Why did he look to heaven that way? He was suffering; why wasn't he angry at being treated thus?

The presence of my mother and her friends—my father was not there, but I do not know where he was, though this was before he left—the comforting presence of the women, the incessant murmur of the priest, the sweet smells, all made up one world that was soft and blurred and safe. The mysterious, terrifying man on the cross made up another.

And then my father disappeared from my life, and my mother was angry. At first I thought Jesus had taken my father away—I knew he had raised the dead and healed the sick—and then I thought my father had become him in some way, that is, that Jesus had absorbed my father. Swallowed him up. I watched him intently every Sunday, looking for a sign. I believed he was looking at me, waiting for me to do something, the right thing, and that he would return my father to me if I only did this one right thing. But I did not know what the right thing was. I stared and stared, waiting. I begged my mother to go early so that I could watch him longer, but she did not like church as much then. I dragged her, unwilling, up to the front where I could see better. I must have embarrassed her; she wanted to sit in the back, but I didn't understand her shame at having been left.

I became more confused. My mother would not take communion at this time. I did not understand this either. I knew she was angry at my father, and I thought she refused communion because she did not want him back. Eating the wafer, eating enough of Jesus, would bring back my father. I hated my mother.

And then we moved to the home of my uncle, and I never saw that church again. My mother became a Lutheran like my uncle. The Lutheran church had a Christ on the cross, but he did not interest me. He was a static object, a statue, nothing more. Not a very good one, at that. I gave up hope. Accustomed now to devoting intense, sustained, visual attention to an object, I turned my focus to the stained glass windows, which at least told stories. It was the beginning of a lifetime of discrimination. The beginning of the development of my critical abilities and my understanding of how feelings interfered.

When I told my mother and my uncle that I wished to go to America, my mother cried and my uncle stormed. "Why America?" he raged. The home of his enemies. No one with a sense of history could like the Americans, who had none and therefore interfered with other people's, as if to steal some for themselves.

I did not cry or argue. I told him I had found something to die for. I would die if I did not go to America.

I did not tell them I had demons inside me. I was determined to escape before the demons won. I needed to remain a virgin if I were going to America; I believed some evil would befall me if I lost my virginity to a German boy behind the school at night, though I was tempted. But I thought sex was not something to die for. The something to die for was not something that made your belly turn over.

This brings me to the first of the three strange things. Last Wednesday I spent the night with Charles Hopper for the first time—that is not the strange thing, but rather an ordinary, unremarkable event that has some poignancy viewed from the outside, perhaps, because I am a widow . . . but for me, playing inside the painting rather than gazing at myself as an element on a canvas, me a vain middle-aged woman who plucks the hairs from her chin and dyes her hair, for me it was fun and silly, and I enjoyed myself thoroughly. I needn't have waited so long. No, the strange thing is this: the morning after I spent the night with Charles Hopper, I bought a painting for Lucy.

I felt witchy. Of course, since coming to Vermont I have had a lot of free time. I've explored galleries in the northern half of the state. There aren't many, by New York standards. I included coffeehouses with shows on the walls, mini-exhibits in the lobbies of banks and the hallways of office complexes. There aren't many of those either. I found several painters I liked: a watercolorist whose work was deceptively simple but strong and fresh, a painter whose semi-abstract oils had animal themes and silly, trendy descriptions, but whose technique and use of color showed an elegant and original gift.

I had bought paintings for Lucy's room before, but never for Lucy herself. I did not know what she liked, other than the religious art I despised. But I thought of her when I saw this painting. Its colors, its mood, something about the composition, spoke to me of Lucy's quirky, dark charm. I had never thought of Lucy this way, that is the extraordinary thing. It was this painting—liking the painting, observing that it was intelligent and original, articulating its personality to myself—every painting has a personality—and then realizing that it somehow reminded me of Lucy—that made me see my daughter in a new light. How is such a thing possible? In the car on the way home I laughed at myself.

I had not bought anything since George died. After my mother died, my buying slowed. My mother never knew anything about art or pretended to. We did not have art in the house when I was very young, I am quite sure, and when we moved to my uncle's house, the walls were bare but for a few heavy, dark prints—Bavarian forests, grim village scenes with church spires. My collecting slowed after my mother's death because I was tired, not because of anything to do with art. George, on the other hand, encouraged me.

I laughed at myself, driving home from the gallery with the painting in the trunk, and then I had second thoughts. Perhaps Lucy would not like the painting after all. She often didn't like presents from me; she felt I was trying to influence her, as of course I was. I believed this to be a mother's duty.

I could just show it to her as if I'd bought it for myself, and then, if she liked it, give it to her. But she was not likely to express joy in any painting I'd bought for myself. Finally I thought I would simply offer it to her, and if she didn't like it, I would sell it. I could sell it in New York for more than I paid for it, I thought. It was a good painting.

It was only later that I realized I'd had an emotional reaction to the painting and had bought it anyway. That is the second strange thing.

I was surprised to find my daughter at home.

"Lucy! What are you doing inside on such a gorgeous summer day?" I didn't mean to be sharp, but I had imagined setting up the painting in her room, privately.

She bristled, started to say something, returned to her book. "I *was* reading." She laid the book beside her, face down.

I hate to see a book bent open that way, it breaks the spine. Over the years I have given Lucy hundreds of bookmarks. She refuses to use them.

"Happy July, Mother. I've hardly seen you."

I took off my hat. It has a broad brim. Removing a hat at the end of a long day, withdrawing the hatpin and shaking out my hair, always makes me feel as though I've slipped for a quiet moment into a nineteenth-century novel. It comforts me.

"I bought you something, Lucy. Would you like to see it?"

She followed me to the car. The painting was in the trunk, wrapped in plastic. We lifted it out together, and Lucy carried it inside. Though she could see colors through the plastic, she said nothing. Inside, she unwrapped it and set it on the couch.

It was a dark watercolor of a woman, abstracted, a woman's shape, inside an oval. The woman looked sculpted rather than painted, elongated, with a swelling at the center where her hips would have been. She was standing, or twirling perhaps, within a seething world of deep reds and blues and purples. Penciled lines encircled her, raced around her, as if she were spinning, or perhaps as if the darkly tumultuous, but beautiful, world were spinning around her. The truth, of course, depends upon where you are standing, within or without a painting.

"Do you like it?"

"I do, actually. I think it's neat. Is it really for me? I mean now, rather than later?"

"It's yours. Do you like the frame?" Suddenly I felt odd. I wanted her to like the painting very much.

"Oh sure, I guess. But the painting is really beautiful."

"The frame is important, too. It adds to the value." I didn't know why I was telling her this. I didn't care about the frame. I was merely nervous and didn't know what to say. To my own daughter. It occurred to me I had never tried to talk to Lucy about art before in a serious fashion, as if she had tastes and opinions of her own. I tried again. "What do you—"

But Lucy had picked up the painting and was carrying it to her room.

"I like the painting, Mom," she said over her shoulder.

I followed her, watched from the doorway as she set the painting on the dresser where it obscured the mirror.

"Is that the best place for it?" I asked.

"I like it there." Lucy turned to me then. "Thanks, Mom. That was really nice. Do you want to go out for dinner?"

But I had plans to meet Charles. I invited Lucy to come along.

"Oh, Charles, Charles. Are you kidding? Thanks but no

thanks. I think he's kind of a flirt, Mother. And a stuffed shirt. No offense."

"I like stuffed shirts." George was something of a stuffed shirt. "They have class."

Lucy rolled her eyes. "I'm going to make dinner here, then. Can I have the car to go to the store?"

"Don't make too much, it will just go to waste."

"No, it won't," Lucy said.

I dressed for dinner. On my way out, I passed Lucy in the kitchen, chopping vegetables. "David's coming over for dinner."

I said I was sorry to miss him, although I wasn't, exactly; it was automatic. "What do you all do together?"

"Mother! I resemble your tone!"

"Lucy, please. Speak English."

"I'm just kidding, Mother. It's a joke. Something kids say. And David is gay, Mother. Homosexual."

"I have many gay friends, Lucy."

"Oh, art people," she said dismissively. Then, in a softer voice, "We talk." She stopped chopping carrots, spoke so softly I could barely hear her. "He likes the way I talk."

I felt stung. "How nice. Have fun, then." I adjusted my hat in the mirror. It was a small, 1940s-style pillbox, black. It gave me courage.

"Will you be back tonight, or tomorrow?"

"Lucy, for heaven's sake."

That was yesterday. Last night, I stood in Charles Hopper's arms while he talked about the museum, and I tried to listen. We had agreed to let alone the question of the paintings for now. He rambled on about vandalism in the round barn, and his concern for the man who takes care of the buildings who was overreacting to it all. His P.R. director was distracted by something, and the board was unruly. "Our very own pity fuck may be going off the deep end—"

"Pity fuck? What is that?"

Charles refilled our wine glasses. "I'm sorry, that's awfully coarse of me. I'd only say it to you, you make me feel honest, and extreme. There's a man we've taken on—you've met him. He's had an odd life but moments of great brilliance. A distant relative of one of the founders. He's made some valuable contributions in the past. Working on something to do with the barn now, some secret scheme. It may even be a good one, it's not impossible. His position is anonymously funded. But—"

I yawned. It was late; I was thinking about Lucy.

"I've talked too much; you encouraged me shamelessly. Tell me about your daughter."

This took me by surprise. I stumbled. *"It does not do to leave a live dragon out of your calculations if you live near him.* I read that in college—Tolkien, the first book I read in English outside school."

He waited.

"Lucy is not really a dragon. More like . . . there is a Monet of the Giverny period. His wife sits on a bench, the gardens are blooming all around, and in the shade at the woman's feet is his daughter. You can look at the painting for several minutes before ever noticing the child in the shade. Why are you looking at me that way? I love my daughter. But we are very different."

"And you wish she were more like you. I used to feel that way about my son."

I could think of nothing to say.

"What I hate most about aging," Charles said then, "is not making babies anymore."

"Why in the world would you want to make babies? My God, you'd be seventy-five when the child was twenty." I knew this was not the point, but did not know what the point was.

"Men and women are impossibly different," I said. "You would make babies while the woman cleans up for twenty years. I too could make babies under those circumstances. A few moments of pleasure, an explosion, presto, a miracle. You remember good sex, while she remembers an ugly bedspread she keeps slipping off." I didn't know what I was saying. I knew I'd had too much to drink.

Charles held me to him. "Sh, sh, sh. It's all right. You're tired."

"My daughter is not really a dragon. She's a—a—"

"A child?"

"A love child." I leaned into him and felt comforted. "You're a flirt. I need to go home."

"Stay with me, Frieda. We'll have a minute of ordinary life, curled up together."

I thought vaguely that I ought to go home for Lucy's sake. Could I leave her three nights in a row? It was odd that I did not feel this protective when Lucy was a child, but then she had governesses, au pairs, mother substitutes, and she had her father. Perhaps I had felt guilty and forgotten it, but I did not think so. I do not think I had felt anything. And now I did.

But I could not leave. "If you want me for my money, it's useless. I've given all I'm going to give."

"Let's pretend neither of us has any money. We're alone on an island. And the dragon is far away."

I liked his smell. I kissed his neck. He touched me. He opened his mouth to mine. I stayed.

part three

36

There is nothing romantic about real grief. It is ugly and exhausting. For six weeks, between the time of her diagnosis in mid-May and the beginning of July, Mary Bailey Daly grieved and raged. She cried until her nose filled up and she couldn't breathe. She cried until her head ached. She cried until her eyes burned from weeping. She got sicker.

In her blue funk, she slept a great deal. She worked in the store almost every day, but not for long. She did not make her special rolls or her sexy sandwiches. She didn't joke with customers. She set out food for lunch, made some ordinary sandwiches, and went home, which all in all was a good thing, thought Jimmy. Despair was not good for business.

It was not only the cancer itself, it was not having known she had it. In the beginning she'd tried to explain.

"But that's how it is with cancer!" Jimmy cried. "No one knows they have it! You can't tell!"

"But I'm a dowser. I put all my eggs in that basket, Jimmy. And I was wrong." She held her husband's hand as they walked a few hundred yards down East Hill Road in mid-June, a rare event even as short as it was.

"So what? So you're wrong, so what? You're going to give up?"

A few nights later, she tried again, as soon as they reached the road.

"Sexy sandwiches are not the answer, Jimmy. Dowsing is not the answer."

"What's the question, Mary? The question is, when are you going to start treatment?" His voice had an edge and she tried to withdraw her hand. He held on more tightly.

"Let go of me!"

He dropped her hand but faced her. "I don't understand what you're doing."

"I know."

They stopped trying to walk.

Now, weeks later, he no longer mentioned treatment. They had argued more than they had ever argued about anything. She was adamant, and he was worn out. Jimmy, too, slept poorly, and felt himself stretched more and more tightly.

He could not speak of his wife's approaching death. He could not say, to himself or anyone else, "My wife is dying." He treated her time left as if it were a period before a long trip, but as he saw her growing thinner and more listless, his anxiety bordered on panic.

It was Friday night, July second, after nine but still somewhat light out. The days had begun their decline toward winter but the difference in the light would not be noticeable for another month. Mary liked to wait until dark to go to sleep, as if she were afraid of missing the daylight—or maybe, missing the transition to night. She and Jimmy sat at their kitchen table in silence, waiting for dark.

"I'm tired. I wonder if I'll fade away like a shadow when the sun goes behind a cloud—just get dimmer and dimmer and then disappear without a trace. What do you think, Jimmy?"

"Mary!" he remembered suddenly. "There's a play in St. Johnsbury. At a church. I got us two tickets."

"A play?" She looked at him blankly. Neither of them had seen a play since high school.

"A girl came in to put a poster in the window and told me about it. What did she call it—a one-woman show."

"What for?"

Jimmy got up, rinsed his coffee mug in the sink. "Why not?" He told her it was tomorrow.

"Is it dress-up?"

He smiled. It was the first joke she had made in weeks.

37

The next afternoon Jimmy left the store in the hands of his new manager, a young woman he'd hired a few weeks earlier, after his part-time help had left. What the future would bring he didn't know, but he couldn't be tied to the store every day, and he couldn't close it. He didn't dare think about money right now. There was no point.

Mary was waiting for him in the red summer dress she wore for weddings and funerals. It hung loosely over her bosom where once it had pulled tightly and ballooned over her belly. But her cheeks had spots of color and her skin had lost its yellowish tinge and turned tan.

"How do I look?"

"Beautiful. The most beautiful woman in the world." He ran his hands over her hair and pulled her to him.

When they entered the vestibule of the church, Mary read the poster. "Is that why you brought me? Because it's a benefit for breast cancer? I don't even have breast cancer."

"I thought you'd like it," he said meekly.

Mary couldn't disguise her interest in everything around her. The sanctuary was full of people, mostly women, many of whom seemed to know each other. Some wore scarves over their bald heads. She led Jimmy boldly down the aisle and squeezed into a pew near the front.

The story was about Eve—that is, Eve's version of what happened in the Garden of Eden. The pulpit area had been cleared of all but a chair, into which the middle-aged actress, having shuffled into the chancel in her bare feet, plopped herself.

She looked like a bag lady. She wore layers of rags, mostly black, and carried paper bags with frayed handles. Settling into the chair, her feet planted wide apart, she said, in a deep, booming voice, "I—love—you."

She paused, scanned the audience. Slowly and deliberately she spoke, as if choosing her words with great care. "Not only because you are beautiful and smart and you bake good bread and do kind deeds." The list went on. Then she leaned forward, dropped her voice conspiratorially, "But also I love you because you are so stupid and stubborn and foolish and petty. You have sometimes cruelty, arrogance, greed. You have made awful mistakes. And you will make more. You get stuck in a rut and you can't get out."

She went on to tell the story of Adam, her wise, annoying husband, and of her one real friend, the snake. Grandmother Snake knew Eve's yearning, her weakness. She told Eve to become very still and listen to the voices of the earth, the creatures, the trees.

Jimmy glanced at his wife. She leaned forward slightly, listening hard.

Eve already knew the loudmouthed, bossy God who yelled, "EVE!" and gave orders. Now she listened, and she heard the voice of God, the many voices of God, in the earth and the trees and the creatures. And now Grandmother Snake told her there was something even more. She could learn to hear the voice of God in her bones. She would need to taste the bittersweetness of the apple, and she would know change, and becoming.

Becoming was what the water did.

When the applause erupted at the end, Mary sat as if frozen, her eyes glued to the woman on stage. When those in front of her stood up, Mary stood, not to clap but because she could no longer see. Suddenly she began to clap wildly.

Jimmy smiled.

"That's it, Jimmy," Mary said animatedly, in the car. "That's what I've always wanted. That's what dowsing is—was. It doesn't matter. That's what I've been looking for, and that's what I'll get from this cancer. What a great way to say it. The still, small voice of God in your bones. The still, small voice of God—who is outside you—inside you, in your bones. Don't you see?"

She took Jimmy's free hand and held it to her chest, wrapping it in both her own. Then she leaned her head against his shoulder.

"Thank you for taking me to a play."

A few moments later she said, "And now I want to talk with you about my death."

38

On Sunday, July 4, Mary awoke with the birds. Never had they sounded so loud, so insistent. Sparrows and wood thrushes and mourning doves. What were they doing? Were they singing or arguing or just doing what birds did because they were birds and it was their nature to make a ruckus at dawn?

Jimmy rolled over against her so she lay under his shelf. She ran a finger along his arm, enjoying the bristly dark hair on his soft skin. In his sleep, his hand slid across her belly and over her hip. How well they fit together. How soft the sheets were, how warm the covers in the cool morning air. One of the best things about summer was sleeping with the windows wide open.

The world embraced her: the chittering house wrens and swallows, the mourning doves calling softly; the bright crisp morning, the soft worn sheets, the old comforter; her big, welcoming husband now turning on his side and wrapping himself around her; the cats racing up and down the stairs and every thump calling, *Still here, still here!* Life was one giant mystery she could not penetrate.

For the past six weeks, she had found it difficult to rouse herself in the morning. When she sensed Jimmy getting up, she had rolled over and gone back to sleep. She was tired and she hurt. One day she had examined her dowsing sticks, wondering whether to burn them or bury them or break them into tiny pieces and throw them into Joe's Pond—but she hadn't had the energy. Who cares, she thought, and left them hanging in the mudroom.

But now. That play! *The voice of God in your bones.*

Jimmy grunted, began his slow ascent into consciousness. He

held her in his sleep. She could tell the moment he awakened, when he stiffened slightly. "How do you feel," he mumbled.

"Fine, Jimmy. I feel fine." This was not strictly speaking true. Her belly hurt, and her back, and she wondered whether the cancer was attacking her bones.

He drew back slightly—was he confused? Alarmed? But she held onto him. "Really," she said. "It's okay. Relax."

She kissed him and snuggled into his arms, and he dropped back to sleep for a few minutes.

She had made a mistake with dowsing. All right. That is, dowsing was right, it had taught her to listen. But she had been wrong to think it was the answer.

"Do you know what's always been my greatest fear, Jimmy?" He murmured his awakeness, with his eyes closed. "That I would find out at the end of my life that I had lived wrong. That I'd go along, living a certain way, and in some flash of deathbed wisdom discover I'd valued the wrong things."

He stroked her back.

"I was right to refuse treatment. I told you last night I wasn't afraid, and I'm not. What I didn't tell you is that I'm curious. I don't want to hurt, and I'll call Dr. Smith this morning; she said she'd help me with the pain. But—I'm going to hear the voice of God in my bones. That's what this is for."

Awake now, Jimmy eyed her quizzically.

"You better get going." She gave him a playful push. "Look what time it is."

After he left, she rolled into his warm spot and stretched. How she loved this run-down old house, with the rotting windowsills and the front porch leaning, and the roof needing replacing. Why they didn't have leaks everywhere she didn't know. The whole inside of the house needed painting, too. She'd always taken it for granted, this ancient house she grew up in. But how fortunate she and Jimmy were to have had it; how lucky that she had this familiar, beloved place to die in.

At the sound of the shower downstairs, Mary threw off the covers. Outside the bathroom, she pulled her nightgown over her head and dropped it on the floor. She paused; she had an idea. She would get it this afternoon, take advantage of a Fourth of July sale.

Jimmy Daly was delighted to see his wife push aside the shower curtain and step into the tub with him. He was surprised, because although she had insisted he take a second shower with her that morning over a month ago, since then he had showered alone, as he had all his life. On the other hand, nothing about her truly surprised him; she was completely unpredictable.

"Let me get under the water." She wrapped her arms around him.

He moved aside and she took the soap from his hand. She began to soap him up briskly, matter-of-factly, beginning with his chest and underarms, moving down his back, turning him around and lathering his privates, where she lingered.

"Hey!"

"Hold still," she commanded.

We should've had kids, he thought absently. *She would've been a good mother.* He didn't know why they hadn't; they'd never had tests. It didn't matter. Only at moments like this, the certainty in her voice, the unspoken enjoyment, the familiar competence in caring for another person, only then did he regret it, for her sake. And maybe, now, for his.

"Now, now," she said. With her slippery hands she stroked him. He turned back to her and held her to him and kissed her neck. The water splashed his face.

"Now do me." She handed him the soap and turned around. He washed her then, from behind. She lifted her face to the spray while he pressed against her. Soaping Mary's round body, he discovered he'd been missing a great pleasure. He slid the soap across her chest, over her breasts. With both hands he circled her breasts, her full belly, inside the folded skin at her waist. His hands slid over her hips and then back over her belly. Holding her to him with one arm, he soaped her gently between her thighs. She opened her legs.

"Not too sexy," she warned. But it was too late. Jimmy stroked her nipple with one finger and caressed her between the legs with the other hand. Soapy water ran off her. She turned to him and he ran his hands over her soft slippery bottom and held her to him with both hands. They kissed. He made as if to kneel in the bathtub.

"Your knees will hurt. Let's go upstairs."

Always a passionate lover, Jimmy felt as excited as an adolescent. He could hardly remember such desire. He knew what mattered. This. Making love to his wife on a cool summer morning after a hot shower. God in heaven knew there was no greater joy. He drew her pleasure out as long as she would let him—he would have buried his face in her forever—and afterward they lay together in silence, and his grief was unspeakable.

Mary arrived at the store a half hour after Jimmy, as she used to, even though this morning he opened the store late. She knew she'd be tired in the afternoon, but she had a task. She measured out the flour, baking powder, soda, and sugar, started the yeast, and mixed the dough for her special rolls. She patted the dough fondly. She had missed them.

When the dough rose, she shaped the rolls—fat and thin, old and young. Small rounded rolls with tiny tips, large full rolls with gumdrop nipples. Flattened, droopy rolls and perky, pointy rolls. She admired each one, for itself and for her own artistry.

What is the voice of God in my bones, she wondered. *What does it say?*

Jimmy had forgotten how much he liked the smell of bread baking. He stepped outside to set out the newspaper rack on the porch and waved to a neighbor passing. If only everything could stay the way it was right now.

By mid-morning, Mary began to fade. She didn't want Jimmy to know. She made an extra effort with customers. *Did you hear the one about the piano player?*

"Hey, Mary, you're looking good."
"All right, Sexy Sandwiches are back."
"Ha, Mary, these aren't half bad, today, huh? I'll take two."
She had wanted to hold out through lunch, the busiest time, but she couldn't. If she were going to drive to town to get her new prescription filled, she had to rest first. During a brief lull, when no one was in the store, she took off her apron.
"I'm sorry, darling. Our morning activity's worn me out," she teased Jimmy.
Jimmy wasn't fooled. Suddenly he looked older and more stooped.
"Don't worry," he said anxiously. "Sarah's coming in at two. It'll be fine. Remember I'm closing early."
He followed her out, opened the truck for her, and as she drove off, she saw him in the rearview mirror watching her.

After sleeping for several hours and then picking up her medicine, Mary bought a bathrobe for Jimmy.
Why a bathrobe? Jimmy wasn't the bathrobe-wearing type. He got up in his shorts, walked to the bathroom, stripped, walked upstairs in a towel, and got dressed. No rigamarole. No lounging around in the morning like a rich person in a magazine ad for coffee. No bathrobes. Nonetheless, she had thought of it this morning and she had done it.
Now it lay in a bag on the seat next to her, a beautiful, blue and green striped bathrobe, the colors of the sea. The warm July air blew through the cab, and Mary drove with her left arm out the window, riding the wind as she used to do as a child.
There was one more thing she had wanted to do today, but it would have to wait. She was a bit worn out. She felt suddenly anxious at the thought of a delay. *It's all right,* she told herself. *East Hill will be here tomorrow. I have the rest of my life for this.* And she smiled at her little joke.

39

Tuesday Bailey had declined to spend July fourth with Sam Desautels and his boisterous family, whom he often joined on holidays. He wanted to see his cousin.

He hadn't spoken to her since the day the silo was moved, back in May—which would not have been unusual under ordinary circumstances. But three weeks had passed since he'd learned from Sam that she had cancer. Three weeks. Where had the time gone? Tuesday had been distracted, more worried than he should have been about the barn and the unexplained vandalism. On the other hand, he had driven past the store a number of times, and past her house, too, and her truck had not been at either place. Where was she? At the hospital? The doctor's? Had she left town? He was going to find her today, one way or another.

For an hour he drove aimlessly around the county. Mid-afternoon he found himself again in front of the store. Mary's truck was not there, but Jimmy's was. Maybe she'd sold it, he thought suddenly. Was that possible, the truck she loved so much? Maybe she'd been inside the store all along.

Tuesday turned off the ignition, but did not leave his truck. The cab became warm quickly, though it was not a hot day but the kind of stunningly cool, cloudless summer day that took your breath away. It was quiet outside, with few cars on the road. A semi roared past, making the ground shake. In the silence afterward, summer sounds floated in—cicadas in the field behind the church across the way, the whirring of the industrial fan from the back of the store, a car door slamming at the garage down the street, a dog barking. A man he didn't know emerged from the store and the screen door slammed. The man drove away. Tuesday knew Mary was not inside. So be it. He would go in anyway.

"Hey, Tuesday." Behind the register, Jimmy was filling out some kind of form.

"Jimmy." Tuesday wandered to the back of the store, returned with a carton of milk, which he set on the counter. "How's Mary?"

Jimmy punched in the price. "Just fine. Doing great."

Tuesday handed him two dollars.

"Lots of life in the old girl yet," Jimmy said. He shut the cash drawer harder than necessary and held out Tuesday's change. Tuesday fingered the candy bars in front of the counter and didn't see him. Jimmy set the change next to the milk.

"Haven't seen you around lately," Jimmy said.

Tuesday didn't know what to say. He glanced around the store. "Store looks good."

"We're doing all right."

Still Tuesday lingered. Jimmy busied himself behind the counter, then seemed to take pity on him. "Look, why don't you come around to the house some time? I know she'd like to see you."

Out on the road, two cars passed. You could hardly see them, the bottom half of the plate-glass window was so filled with posters—local groups advertising car washes and summer bingo, Bible study and a play in St. Johnsbury. The standing rack of paperbacks next to the door hadn't changed since the last time he was here; who ordered them? Did the same distributor who brought those little pencils with vegetable erasers bring the books? He rubbed his chest absently.

"Is she in pain?"

"Yeah, she's in pain. But you know Mary, she don't complain. She went to get her morphine today for the first time." Jimmy put his hands on the counter and gave his full attention to Tuesday. "She's had a bad month. But she's better. Where've you been?"

Tuesday stepped back as if he'd been struck.

"Tell Mary I asked about her. Tell her we've had some trouble at the museum, but I heard she was sick and I've been thinking about her." Tuesday stood in the doorway with his eyes fixed on the road. "Tell her I'll come by soon."

He closed the screen door behind him carefully.

"Bailey! You forgot your milk!"

Either Tuesday didn't hear or he ignored the call.

Jimmy shook his head, replaced the milk in the cooler. He set Tuesday's change back in the drawer, rang up a credit, withdrew two bills and attached a note to them with a paperclip: *T. Bailey.* He slid the folded bills under the edge of the register. Then he phoned home for the third time in an hour to see if Mary had arrived yet, to reassure himself that she was indeed okay.

Tuesday's house sat halfway up a low hill. At the top of a long driveway, the land flattened out. To the right was the old farmhouse, a large, white-clapboard Vermont-style collection of attached buildings, without the barn, which stood alone on the other side of the driveway. No longer used as a working barn, it held Tuesday's tools as well as several generations of junk—in the farthest back, old rusty farming equipment piled together, a sprinkler cart and hoses, a broken rotary tedder, a trailer attachment. Squeezed in front were an old sink, a ladder, aluminum cans of various sizes, pipes and coils of wire, old boards and wire mesh, old windowframes with the glass partially intact, a broken refrigerator, a riding mower, rakes and shovels, two old kitchen chairs.

Tuesday opened wide the barn door, half falling off its hinges, and surveyed his holdings. He would clean out the barn; it was time. He didn't want any of this stuff. He would take all of it to the dump, one truckload at a time. Never mind the cost.

Then he saw, overhead in the rafters where he had stashed it years ago, the gun. His old rifle. He climbed through the junk, onto the forty-year-old tractor he had probably climbed onto back when he first wedged it up there, just before he went to Maine.

He brought it outside. It was a two-seventy he'd bought in Barre with Sam, the year Sam invited him to go to deer camp. Sam had nearly fallen over when he found out Tuesday didn't have a rifle of his own. He must have been the only eighteen-year-old Vermont kid who didn't. Tuesday didn't tell him he didn't want one; it was all he could do to make sure his father's was unloaded every Friday night.

Tuesday had kept to himself in high school, the way a big man can without being bothered—like now, he thought—but Sam had always had lots of friends. Sam and Jimmy Daly and two other buddies had gone to deer camp every year since they were fifteen—

Pop's Camp, they called it, though Sam's father no longer used it. It was a small camp in the woods that slept four on the floor. Sam's father had always maintained that hunting was about roughing it anyway, that it made you more sensitive to animals if you shared their ways. But then Jimmy's father fell off a roof and broke his leg that November and Jimmy had to help out in the store—deer season being especially busy—and Sam had asked Tuesday to make their fourth, for poker, poker and beer being as important as stalking deer. Sam had explained about Jimmy so Tuesday wouldn't feel hurt when he wasn't invited the next year. That was like Sam.

Tuesday sat outside the barn in the July sun with the gun across his thighs. It was how he had sat in the woods that day nearly thirty years ago.

Sam had cheerfully driven him to the gun shop, enjoying his role as the one in the know, since he was a year younger. On the way, just down the street, or maybe next door, they'd passed a pawn shop full of the most amazing collection of stuff Tuesday had ever seen—the contents of ten sheds and ten attics dumped in one place, every which way and full of dust. In the window stood an old desk, a box of books, dishes, a smudged, one-armed doll propped up naked on the desk, milk cans, tools, crates of mixed-up junk, and a hand-painted sign saying More Inside. What caught Tuesday's eye, what made him want to stop and look, was a painted wooden chair. Half covered with a moth-eaten, embroidered cloth, with a stack of dishes on the seat, the only part he could clearly see was a section of the top, where a bright red snake dotted with yellow and green and purple splotches curled around toward the back.

"That's cool," he'd said, but Sam had dragged him along.

In the gun shop, a tall Lincoln look-alike waited behind the counter. He moved slowly and deliberately, like a great blue heron, thought Tuesday. The guy could probably move real quick with a gun if he had to, the way a heron snatched a fish. He spread his long arms over the cases as if they were wings shading a pond, making a cool place for his prey before grabbing it. The man was proud of his guns, but Tuesday only wanted the simplest, easiest rifle to shoot and take care of.

The man was also proud of his trophies that lined the back wall—deer and bear and elk. Tuesday didn't like the heads of dead animals.

"Seems to me when you're dead you'd want all your parts together," he said.

The man only laughed. "I got their butts stuffed on the other side of the wall." He moved slowly and easily, wrapping up the gun Tuesday didn't really want as if he knew the worst things about Tuesday and was just waiting to tell him. Tuesday was glad to get out the door.

"Ever worry you're going to kill someone?" he asked Sam on the way home, in an uncharacteristic burst of friendliness.

Sam didn't. He was real careful, he said. It wasn't what Tuesday meant.

All Tuesday's siblings were older. By the time he was ten, they had all left home, one by one, except his next brother, seven years older, who took him aside one night.

"I'm leaving tomorrow," he said. "One thing you got to do is empty the gun every Friday afternoon when you come home from school. You got to come home from school right away on Friday. Don't forget. That's your job now." He'd done it, too, every day, until he went to Maine. And after all that, his parents had been killed in a boating accident. Life was funny.

He'd told Mary this once—she was the only one. She'd said, "Give it up, Tuesday." And he had. But it didn't make him like guns.

He wasn't too popular as a hunting companion. He was too noisy. *Jeez, you got a heavy tread, man.* But he liked the nights, sitting around playing rummy and blackjack, drinking beer, strategizing as if for a world war, trying to outguess the enemy. Where the deer had been the year before, where they were likely to turn up this year. Who was going to flush them out and who was going to wait to ambush them when they appeared. The deer were like partners in the game, only they didn't ask to play.

Tuesday could walk over the gravel paths in the museum in the dead of night with barely a sound. He felt at home there, as if it were his. *Wild mine.* Not as if he owned it exactly, but because he cared for it, and he had given himself to it . . . But no one owned the woods. He liked to go stomping through them in his own way, scattering squirrels and chipmunks that turned and scolded him furiously. There was enough room here for everyone, enough air for everyone to breathe, enough space to make a commotion without worrying about waking up an old drunk who might do who knew what.

He liked living alone and he liked walking in the woods alone. Which suited his new hunting buddies just fine.

On the last of four mornings, he'd awakened before dawn as usual, freezing in the dark cabin, the fire out in the fireplace. But it was his turn so he dragged himself out of his sleeping bag to start the fire and light the kerosene lamp. The other guys groaned and cursed under their breath as they woke up, the dark hushing their normally loud, blustery voices. Dawn was a humbling time for hunters, full of soft hope.

As prearranged, Tuesday clomped off alone. He felt friendly and waved back at the three scowling after him. When he came to a small meadow, ringed by low spruce, he kicked away the top frosty layer of leaves at the base of a large maple, removed his orange hunter's vest and sat on it. No one was going to shoot him here, and he was more concerned about a freezing, wet ass. He lay his gun across his lap like a good hunter. It was a chilly November morning; he could see his breath, and the woods were quiet, but not silent. There was only a light frost; the sun would be warm, and by mid-morning he would feel downright cheerful. He closed his eyes to listen better.

Tuesday had no intention of shooting anything. He planned simply to enjoy the morning. His life sucked right now—he'd just graduated from high school, he'd been promoted from maintenance to security at the museum an hour away, but it was boring, and the girl he loved was going out with Jimmy Daly. The future looked pathetic. Worst of all, he didn't know what to do about it. But Jimmy Daly wasn't here, and Tuesday had taken his place, and it made him feel hopeful. Once in a blue moon—as Mary used to say—came a gift, an unexpected moment of happiness. *Don't blow it,* she would have said. And he wasn't going to.

He sat and listened to birds call here and there, and a rodent skitter over crunchy leaves. He dozed. And then he heard a shot. A few seconds later, into the meadow in front of him leaped a young buck. A spikehorn, a two-pointer, about eighty or ninety pounds. Steam rose off its back. There was another shot, and the buck fell.

Hidden in the brush, Tuesday Bailey sat stiff and alert as a deer himself. His heart beat crazily, as if it was his own mate just been killed. He gripped the gun. The ridges of the tree pressed into his back.

A man crashed through the woods on his left, into the meadow. He wore an orange vest over his denim jacket and an orange wool cap. He was panting hard. He stood over the buck, then knelt beside him. It was Jimmy Daly, the fuckhead, who was supposed to be minding his father's store.

Slowly, more slowly than he had ever moved in his life, as a seasoned hunter takes care not to frighten its prey, as if he had all the time in the world, Tuesday Bailey raised his gun. All the time in the world. Just Jimmy Daly and he, and the woods, and a dead buck barely thirty feet away. Everything else was still, and waiting. Everything else was knocked quiet by sudden death, death come and gone and death about to be, and Jimmy barely thirty feet away, clear now in the sights of the rifle lying lightly against Tuesday's shoulder. So lightly he could barely feel it. No weight at all in that rifle, it was a part of him now. No tension in the trigger.

It was the air that was heavy and still, pressing the voices of tiny birds back into their throats. The sound had gone out of the day, and the light. There was only Jimmy Daly bending over the dead buck. Everything else was holding its breath.

Tuesday gazed through the sights of his new rife at Jimmy Daly's orange back. He removed the safety. His finger lay lightly on the trigger, the trigger that was an extension of his own finger.

A leaf fell soundlessly in the clearing. A drop of sweat rolled down Tuesday's side. He watched Jimmy Daly through the sights of his gun, and he had no thoughts but one, a mind free of thoughts for once, almost, in this no time, almost but for one: that he could see Jimmy Daly, and Jimmy couldn't see him.

Tuesday stashed the empty gun carefully where he had found it. It was early evening but dusk would not fall for several hours. He no longer wanted to clean the barn; it would wait. He had another idea.

In the barn, the two old kitchen chairs were stacked on top of each other next to the dead refrigerator. Once he had extricated them from the surrounding junk, he carried them over his head out onto the gravel driveway. They were scratched and covered with dust but they weren't broken. He would buy paints and he would paint a chair for Mary.

It was the only thing he could think of, besides killing her husband.

40

After Jimmy left for the store on Monday morning, Mary made phone calls. She arranged for the Fishwives to bring meals for Jimmy once she could no longer cook; after all, she was still on the Life Passages committee. Anne Marie Desautels would do the scheduling. She arranged to have the visiting nurse come once a day after she couldn't get out of bed. She talked to the hospice people. She talked to the woman at the managed care place who knew her condition.

She knew she would have good days and bad days as her strength ebbed. And increasing pain. Already it hurt to sit and hurt to move, although the morphine she'd started yesterday helped a lot. She was thirsty all the time. The cancer was in her bones and her liver and it could go into her lungs. She would probably go in and out of consciousness at the end. And then she would die.

She slept then, and awoke before noon. She wasn't hungry. She thought of the young woman Jimmy had hired to help in the store—what was her name? Sarah?—making sandwiches on the extra rolls Mary had left yesterday. She shook her head: that thin little thing, what did she know about love and life? But she'd need to start somewhere. Lucky girl to make sandwiches on Mary's rolls! Mary smiled to herself.

She called Jimmy to tell him where she was going. She'd never been very good at doing that, and she had to start. He was so worried about her.

Ten minutes later she pulled onto Fletcher's field, the site of the old round barn. The sighs and clicks of the engine, the rhythmic clacketty buzz of cicadas—from within the truck she listened. If any heart was open in Mudville that day, she thought, it was hers. It was hot, and she fell asleep.

41

Tuesday Bailey was waiting on the porch of the general store early the next morning when Mary drove up in her red truck.

"Hey, cousin!" she called cheerfully.

He folded his newspaper and set it on the bench beside him to keep from running to her as she climbed down from the cab. My God, she looked wasted. As she negotiated the two steps to the porch, holding onto the handrail, he leaped toward her.

"Let me go, silly. I'm not ninety, you know."

He dropped her arm. He wanted to swoop her up and carry her off at a run, to somewhere lush and abundant. He wanted to fatten her up.

"What are you doing here at this hour anyway? The store's not open. Why aren't you at work?"

He smiled in spite of himself. It was like when they played school when they were kids, and she was the stern schoolmistress. Now Mary sat on the bench, patted the space next to her, gesturing for him to join her.

"I heard you were sick. How's—"

"It's shit, Tuesday. It's way too fast. I feel like I barely got here."

Jimmy stuck his head out the door, looking worried.

"I'll be in in a minute," she said.

"You having radiation, chemo, all that?"

Mary looked at him sideways. "No, cousin. I am not."

He was silenced by her tone. She seemed to soften.

"You know something? I don't argue anymore. Trust me, it's the right thing."

Tuesday rubbed his palms on his slacks, thinking madly. Mary leaned into his shoulder briefly. "You need to get married, cousin."

Tuesday shook his head.

"I used to think there were lines of power under the house, remember? I told you about it once. They have to do with water, the flow of the sea under the earth. I believe the continents float on the sea. Oh, I know they don't really, the earth is solid, but that's how I imagine it. I feel it that way. Far below us flow energy streams that are related to water. I thought if I could hear them, hear the water, I'd understand something important."

Tuesday nodded.

"But that was silly."

He waited.

"But it doesn't mean I was stupid or empty-headed, you know. I can hear things."

They sat in silence. Tuesday wished—he wished so many things.

"What can I do for you?" he asked finally.

Mary leaned her head back against the window. Above her a neon sign advertised a light beer. "I don't know how the end is going to be, the next few months. It's rushing at me."

Tuesday leaned forward in alarm. The next few months?

"I don't know how much I'll be able to do. I've made some arrangements. What can you do? Take care of Jimmy for me." She added, almost as an afterthought, "He's drinking too much."

Take care of Jimmy?

"Oh, for heaven's sake. Don't look so stricken." She patted his knee. "I'm sorry, Tuesday, I thought you knew. I've always thought you could see inside my head. I thought you were magic, ever since we were little. Look, come and see me in a few days and we'll talk. Come in the afternoon, after I've slept. I sleep a lot," she added apologetically.

The screen door slammed behind her. Mary had never been afraid of loud noises. Tuesday heard Jimmy's earnest, worried voice behind him as he left.

42

The last few days, ever since the play, Mary's wanted to walk again. Before that, after she found out she really did have cancer, it was like she crawled into a ball except to go to the store for a few hours or drive up to East Hill where the round barn used to be. The rest of the time she slept, or thought, maybe.

We don't walk as far, or as fast, but she insists on it. It's like the days before cancer. Sort of. Except sometimes we just make it to the end of the driveway.

"I wish I believed in God," she says tonight. She's had a good day and we're shuffling up the hill. "But I don't. There's got to be something else."

In Vermont in July, at least in the mountains, the temperature can drop into the forties once the sun goes down. When I take her hand, I am surprised at how warm it is.

"What about the voice of God in your bones?"

She waves her hand, as if that is something else entirely. "I remember the first time I found out that fillings didn't last. What a shock! I thought they were permanent. I was probably twenty. Now it seems funny, but then! That was the first time I knew nothing lasts forever."

The days are still so long, full dark settles in about nine-thirty—a beautiful night. The stars have come out, but the moon hasn't risen yet. Where we live, up in the mountains, the woods alongside the road make it pretty damn dark unless there's a moon. We reach the crest of the first hill. Slow, but we're there.

"Let's turn back," I say as I always used to, only this time it's half as far. I used to wonder if Mary would keep walking if I didn't say anything. We drop hands, turn around, and she reaches for my hand again. This pleases me.

"Nothing is forever," she says now. "There is no hole that can ever be completely filled up, no flaw that can be completely fixed. Do you think that's sad?"

"I guess not, because then you'd be perfect," I try to tease her but it falls a little flat.

"Do you ever mind that I'm not a better gardener?"

"I don't care about the garden."

"Or a better cook? Do you wish I did the laundry more often? Or changed the oil in the truck more often?"

"I like to change the oil."

"Do you think when I get to the end of my life, I'll discover I lived wrong?"

"No."

I squeeze her hand, but shit, Mary, what do I know?

Mary has always liked being out of doors. At certain times of the year, like in spring before the blackflies come out, or late fall when the mosquitoes are too sluggish to bite, or in the winter—she loves the winter—she likes to walk where the snow is not too deep and listen to the silence. She'll come back from a walk on a Sunday, all rosy-cheeked like a child, and I'll say how was it, and she always says, "It's so quiet."

Sometimes she'll tell me she's seen a fox, or a fisher, or a deer, or heard a couple of raccoons fighting when they should have been asleep. One Sunday just last winter, she came in all snowy, stomped the snow off her boots in the mudroom, hung up her coat—I was in the kitchen doing the supper dishes—and she didn't say anything. Usually she's full of little talk.

"Have a nice time?"

She came and hugged me from behind. "I'm a silly woman." I felt her cold cheek through my shirt. I turned off the water and stood there with her holding onto me. She said, "I thought I heard the water under the earth. I really did." I turned around then; she let go of me, and turned away, as if what she had to say was too private to say to my face. She ran cold water over her hands, then hot.

"I was walking along the brook, listening. It was perfectly still. I could hear my own footsteps. The brook is frozen over, covered with snow. You know how it looks, like a white, rolling road full of soft bumps. Then all of a sudden I heard this sound, sort of muffled, and I thought for a moment that was it." She dried her hands. "I thought I might burst." She turned on the faucet with one hand, watched it run, then turned it off.

"Of course it was only the brook, where the ice had broken through and the snow fallen in. A dip in the streambed where the water fell about a foot, a little tiny waterfall in the middle of winter. Silly me."

She seemed like she'd just lost her best friend and was trying to be matter of fact about it.

"What about the lines of power?" I ask her now. We're almost home. We stop to rest at the foot of the driveway that curves up toward our house, where the light is spilling out of the kitchen windows.

"I've been thinking that ascites sounds like a Greek hero," she says. "Remember that TV show about myths? Ascites would be the guy who crosses the water to bring back the golden fleece or something."

We start up the driveway. "Mary," I say. "Remember the first time we went skinny dipping in Joe's Pond?"

"You were after me, trying to get your little weenie in me."

"You nearly drowned me." I remember it like it was yesterday, how she wrapped her legs around me. She teased me like crazy. It was our first time. "It was your idea," I remind her.

When we get into bed later, I get in first and she scrambles in and climbs on top of me because the sheets are cold and she's sleeping naked, ever since the day after the play. That was when she started taking a shower with me every day. The day she started taking morphine and stopped hurting so much. She took off her nightgown Sunday morning and hasn't had it on since. I've always slept without a shirt—I sleep hot, and I don't like all that material getting twisted up, makes sleeping too complicated. But Mary—she liked a soft nightgown. But now, she lies on top of me to escape from the cold, and she's so soft and warm, it's my favorite part of the day.

"I should have been sleeping naked all my life," she says now. She slides around to get off her belly. "All those nights I could have felt your skin next to me."

I tell her I love her, but she's already asleep, that's how exhausted she is. And I'm glad she's fallen asleep so she can't see me.

There are times when the universe asks of you more than you can give, and you give it anyway because you have no choice. You aren't asked if you want your fillings to fall out, or a life without children, or maggots to eat your carcass. You aren't asked if you want your wife to get sick.

I don't understand what Mary is trying to learn from the universe, as she puts it, what it is she is trying to hear, some mysterious message that matters more than anything else. I don't understand it, but she was cold, and I held her and tried to warm her up.

43

Shortly after three the next morning, Tuesday Bailey got a call. A security guard making his rounds had discovered more chaos in the round barn. The police were on their way.

"Thought you'd want to know."

Tuesday barked instructions as he buttoned his pants. He was out the door in minutes. Furious, he drove dangerously fast over the back roads. More vandalism? How could it be? What was wrong with the alarm system? Someone had to be tampering with it. It had to be someone on the staff. It couldn't be *his* staff, he'd vouch for them all. It had to be someone else. That kid, David, who had access to Didi's keys, and weren't kids these days capable of any technological feat? But that wasn't likely. More likely that crazy Dean Allen.

It enraged him. Why would anyone break things for no reason?

He himself wanted to break things sometimes, but he always had a reason. What did Allen have against the museum? If it was Allen. If not, who?

The more he thought about it, the angrier he became. He envisioned a shadowy man creeping about, a man who didn't belong there, who had broken in one way or another, with a key or without, through a locked door or a door left open, who found himself delighted to be inside a beautiful, solid structure that he was not allowed to be in, in that time, in that way. A man full of evil, a dark force gleefully gobbling up the light, salivating at his power to destroy.

But that was a cartoon. A real invader would work slowly and methodically, grim, not joyful, with spasms of rage, not glee, desperate but with underlying purpose, wrecking first this, then that. It didn't even matter what—Tuesday couldn't see that far. It was the idea of an alien invader breaking through the safety system in the first place. He pounded the steering wheel. The tires squealed on the curves.

He roared into the visitors' parking lot close to the barn, deserted but for the empty police cruiser with its motor running and its lights still flashing—why did they do that, it was such an intrusion—and Charles Hopper's little sportscar. The night guards would have parked in the staff lot.

The main door to the barn was open. The police chief was shaking hands with Charles, the police photographer already on his way out. The hapless security guard stood to the side. They greeted Tuesday. Charles looked old and tired; the guard looked dejected and glanced at his watch as if anxious to go home.

"It's all over, Bailey," joked the chief. Tuesday didn't smile.

After the two officers left, Charles led the way down the stairs to the dairy floor. "Same thing," he said wearily. "No sign of forced entry. The alarms are functioning but never went off—or were turned off and then on again, I suppose we have to consider every possibility. Artifacts thrown from the wall, turned over, minor upsets. Nothing seriously damaged. Nothing is smashed or shattered. It's more like someone got pissed and threw things. Like before."

Now Tuesday saw for himself. On the floor were strewn pieces from one of the hanging exhibits: maple sugar molds and trays. The tapping gouge and troughs lay on their sides. Scattered across the room were the wooden carrying yokes, the strainer and scoop used in sugaring. The sample wedge of a maple tree lay across the room as if someone had heaved it against the wall in a rage.

But Charles was right. The brace and drill bit weren't broken. A kettle was dented. A pruning hook was jammed hard into the side of the silo, but nothing was actually broken.

"What is going on?" he asked, more bewildered than angry.

"We've got a problem," Charles acknowledged, rubbed the back of his neck. "We'll close the floor for the morning, get the curators in first thing to do an inventory and a formal assessment—and then set things back up. Meanwhile, let's have a meeting as soon as everyone gets here—senior staff—and figure out what to do. Which may be nothing." He led the way back upstairs.

"Wha—?"

"Listen, Tuesday," Charles put his hand on Tuesday's arm, which Tuesday disliked. "Sometimes it's best to wait. And don't go judging someone without cause. We have no evidence, no suspects. You got that?"

Tuesday pulled himself up. He was taller than Charles.

"You'd be surprised how people reveal themselves," Charles said mildly, with a wave of his hand toward the museum grounds.

They stood outside the barn, in the oblong shaft of light that fell onto the ramp. It was a clear, moonless night, full of stars. "See you in the morning," Charles said, then amended ruefully, "in a few hours." With another wave he headed for his car.

Tuesday sent the guard to finish his rounds, locked the barn door from the inside, and returned to the second floor. Slowly, painstakingly, he examined the walls, windows, doors, every object without touching it. He did not expect to turn up any clue, but he could think of nothing else to do. He was relieved that nothing was destroyed, but only slightly. The fact was, someone had broken in. He couldn't let it go.

An hour later he left the barn. It was nearly six, the sky beginning to lighten. A gray film of dew covered the grassy lawns between the buildings. He kept to the paths; the gravel crunched quietly under his feet. Shadows lurked behind every lilac bush and in the entryway to every building.

The senior staff meeting was a briefing, not a time for discussion. Afterward, Tuesday caught up with Didi. "What are you going to do?" he asked.

"I'm not going to do anything. You heard what Charles said. The police filed their report, there are no suspects, no one to press charges against."

"We should send out a press release or something. Try to flush them out."

"This isn't a police movie, it's real life!" Didi considered him seriously. "I know you're upset, but I don't think we're being dishonest in not saying anything. The truth is, we have no story to tell."

"But we should let people know what a big deal it is."

"Tuesday, it's not that significant. A few artifacts knocked off a wall. I'm afraid the papers will make too big a deal out of it already. They pick it up from the police dispatch. The Free Press already called and so did the AP. It's too much!"

"It's never happened before. Before this summer. It's an unbelievable violation."

"A violation?" Didi shrugged. "It's a violation to have reporters swarming all over you making a mountain out of a—it's not even a molehill."

Tuesday got no further with Charles Hopper, whom he found in his office.

"I'm concerned about the vandalism."

"Of course. So am I."

"I'm going to put in for a new security system to replace the old one."

"Well, all right, but before you do that, Tuesday, I'd like to see an analysis of the old one, its strengths and weaknesses. It's worked fine until now and it may still work fine, if it turns out this was a little inside prank, which I suspect it was."

"Allen's lost his nut, but he wouldn't hurt the barn."

"I agree with you. I'll be speaking with every member of the staff." Charles stood up. It was Tuesday's cue to go. He felt hot with frustration.

"And meanwhile?"

"Meanwhile, do your job, keeping the museum safe and in tip top shape for our visitors. This too will pass." Charles spoke mildly, but massaged the back of his neck with one hand.

Tuesday trudged scowling through the museum grounds. The wind was picking up, clouds rolling in. Good. It should be thundering and lightning, or at least raining. Was he overreacting? No! But he could not explain his grief.

He passed Dean Allen sitting on a bench. The museum would open in a few minutes, but Allen might sit there all day, as much a fixture as the cigar store Indian in front of the general store nearby.

"It wasn't me," Dean said.

Tuesday stopped a few feet away. "I know."

"They'd like to blame me. They'd like to have a reason to get rid of me. They think I'm useless. I am useless in fact if no one listens. A fish without its tail, a barn without its silo, a hangman without his rope, a boy without his, without his . . ."

Tuesday waited. The weeping willows lining the pond across the way draped their leaves in the water.

"It was the ghost that did it. He's unhappy. He wants to go

back—to Eustis, to the garden, to where it's bright and open. To life before the fall, before his lover slipped and fell into the foamy brine. No one believes me, of course. Except that boy, who laps at my heels, poor thing. My David. Michelangelo had his David, Donatello had his, and I have mine, a poor imitation but he'll do. Sweet, besides."

"Not yours," Tuesday said abruptly and strode off.

"No," came the faint agreement. Tuesday imagined him smiling his loopy, unpredictable smile at no one.

44

Dear Cynthia,

The women are in cahoots. My only consolation is that boy. He actually told me in his shy way that I was charming. I've taken him on as a sort of informal assistant in the afternoons, for my latest project in the round barn. It is a secret. He follows me around, my sweet little shadow, and listens to me and laughs at my jokes. He arouses in me a desire . . . to live. Is that a funny thing to say? We are David and Goliath, only I am a gentle giant, a Big Friendly Giant, a servant of God. And I am Saul. The nemesis and the beloved. He is—

He wants so badly to create. I see myself in him. After a while you learn that some are meant to create and some to destroy. I am one of the latter. I do not mean to destroy the boy.

What is goodness and what evil?

In sickness and in health.

45

Maude had been gone nearly five weeks. Didi found the last poem on Friday morning, attached to the last page of her calendar.

dear sensuous universe / thighs open / to the moon

What was Maude saying? Thighs open to the moon? Did she have any idea? Didi thrust the poem into a desk drawer with the others and shoved it shut as if the little poems could escape and do wild, forbidden things.

Maude was thriving, Maude was ecstatic, Maude called last weekend in a heat about the work.

"The celebration of femaleness is not just about giving," Maude had said on the phone. "It's about a fullness of being." She described how she was connecting great swatches of purple and red and blue satin, and darkly patterned cottons, and ropes of different thickness, and transparent gauzy materials, and photographs covered with cheesecloth soaked in a thin solution of glue. "The piece is rough and harsh on the one hand, with the rope and the torn places and the way it hangs, and it's full of soft light and silky textures on the other. It's three pieces together now. They're called 'Woman Interrupted,' 'In Flagrante Delicto,' and 'Home.'"

Didi had been silent.

"Didi? Do you think it sounds good? I need you to think I can do it!"

"Of course, darling. It's just that I miss you."

"Oh, I know, it's way too long, and we won't do this again. But you're still glad I'm here, aren't you? It means so much to me."

"I'm a painter, really," Maude had said, soon after they first met. "Who are you?"

"I'm a poet," Didi answered, because she had aspirations.

"The painter and the poet," Maude said. And that became who they were. But it wasn't true. The poetry she wrote when she met Maude was awful. Calling herself a poet was like someone who stove in a man's skull with a meat cleaver calling himself a brain surgeon. And that was her best image of the year.

Didi met Adrian that afternoon for a late lunch in Montpelier, in the restaurant-bar of the local hotel, a cool, dark place with unobtrusive waiters and booths that were nearly empty at this time of day. She felt as though she were someone else.

They spoke of the barn and of her nephew's theory that the vandalism was caused by a ghost. And how would she tell *that* story, committed as she was to the truth?

Adrian laughed, as if she weren't serious—as if she were flirting. And who knew? Maybe she was. It crossed her mind that Maude would know whether she were teasing or not. But maybe that was how it was with men and women. Around the perimeter of the room, just below the ceiling, ran a model train. The glare from the sun behind Adrian's head made it hard for her to see his face clearly. *Tell all the truth but tell it slant.*

Adrian was saying how happy she made him. "You're the best thing that's happened to me in years. It's not every day you make a new friend, or when you can connect on so many different levels."

Intellectual? Emotional? Sexual? Neither one broke the gaze between them. Didi thought they would kiss had they not been in a restaurant in the middle of the day. She reached across the table and he intertwined his fingers with hers. He caressed her palm with his thumb.

"I had to run a story. You understand, don't you?"

Didi withdrew her hand. "Of course. I appreciated how low-key it was." She'd seen it first thing this morning. "What is it?" she asked now. He was looking at her so intensely. He didn't answer.

"Do you ever wonder about what's important?" she asked, sitting back in the booth, her arms folded across her chest.

"No. I've got that figured out." He smiled. How could a man's arrogance be so charming? Was it the hint of self-deprecation in his tone? The twinkle in his eye? Maude would be so surprised at her! He ticked them off—his work, his family, friends. Her, of course. "Not in that order."

"I mean ethical questions. Moral dilemmas. Truth versus fantasy, that kind of thing."

"Ah. Like when someone—an important source, say—tells you in confidence, off the record, that he's going to commit a crime. Like that?"

"Sure, for starters." Finally the waiter brought their meals, offered Didi fresh pepper on her spinach salad.

"It depends, of course."

"On what?" Didi poked at her salad. She was too keyed up to be hungry.

"On what you stand to gain or lose in either case."

"Purely utilitarian."

"More or less."

Adrian dug into his pasta with gusto. She watched him eat.

"Do you ever wonder what's . . . real? Like—" she hesitated, changed her mind. "Like the desire to play music versus the need to make a living. Conflicting desires."

"Oh, that." Adrian shrugged. "I'm an honorable guy. I've got a family to support, so I go to work every day. You can always screw around on the side." He grinned at her. "We're talking about music here, right?"

Oh, dear. Didi looked at her plate. What was she doing here anyway? How could she have thought this guy was a friend? Shit.

"I'm sorry, Didi. I shouldn't tease you. I forget how serious you are. Do you want to go?" She nodded. He signaled the waiter. He would pay; they took turns. She excused herself.

Upon her return, she found him standing beside the booth, waiting.

"I love you," he said.

Now? Right here in the middle of the restaurant? What a nut.

He followed her out. But in the small entry, away from public view, she turned back to him and embraced him quickly. His lips brushed her ear. She leaned her head a moment on his chest. He kissed her hair.

"Come on, pal," he said. He took her hand for a moment, but dropped it as they stepped outside. He walked her to her car, recounting an anecdote from his band that made her laugh. She did not want to talk, herself, only to listen to his voice and feel him next to her. What was it? His smell, registering below her awareness, some animal scent?

"Didi, forgive me."

"For what?"

"It's just the natural push-pull of two people in our situation.

It's not easy to figure out. But we're being good. We can do it. We can be close, without—hurting anyone else. Please don't go away."

What was it about men? So full of themselves sometimes, and so open and revealing at others? She slid her arms around his neck. "It's all right," she whispered.

He held her tightly, made a soft sound at the touch of her body pressed the length of his. They held each other.

She released him first. He kissed her lightly, his soft butterfly kiss. She kissed him a second time, harder.

Driving home full of heat, she wondered at herself. She needed to do this. She shouldn't, but she needed to see it through, she didn't know why. So it was all right. She wasn't doing anything wrong. She loved him. She loved Maude, too—much more. But Maude wasn't here, Maude was doing her art. Maude didn't need her. She depended on Maude too much.

Oh, fuck it.

46

Tuesday Bailey could count on one hand the number of times he'd been inside Mary's house as an adult. There were times when, as a child, he'd played here weekly, if not every day. Playing pirates in his aunt and uncle's room, jumping on their bed, sneaking up to the attic, hiding in their closets. Playing outside, hiding under the front porch and eavesdropping on the grown-ups, or once on her older brothers as they told stories about girls. Tuesday's ears had burned, and he dragged Mary out the side to make a run for it before her brothers could catch them.

Those same brothers had stuck her up in the apple tree—his first memory of her. He'd come across her singing and swinging her legs way up in the blossoms, sweet little white flowers humming with bees. There she sat in her bright red overalls, the only ones not hand-me-downs from her brothers, she'd told him later, hence her favorite. What was she doing up there? Just singing and swinging her legs—but obviously unable to come down on her own.

"What are you waiting for?" he'd called up.

"For you to come and help me down." She was four and he six.

What's a cousin? Part of the scenery like anyone else. She lived just down the road but so what, he remembered her older brothers better than he did her, until then. There was something about the way she sat in the tree, so patient and confident of rescue, knowing what she could and couldn't do, and unafraid. Unable to get down on her own, but happy to wait. Enjoying herself. Singing away in her clear little voice, sure help would come. Always sure everything would come out all right in the end.

It was Saturday. Tuesday felt an almost desperate, if inexplicable need to talk to Mary about the vandalism in the round barn last Wednesday night. He took a chance and drove straight to her house. It was nine in the morning. Her truck was in the driveway, but what was Jimmy's truck doing there, next to hers?

Tuesday knocked tentatively, then loudly, on the mudroom door. Jimmy opened it.

"Hey, Tuesday." He didn't seem surprised. "Mary's sleeping. She had a bad night." He hesitated. "Want to come in?"

"No, thanks. I didn't come for a visit, anyway. I came by to see if you folks needed anything."

"No, thanks. Nothing you can give us." He smiled awkwardly, to show he meant no offense.

"All right, then." Tuesday hesitated, as if he had something more to say. Jimmy waited in the doorway. Whatever it was, Tuesday appeared to think better of it, and left without a word.

Back home, he pulled out the four jars of paint he had bought on Monday. He'd tried the paint store first but the girl behind the counter directed him to an art supply store. Tuesday had supervised dozens of painting projects at the museum over the years, but he had never tried to buy paint in two-ounce jars.

He set the two chairs once more in the driveway. They needed washing and sanding; he brought a pot full of soapy water from the kitchen and an old sponge. Forget his usual Saturday morning errands, he needed a distraction, something else to think about. Was it only two days ago? It felt like weeks. He probably should have gone in today just to hang around and watch; yesterday he hadn't been able to devote his full attention to it but instead had to deal with scheduling problems, a new hire, meetings about the replacement plumbing in the cafeteria, the upcoming budget review. Protect and guard the museum, hah! A fine job he was doing.

Tuesday washed the chairs carefully. The morning sun felt good on his back. Anyone glancing up from the road would have seen a burly, middle-aged man in jeans and a white T-shirt and imagined a happy, domestic life—a family chore perhaps, a father making a present for a young daughter. *Wild mind,* thought Tuesday. What Liza used to say—Liza, his only real girlfriend, besides Mary of course, who was never his girlfriend.

He sanded both chairs, first with coarse-grained paper, then with fine-grained.

The closest he'd ever come to making Mary his girlfriend was on the day of his grandfather's funeral, a happy day, except for Tuesday's colossal failure.

Mary and Tuesday, teenagers at the time, were not sorry to see Old Fuck Bailey go. At the funeral, when the minister had spoken of Grandpa Bailey dancing in God's mansion in the sky, Mary, sitting two rows in front, had glanced back at him and made a face and he'd laughed out loud. Afterward, they walked down the road together, something they hadn't done in a while. Tuesday had graduated from high school; Mary was about to be a senior. She'd been going out with Jimmy Daly the year before and then had abruptly stopped. Something about their grandfather's death—the old guy was a jerk, but it made you think about life being short—and the fact that Mary wasn't seeing Jimmy anymore, must have made him a little crazy.

"Remember that song you used to sing about Harry Houdini? You still want to marry him?"

Mary had laughed, elbowed him in the side.

"You could marry me instead." He hadn't planned to say it, it just slipped out. *Marry me instead.*

Mary looked up the road. "We're friends, you and me."

Tuesday had nothing to say to that beyond the obvious. She knew he wanted to be more than friends, he'd just told her so.

"You can't give me what I want, Tuesday."

"What do you want, Mary? I'll give you anything!"

Mary frowned. "It's not a thing, it's different. I don't know what it is yet. You—you're like a part of me. I can't marry you. I don't know if I can marry anybody."

"Sounds like an old movie."

She laughed, smiled at him quickly, a burst of warmth. If it had been an old movie, he would have taken her in his arms, but he didn't.

You've got to! he thought desperately.

"I want bluebirds of happiness flying around my head."

That's what he would put on the chair. Bluebirds of happiness. Bluebirds of happiness for Mary. What did they look like? He'd make them up. But first he laid on a base coat of red—red, the color of life. He painted with long, even strokes that calmed him. The paint dried quickly.

When he went to Maine that fall, he didn't tell her he was going. How could he? Ten years he'd stayed away, without a visit home. When he came back, only because his parents were killed in that boating accident, Mary was married to Jimmy, and living with him in the house she'd lived in all her life, just up the road. The house Tuesday had played in, the house whose front steps he and Mary had sat on, talking endlessly, for hours, years. Jimmy Daly! What did she see in him? What did he give her that was different? What a joke. Jimmy Daly had crows and ravens nestling in his hair.

He couldn't think she might have married him if he'd stayed around.

He finished painting the first chair red. Maybe he'd paint the second one blue, for Liza. He hadn't thought of her for a while. But then, what could he do with it? It would be an artifact, dead, and he was already an artifact himself, stuck in one position all his life. No, he'd paint both chairs for Mary. Mary and Jimmy. At least they'd be useful.

He'd paint bluebirds of happiness across the top of one, and wild whistling blackbirds across the other, from that poem. And the river, *Flow gently sweet Afton,* down one side.

He'd paint white flowering apple trees along the sides of the other.

Careful what you wish for, Mary used to say, when they were young and talked a lot. She always seemed to know what she wanted. But he didn't know. He'd left Liza and her wonderful crazy farm with the chickens and blueberries and slugs and the little cabin where their lovemaking never grew stale, and he didn't go back. He moved into his dead parents' house, and it was as if he'd never left. He got his old job back at the museum. Five years later he was head of security, then assistant director of buildings and grounds, and then director.

He'd missed Liza in the beginning, but the first year after his parents' deaths passed quickly, and then he'd fallen into a new routine. And there was Mary. He didn't see her much, though he dreamed of stealing her away from Jimmy at first. He took up with various women for short periods, but he'd spend Saturday night with them, and leave them on Sunday to stop at the store to have a cup of coffee with Mary behind the counter. If he didn't find her laughing with someone, he found her singing.

Tuesday turned over the second chair to paint its underside. Those were hard years. He used to sit in his darkened kitchen by the big picture window and watch for her truck—listening to the crickets in the summer with the windows open, hearing the sounds of the house in the winter, the emptiness, the silence. Listening always for the rumble of a truck on the road, her truck, a particular rumbling clatter, always going too fast, bumping over the hill. Watching to see whether she'd glance in his direction. She never did. It was not her way to wave at ghosts or to give a dark, empty house a second thought.

He stared at the road the way other people watched TV, sipping a beer. He had his own show, endless reruns of old memories—Mary leaning into him on her porch when they sat shoulder to shoulder talking about nothing, Mary driving her new truck all over the Northeast Kingdom flushed with excitement, Mary consoling him after Harrietty died, and assuring him she'd come help. Most of his images were happy; he'd rarely seen her angry. Well, there was the time he'd let go of the seesaw so her end dropped hard, when she wouldn't speak to him for a week.

He would paint a seesaw on the chair. And he would paint his name, misspelled. That was the other time she'd been angry with him. He was perhaps in fourth grade, she in third. She'd come stomping up to him one morning, in the back of the schoolroom they shared, waving a note she'd found in her desk, shaking it in his face. "Did you write this?

Dear Mary, I love you. I want to mary you. Teusday Bailey, read the note.

He felt himself turning red. "You think I'm crazy? I can spell my own name!"

"Well, who did?"

"How do I know?"

She crumpled it into a wad and marched off. Some boys hanging around in the back with him mimicked her. *Did you write this? You better not've!* They pummeled and bumped each other. Across the room with kids her own age, Mary ignored them.

On the way home, she sat next to him on the bus as usual. "You didn't see what Sam Desautels had for lunch," she said amiably.

"What?"

"A mouse sandwich."

"He did not."

"He did. Two pieces of bread and a mouse right between them, and he ate it."

"I don't believe you."

"He found it on his driveway. No cat marks. It died of old age."

"He ate a *old* mouse? Gross!"

Tuesday would paint a mouse peeking out between two slabs of bread. Would she remember? Should he paint something current—her special rolls, maybe—instead? No, he couldn't.

Could he have said something different that day so long ago? What if he'd said, *Nah, I didn't write the note, but what if I did?*

What if I did want to marry you? Would things be any different? Would he be downstairs fixing her soup or calling the doctor or sitting by her bedside, instead of Jimmy Daly?

The undercoats of red were done. They needed twenty-four hours to dry. Tuesday went inside and lay on his bed with his hands behind his head.

47

Dear C—

I will be a hero. Odysseus coming out of the brush, naked, sleek and strong as a lion after weeks at sea and nearly drowned, and only one stands her ground. Only one is not afraid of him. Nausicaa. She falls in love with him, desires him, but his heart is elsewhere. There is the possibility of love between them, but he holds back. My Nausicaa is that boy who desires my friendship, wants me to absorb him into myself. I feel it, know the feeling all too well, the yearning for dissolution. My heart goes out to him.

48

Tuesday woke up at mid-afternoon, his heart racing from a dream in which he had been screaming at his father. Screaming without restraint, as one only does in a dream. He'd caught his father in the round barn; his father was the vandal. He was systematically breaking one artifact after another, snapping them in two across his knee, with an expression of defiance and rage, like a child purposefully destroying something his parent loves. Tuesday was surprised to find he'd slept several hours.

Could he try again to see Mary? If Jimmy's truck were there, he wouldn't stop, but if she were home alone . . .

Tuesday thought very little about his father. Who knew why

the man had come back to haunt him today? Never mind, he wanted to talk to Mary about the vandalism. She had always made him feel gentle, when he knew he wasn't. He alone knew how close he'd come to killing Jimmy Daly, and how often he wished he had. He'd wanted to kill his father lots of times.

He'd only fought his father once. What was it about? He couldn't remember now. Maybe about his doing something with his life besides cleaning grounds at the museum. He'd been working as a custodian for two years after school and was only promoted to security guard a few weeks before he left for Maine. For two years he'd been driving an hour away to empty a hundred trash cans and pick up litter after slobs. There he was, feeling down already, feeling like shit actually, wanting more for his life and not knowing how to get it, and Pop was nagging him. It wasn't right. Pop had given up years ago, and at least Tuesday was still trying. It wasn't fair. Something snapped.

They were standing in the kitchen. Maybe it was about work, maybe something else. It could have been anything really. Tuesday saw red. People said that, and it was true. Blood filled your eyes. He didn't know exactly what he was doing. He picked up an old wooden kitchen chair—for what? To smash against the floor? Throw across the room? Throw at Pop? He didn't know. Grabbed it in a fury, as some kind of weapon. It was enough to set off Pop. As if Pop were waiting. Pop lunged at him. Tuesday heaved the chair, Pop knocked it away, went for him. It happened fast. They fell to the ground, struggling. They wrestled on the floor. It only took seconds, though it felt like hours, and suddenly Tuesday knew: *I'm the winner. Stronger than my father. Going to win this fight.* But then what? He had no time to figure anything out. He thought only, *then what?* And there was no answer. Only, *I can win.* And Pop knew it, too.

And then it was over. Tuesday gave up, let Pop win. Knowing that in fact he'd won. Both of them knew he'd won. Both of them pretending Pop had won, so things could stay the same for a little while. But not really. Tuesday left for Maine soon after. After Jimmy in the woods.

Mary was sitting outside in a webbed lawn chair when he drove up, with her face to the sun. He sat on the grass next to her.

"You know the round barn?" he began.

"Sure. I go up there often. Something speaks to me, some unfinished business about the place."

He told her about the vandals. "I can't stop thinking about it. Someone invading the barn. Why would anyone do that? I don't get it."

"Let it go, Tuesday. You didn't do it. You're not even responsible."

"It's like it's my barn, though."

"But it's not, is it? It's important to know what's yours and what ain't. Remember when we learned not to say ain't?"

He didn't.

"No? That substitute in third grade? You were in fourth. Every time she came that year, she kept harping on it—and it worked. For some of us. That's when I learned that what you learn at home ain't always right."

Tuesday didn't smile. "When you love something," he began.

Mary flared up. "What? When you love something, what? You hold on as hard as you can so you squeeze the life out of it? Or you let it go? It's just a building, for God's sake." She slumped in the chair, worn out. "I'm on my way out, cousin. Find yourself a good woman and get married."

There was a long pause. "I'll do that."

Mary sighed, and touched his scowling face with the fingertips of one hand. "You're getting middle-aged, cousin. Don't worry so much. You're too much like me. Listen—"

Too much like her? How? He'd give anything to be more like her! Even though at the moment he hated her.

"—somebody told me once that forgiveness was the gift of the old. I've been thinking about that. I'm not going to be old, so I want you to know I forgive you."

"For what?"

She smiled. "Hey, it's all right! Whatever your deep dark secrets are, they're yours to keep. I forgive you for jumping off the seesaw and landing me in the dirt. For putting a spider in my hair on the bus that time. For writing me a love note in third grade. You were in fourth I guess."

"Told you that wasn't me. Remember?"

"All right. For not writing me a love note, then." She was teasing him—like old times. She leaned back in her chair and closed her eyes, as if she were drifting off to some private place, of forgiveness and old times and her own secret disappointments.

The sun played across her face. Thinner though she was, her face had the same softness it always had. The faintest lines had appeared recently around her eyes; he hadn't seen them before. He'd thought of her the same way for years—and in fact, she'd changed but little. Or maybe he just hadn't noticed. He never got to look at her face like this. Her cheeks had always been round, slightly flushed, shitty Irish skin as she called it framed by dark curly hair from her Italian stonemason grandfather. Now her cheeks were less round, and her overalls didn't pull across her belly or her chest. She'd said she had fluid in her abdomen, and it was uncomfortable.

But her lips were full and relaxed in sleep, and if she was in pain, he couldn't tell. He couldn't keep her safe, no. He couldn't even keep the museum safe—and she was right, it was just a building. Never mind. There was nothing he would rather do than watch over this woman. *Flow gently, sweet Afton. Disturb not her dream.*

49

Sunday, July 11
Dear Cynthia,

What is the difference between good and evil and how can you tell? Someone came into my room at night long ago and comforted me, loved me, gave me a sweetness I've never known since. And then she left. She left me. I have longed for her, I have forgotten her, I have wished her dead and yet I would give my life for a taste of that early joy. Never was anyone, any time, so tender, so sweet, so dispassionate.

There are questions that torture me. I wander the museum, I touch things to make them real and if they are real I think I must be real and then everything is real and I am pressed down by a weight so ponderous I can hardly speak. The docent wants to tell me every detail about a building I would just as soon burn down and when I escape I can breathe again. What a stultifying place. Or is it me. I suffocate myself. The flame in me has used up all the oxygen and what is left?

This boy-child who craves to be like me, or perhaps just near me, or just in the space I'm in. Maybe he just likes to be in the round barn and I am the one with the key. I am always the one with the key.

I am in charge. I will make this exhibit come to life. It will not be a stagnant pool where no fish live, choked with foreign plants. It will live. Ghosts from the past will materialize, breathe life into scenes. Visitors will tremble against the brightness, the pulse of what others call history, that sleepy, dusty word. I want people to come into the round barn and feel their skin tingle, feel a shiver along their backbones. Something is different.

I don't know how to do it. I'm thinking.

Great plans take time. I will create a vision that will transform the museum, as I did with the circus building years ago. No one can deny that. I am a man of extraordinary ideas. I will bring that boy along. No one will share in my glory but he, this dear reflection of my younger self, this sweet young man so open and full of longing he is irresistible.

50

Before her cancer, Mary had followed a certain morning habit: she got up before Jimmy, fed the cats, made herself a cup of instant coffee, wrapped herself in the blue and white Eternal Triangle quilt the Fishwives made, and sat on the overstuffed, cat-hair-covered couch in the great kitchen and read the paper. The noisy red cat, the sociable, demanding one, always came meowing over to her and snuggled in smack against her thigh and purred madly. Jimmy got up a half an hour or so later; it took him that long to wake up. Mary had liked that private time, alone. A half an hour—it was all she needed.

But then for those many weeks she had not wanted to get out of bed at all. And she had stopped reading the paper. There was nothing there anymore that she cared about. She knew what she knew. Now, since the play, her routine had changed again. Instead of hopping out of bed at once, as she had most of her life, she lay quietly next to Jimmy and thought. She was alone enough now, felt alone, didn't need physical distance. She wasn't sure whether or not she really was alone in that fundamental way gloomy people talked about. She didn't know yet—that is, she hadn't decided, though it was a possibility. She had always been willing to consider that the way she saw the world was a matter of perspective, not truth. Dowsing, sensing the earth's secrets, was as close to the truth as she'd suspected she was ever going to get—until the moment of her death. And strangely, perversely perhaps, that was something to look forward to. If that's what it took, she was willing.

The medicines she was taking for her comfort, in addition to the morphine, made her forgetful, made her repeat herself. But she was not unhappy. Sad, yes, but not profoundly discontented. Not despairing. There was a difference.

In any case, she knew what she needed, and she no longer needed to have a tiny space in which she did exactly what she felt like, reading the paper by herself in the morning before Jimmy got up. Her needs now became both all-consuming and surprisingly moderate. She didn't want much, but what she wanted, she wanted with a passion that surpassed anything she had known before. She stayed in bed because she wanted to feel Jimmy's strength, the rightness of him. For the next half-hour after she awoke, she observed Jimmy, with her body more than her eyes, as he struggled to leave sleep behind, felt his silent effort as if it were coursing through her own body, an effort to gather tension, to pull it into himself from somewhere, wherever it came from, a tension she herself never completely let go of—when she woke up, she was awake—but that he surrendered entirely upon sleeping. She was more attuned to him now than she had ever been.

When he finally climbed out of the darkness, which she was certain didn't feel like darkness to him but soft and liquid, neither dark nor light but safe, endlessly, deeply safe, she got up with him. She put on his new bathrobe.

The afternoon after the play, she had bought Jimmy a bathrobe, which he considered pure extravagance, though in a few months he would wear it every morning for the short trip from the bed to the bathroom.

Mary bought Jimmy a bathrobe because she was too practical to buy one for herself for the little time she had left. Who cared about such a stupid thing as a bathrobe, after all? Why did she want one? But of course some little things mattered more now than ever, and what Mary loved, once she discovered it, was standing in the hallway outside the bathroom, feeling the wide floorboards of the old house beneath her feet, loosening the bathrobe around her shoulders, and dropping it to the floor. First she had done it with her nightgown, beginning the day after she stopped reading the newspaper, the day after Jimmy gave her the sweet gift of a second shower after she removed her nightgown in the living room for perhaps the first time ever, the first time she had thought to undress in the living room before showering. Not that she particularly thought of it even then. Say, rather, that it was the first time her instincts had led her to this particular act. Following her instincts was one of Mary's reasons for living and she would do it from now on.

On July fourth she bought the bathrobe. Was it only a week ago? Not a month? She no longer wore a nightgown for sleeping. She slept naked, and wondered why she hadn't slept naked all her life. She regretted all the nights she could have felt Jimmy's skin close to hers and didn't; she argued with herself about regrets, why waste the energy, and decided it was all right. She discovered she regretted many things.

When Mary Bailey Daly dropped the bathrobe slowly from around her shoulders, she felt as though she were shedding a skin. The bathrobe was blue and green striped flannel, not too thick for summer mornings in northern Vermont. When she wore it—and she was the only one to wear it that July—it reached to the floor, skimmed the floor so she had to hike it up in front in order not to trip. She had wanted a floor-length bathrobe for Jimmy but for some inexplicable reason the men's bathrobes were designed to come just below the knee, as this one would. She was sorry it wasn't the other way around, so that short men and tall men both had choices. Mary was not much of a shopper, but she nonetheless was perplexed that manufacturers of bathrobes wouldn't find it in their interest to offer more choices. It made her feel out of synch—again—and she was glad she had not spent much time in her life shopping. That, at least, was something.

In her new bathrobe, Mary walked like a queen down the stairs after her husband. She stood up straight; in the past month she had begun to stoop. While he disappeared into the bathroom, she, with back straight and head up, made a small sweep of the living room. It was important to do things just right, now. Once she had become a queen, or someone in a Greek myth—Athena or Hera, or her new favorite, Ascites—or an imaginary person of legend, outside history, someone whose spirit was immortal—once she became this special soul for only a few seconds, she was ready. She stood outside the bathroom door, shed her striped flannel bathrobe, and listened to the sounds of the house—the rushing of the shower, the click of the kitchen clock with the cracked face, the bumping of the cats as they raced up and down stairs in their morning romp. She listened out of habit for the sound no one could hear, the sound of water running under the house dozens, or even thousands, of feet below, the water that determined the lines of power through her house, her life, her Self, the lines of power that determined the rightness of the world.

She didn't hear it, but it didn't matter anymore. Now she listened for something else—the voice of God in her bones. She listened for laughter.

Mary's naked, ritual listening took only a few seconds, long though they were, but when she stepped inside the bathroom, the steam had already begun to cloud the mirror. Jimmy liked a good hot shower.

51

"Give it up, Tuesday," Mary had said about the vandalism, just as she had throughout their youth whenever he had tended to brood. He couldn't "give it up," as she urged, but he heard her voice in his head chiding him as he interrupted his work in order to walk through the round barn several times a day.

On Tuesday afternoon, during his wary inspection of the top floor, he encountered the new board member to whom he had been introduced on several occasions this summer. She had been there when they moved the silo, before his cousin got sick. Or before she knew she was sick.

"Mrs. Maxwell," he said.

"Remind me of your name," she said pleasantly. He told her.

"Yes, yes, you were involved in getting this barn here. From the countryside to this great metropolis. I find it all very perplexing."

"Ma'am?" He had to admit she was a handsome woman. It wasn't her silk suit or her traditionally beautiful face, aging well—she was probably ten years older than he and didn't look it. It was the way she held herself. She was confident, even stately, but there was something provocative about her—as if under that formal exterior was a woman who liked sex.

"Here you have this wonderful museum, with some truly exquisite paintings, some of the finest art of the century, and you place ten times more emphasis, you admire ten times more—a barn! Oh, I don't expect you to understand, but it puzzles me."

"The paintings are very beautiful," he acknowledged. He wasn't the one to argue the relative merits of one part of the museum over another. He loved the paintings.

She waved a hand in the air. He saw she wore no rings. "Of course, of course. But the to-do, the hoopla over a little vandalism, compared to the complete loss of several Impressionists—it doesn't make sense. Oh, forgive me for going on like this. I told Charles I would come look at the barn for once, to try to see its merits. What are its merits, Mr. Bailey?"

Tuesday waited. Was she done? Did she want an answer?

"The panels on this floor explain how the barn was acquired and why," he explained politely. "I'm sure you'll find the exhibit very informative."

He excused himself. He was too tightly wound to suffer fools, even beautiful ones—although in this state if he came upon a vandal, he would relish a fight. Maybe that was the real reason for his repeated trips to the barn.

Ten minutes later, Frieda Maxwell had concluded her tour through the barn. She was disappointed. She surveyed the bottom floor one last time: yes, it was interesting, mildly. The concept of arranging the stanchions on the dairy floor in a circle around a central silo, with trap doors to drop the manure down to this level, was pleasingly efficient. But for heaven's sake, it was still a barn. How could it compare with art? What profound statement about life was contained within it? It was distracting Charles from the real issue she was here to help with—the potential selling of the paintings, or an alternative solution to the museum's financial woes.

"They might as well burn it down," she muttered.

"Burn it down, madam?" said a voice at her elbow.

She jumped. It was Dean Allen, who stood motionless, in contrast to his usual fluidity. Although he tended to hunch and lurk, drifting from place to place like a rain cloud, now he stood transfixed, gazing wide-eyed at the wall of the silo a few yards away. His unexpected intensity, his inexplicable dismay, disconcerted her.

"What an idea!" he said with an effort. "Even when Icarus flew too close to the sun, he was not burned up for his sins. He merely had his wings melted, a much more fitting punishment."

Frieda fled. What a strange place. Outside the barn she collected herself and walked quickly through the museum grounds to her temporary home nearby.

52

Dear Cynthia,

What is it? What is evil, what is light? Desire

I want, no, I

I remember longing. I remember

Some things are outlawed that shouldn't be. We used to put people in the stocks. Punish them. Humiliate them. People should not be humiliated. Evil people should go in circus cages and be paraded around the world where we can throw stones at them. Stones would hurt. Not stones. Food. Don't punish

It is not I who need punishing, it is that boy. He

No, no. That woman is bad, burn her up like a witch. She is a witch. They are all witches. I am a witch. A bad

53

The third strange thing happened yesterday, Bastille Day, which is irrelevant, except I always loved the image of revolutionaries storming the Bastille. They knew what was worth dying for.

I spent much of the day walking. It is an odd thing about Vermont that people do not walk a great deal, not walking from place to place to get somewhere as we do in New York. They drive somewhere in order to hike. Yesterday I avoided the museum and its dreadful characters. Instead, I walked for hours, along my road that runs through the valley, with the Green Mountains on one side and the Adirondacks on the other. I returned home late in the afternoon. Lucy was not there.

I sat on the bed in her room to look at the painting; it was the best place to see it. Where was Lucy? With her friend, David? And where was George? Did he know I had spent the night with another man? *I was faithful to you, George. I still love you.* I wanted to talk with him about Lucy, something we had never done much of. I hadn't wanted to; I let George make all the major decisions regarding her, and she always went to him for permission to go somewhere or do something.

Who was this person? I'd always considered her an extension of myself, a part of me I didn't like, a part that was best left ignored.

Books were stacked up next to the bed. There was a book about goat farming, and one about barns. There was a thriller about a law firm, a historical novel about Nazi Germany, a prize-winning novel about a community of black women. I read the jackets to find out that much: I didn't know the books. I don't read contemporary fiction, only classics, when I read novels at all. I prefer biographies of artists and collectors, and art magazines. I was surprised at her choices. What else had she read since entering college? I did not think she had read much in high school, but then, perhaps I didn't know. She never spoke about her assignments. I had assumed she didn't have any, or had nothing to say about them. I had thought she was a boring child.

I was seized then by an intense curiosity. Lucy had some kind of project in the basement. I had ignored it as I tended to ignore most of her activities. I do not say this proudly. I had not realized it until that moment. The awareness came to me with pain.

I have said that I do not like damp, cold places, or dark places, or places where things are hidden. I am afraid of being underground the same way some people are afraid of heights. When I am in Paris, I love to climb to the parapet of Notre Dame and look out over the city and feel the wind. I never have been to the crypt. I never went into the basement of our New York apartment when George was alive, though you could get directly into the car that way. I went out the front door and had George drive around to pick me up. Now I walk or take cabs.

But last evening I didn't even think of the basement. I wanted to know something about the mysterious person I'd always considered a part of myself and thus unworthy of special attention. What was she up to?

I switched on the light from just inside the stairway. A bare bulb burned below. The stairs felt unsteady to me; I held onto the handrail.

The basement was empty, neat. It smelled like wet cement. There was an old furnace, an oil tank, a water heater, the washing machine and dryer I did not use, an empty worktable against one wall. It was not what most people find creepy, but my skin crawled nonetheless. In one corner was what looked like Lucy's project. Newspapers were spread neatly on the cement floor. In the center of the newspapers was a brown, plastic box. I came closer, saw it had tiny holes in the sides and top.

Imagine the dim basement, lit by the one bulb, dank and cool as any crypt, the walls crumbly from moisture, the cement floor crisscrossed by a dozen jagged cracks. A brown plastic box separated off to one side like an altar. Imagine my discomfort, I who have nightmares about being lost or imprisoned in a crypt, or the catacombs of Paris, left to rot like a medieval prisoner in a place where starving rats emerge from hidden holes and eat human flesh.

And yet I was curious. Slowly, a middle-aged Pandora who perhaps should have known better, I opened the box.

It was full of dirt, and bits of garbage—old lettuce, eggshells, an apple core, mostly unrecognizable. Puzzled, I picked up a slotted metal instrument, a sort of spoon, a gardening tool I supposed, lying next to the box, and poked around gingerly in the muck. Had she buried something? Was she growing something that required only darkness? I half expected to find tiny body parts, or shrunken heads, some unsavory talisman, something impossibly foul.

The dirt moved. I turned it over and strings of it wiggled.

Worms.

There were hundreds of them, thousands perhaps, it was hard to tell in the dark. Blind, slow, sluggish. Worms and dirt shifted uneasily before me, a slithering, shape-shifting, infested mess. Worms? Whatever for? Was she poisoning them? Doing experiments?

Then I saw next to the box, in the shadows, a little book—about composting with worms. Composting.

My daughter the gardener.

I did not touch the book. I replaced the lid, carefully, making sure it snapped down tight.

What would George have thought, George who was more fastidious than I, about his daughter feeding garbage to worms, with her gay boyfriend, in a basement in Vermont. Our daughter. It was so innocent.

I laughed. I wanted to cry.

I so wanted to talk to him.

I went upstairs and poured myself a glass of wine.

Why Frieda, I love you.

My mother loved me, but I was not my mother.

I waited for Lucy for a long time. I did not worry about her. It's not that I wasn't interested. I was, terribly, more than I had ever been. But I believed, then, perhaps for the first time, that she could take care of herself. I wrote her a note. Another first. And then I went to bed.

I did not fall immediately asleep, exhausted as I was. I remembered I hadn't called Charles as I'd said I would. I'd forgotten all about him!

It was as if the old man on the bicycle had just ridden by, I saw things so clearly.

I would continue to enjoy Charles for another few weeks, but then I would return to New York and get on with my life. I would use my contacts to help the museum sell the paintings—and fill the round barn with rakes and hoes and other silly tools if they wished. It didn't matter. My summer romance pleased me; it was fun. I didn't think George would mind. He would see it for what it was. George would understand that the person I was truly interested in, the one I sought to know as intensely as a lover seeks to know the beloved, but with feelings I'd never had before, feelings one might call maternal, perhaps, though I wasn't certain, as such feelings were new to me, the person to whom I would open my heart, such heart as I had, was Lucy.

54

On Thursday, Dean Allen was having one of his gloomy days. David had heard about them from his aunt.

"I had a good idea. A simple, brilliant idea. To open the museum up to the people one day a week, each day for a different county. Vermont Days. I did the hard part. I thought of it. And no one followed up on it. I did my part, where is everyone else? I am always alone."

David fiddled with a pulley, wondered what it was used for.

"Have you talked with your ghost today?" Dean asked. His voice was surprisingly hopeful, almost like a child's, David thought, and wished he *could* talk to a ghost.

"Trying to."

"Look, David, I think it best you forget everything I've told you. I am not cut out to be a mentor. I'm a ghost myself. I'll leave now; I have other things to do. When I come back, you and I can take a nice walk and I'll show you some things you haven't seen yet. In silence. No more words today."

55

But David could not wait for Dean Allen. He spent the rest of the morning in the museum's library, researching the round barn. Didi showed him several fat files full of notes and photographs, and photocopies of old documents. She told him to come find her at lunchtime.

“I can’t, auntie. I’m on a mission. I’ve got to go up there, to the place where the round barn came from.”

“What are you looking for?”

He wasn’t sure. She lent him her car.

It was the kind of bright, warm, breezy summer day during which Vermonters say, “This is what summer is like in Vermont.” He’d heard it twice today already, from Didi and from the man at the gas station. He drove east and north for two hours and then circled back to his destination. His aunt had told him that family farms in Vermont were dying out; he couldn’t believe it. He saw picture-postcard charm all around. Where was its seamy underside? Or was it simply that no matter how run-down the trailer, and how much junk filled a yard, the lush backdrop made everything beautiful? How did you find what was below the surface? He knew how to do it with his birdhouses—you just waited, and listened—but how did you do it in real life?

In Eustis he stopped at Daly’s General Store. He didn’t find it quaint, only small. Behind the cash register hung key chains and nail clippers and batteries. Overhead was a plastic dispenser of lottery tickets—at least five different kinds. On the counter sat a box of brightly colored lip gloss for chapped lips, and a fat jar of beef jerky, and a display of pencils with pastel-pink rubber animals stuck over the erasers.

David bought a bag of potato chips, a national brand. The store didn’t carry the special Vermont chips his aunt bought. “There used to be a round barn around here,” he said to the man behind the register.

“That’s right.”

“Do you know where it was?”

“Yep.”

David smiled. “Is this a joke? Will you tell me where it is?”

The man, who looked as though he were perpetually worried about something, didn’t smile back. “On East Hill Road.”

“Where’s that?”

The man gave him directions.

David hesitated, not wanting to seem like too much of a dumb city kid, but not wanting to get shot for trespassing, either. "Can I just go up there and look around? Would anyone mind?"

"What are you looking for?" A small woman he hadn't noticed behind the counter rose with difficulty from her stool. She smiled at him warmly.

"I don't know. A grave maybe. Have you ever heard of a man named Hoke Smith?"

"Yeah."

"Really?"

"He hung himself in the round barn a hundred years ago. Everyone knows that around here."

"Why did he?"

"Don't know. There are stories. I don't suppose anyone really knows why somebody kills himself, do you?"

"Do you know where he's buried?"

"No." She considered this. "It would be interesting to find out." She glanced at the man behind the register.

"Mary—," he began.

"It's one of my good days," she said, reassuringly. The man squinted in concern, but said nothing more. "If you're going to go to East Hill," she said to David, "I might as well show you where it is."

She folded her apron and lay it on the counter. The man turned to help another customer. "I think I might stop by the house and get my sticks," she said. The man raised his eyebrows, in the middle of counting out change. "You never know," she went on. "You got a truck?" she asked David.

"Sorry. Just a little car." He followed her toward the door.

"Why are you sorry? It drives, doesn't it? But we'll take the truck."

Again she and the man exchanged looks, and he nodded. David was struck by the depth of connection in such an ordinary exchange between two people and wondered whether he would ever have that link with another, whether anyone would ever look at him the way that man, in all his worry and distractedness, looked at Mary.

Mary held onto the banister descending the two steps of the store porch.

"Can I help you?"

"No, no, no."

But she didn't object to his giving her a small lift under the arm up into the truck.

There was no hesitation in the way Mary drove, fast and sure, over the hills, the truck flying like a racecar with no shocks, and David's head bumped the roof more than a few times. They stopped at an L-shaped farmhouse.

"My sticks are just inside the back door, on a hook. It's not locked. Would you mind?"

"What are they for?" he asked upon his return. He held the two-pronged stick out to her.

"Dowsing. You can hold onto these. It's called a Y-rod. I used to be a dowser."

"You're kidding."

"What do you suppose dowsers do?" she demanded, but her voice was friendly. "It's not hocus pocus, you know."

"What is it?"

"An ancient spiritual calling. You laugh. You think it's a stick that bends down to find water, right? And you have a scientific explanation for it, having to do with the chemical components of the kind of wood used, right? Like a barometer."

"Actually I don't know anything about it"

"What a surprise." When Mary smiled, it was like the sun breaking through the clouds.

"They'll help you find where the round barn was?"

"I know where the round barn was. They just moved it a few months ago. Besides that, I can see its outline in the sky. But like I said, I don't dowse anymore. The sticks are for you."

Curious, David rode in silence, the stick inert in his lap. Five minutes later, she pulled into what looked like a mere break in the trees. She drove right onto the field. "Here we are. Hop out."

"It's so quiet."

She glanced at him.

"I mean, underneath that buzzing—what are they, bees? Flies? Underneath that, it's so still."

She asked him his name. He told her. She seemed energized by the ride, but nonetheless she accepted his arm. With his help, she picked her way through foot-high grasses and wildflowers. David was drawn to the woods a few hundred yards away.

At the edge of the field, in the shadows under overhanging trees but before the actual woods began, the grass gave way to a patch of lichen, out of which sprouted a small gathering of tombstones. David bent to read them.

"These are all Fletchers," he said.

"Thomas Fletcher built the barn."

"Oh, right." He'd read that this morning. "But . . . this says Thomas Fletcher died in 1887, and the barn wasn't built till 1889."

"That's Thomas Fletcher, the father. Young Thomas built the barn. The first Thomas Fletcher's son."

"But where's *his* grave?"

Mary stepped out of the shadows to stand in the sunlight where it was warmer. She tilted her head as if listening, rubbed her hands absently on her round hips.

"In the woods. By the river."

The undergrowth was sparse; David followed Mary over soft, piney earth about thirty feet down a gentle incline toward a brook. She stopped. "Here."

"Where?"

"Somewhere in here. Unmarked, it looks like."

"What did he die of?"

Mary tilted her head. Then, "He drowned."

"Here? You couldn't drown in this."

"Not now, no, unless you were drunk or somebody knocked you out first. But look at the bank. The spring runoff raises all the little brooks around here and turns them into raging rivers. Freezing cold, too."

David was unconvinced. Was she pulling his leg?

"All right, not a river, but a mighty stream you wouldn't want to have to cross if a bear was after you."

David laughed. "Oh, come on. Bears?"

"Anyway, he drowned. Don't ask me how I know, I didn't think I could do it anymore. What do you know." She started back up the incline, smiling as if he had just given her a present. He jumped to help her. "I'm going to take a little rest in the sun." When they got to the top, she waved him off. "Use the sticks to help you concentrate. But don't think about the sticks, concentrate on the question. The answer is in the question."

David meandered through the woods. What was he looking for? A rise in the earth? An overgrown tombstone? A mark on a tree? He held out Mary's stick but felt foolish and shoved it into his back pocket. Could this be the grave, this space between two older trees? What were they, hemlocks? Cedar? He'd have to learn trees. The thick, gnarled bark meant they'd been there a while; it also made a good birdhouse wall. David crisscrossed the spot, closed his eyes and called upon Thomas Fletcher. Nothing happened. And yet, there was something about this place—he felt it, too. He sighed. Silly boy. He believed this was the place—or at least it might be—but if he expected a ghost to appear, to whisper a passionate love story into his ear upon a breath of wind, he was misguided.

There was nothing left to do but collect. He found two thin, closed, pine cones, and gathered a bundle of twigs and one of small sticks, wrapping them carefully in bandanas before stashing them in his backpack. He collected handfuls of miniature cones and, from the edge of the river, several flat stones. He was about to leave when a spot of green-gray next to a fallen log caught his eye. It was a puffball, of the kind his childhood friend John Barenholz once showed him. *It's an apple of mystery.* What would John Barenholz, with his preoccupation with science, think of David's current obsession with ghosts?

It was when he picked the puffball that he found the stone. Later, he couldn't remember exactly how. Was it that the ground was too hard beneath his knee? Did his foot catch the edge of it? Did the sticks have anything to do with it?

With his fingers and the butt of his knife, he brushed away the leaves and dirt that covered the stone.

Thomas Fletcher
1865–1890
Beloved Friend

The letters were uneven, as if chiseled by a family member rather than a skilled craftsman. But all Thomas's family was dead. Perhaps done by the beloved friend.

When he returned to the lichen-padded circle at the edge of the woods, he found Mary on her side, asleep. He set the Y-rod next to her and lay down to wait. Now and then he waved the puffball in front of his face to see it emit a thread of greenish smoke. The answer was in the question, but what was the right question?

A half-hour later, Mary sat up. "Find what you're after?"

"Sort of."

"That's a start. Look. See over there? Where the ground is flat and there's a little rise? That's where the round barn was. That's a high-drive ramp up to the main floor. There are other outbuildings and a house on the other side of those trees, you just can't see them from here. But look against the sky—"

"Wait a minute!" David jumped up. "The round barn is there. Thomas Fletcher built the barn and a year later he drowned in the river. Hoke Smith hung himself in the barn. What's his connection to Thomas Fletcher?"

"He helped Thomas build the barn," she offered slowly, as if pulling the words from the air.

David paced in front of her in excitement. "Okay. Okay. And why did Hoke hang himself in the barn, the same year?"

Something crossed Mary's face. She started to answer and then stopped, and leaned back on her hands. "Why?"

"Do you know?"

She shook her head.

"Don't you see? Thomas Fletcher drowned accidentally. He was standing on that big rock feeling good because it's spring and he's happy. He's in love for the first time in his life—the first time it's returned, anyway—and everything is wonderful, and he slips and cracks his head, and drowns. Who's he in love with? Who's left to bury him and put up a stone? His beloved friend. His lover. Hoke! Who helped him build the barn."

Mary nodded.

"They built the barn together, and they fell in love. And when Thomas died, Hoke was inconsolable. He didn't know what to do with himself, and it wasn't his barn anymore, maybe someone else was about to buy it—but he felt like it was his barn, his and Thomas's, it was what they'd built together—and now he has no place to go, and no lover, and . . . well, that's it." David flopped onto the ground, onto his back. "Oh, man. Oh, man."

Mary's face was lit up. "I heard the grief," she murmured so he could hardly hear her. "But I thought—." She turned her open, wondering smile to him. "How—how did you hear the story?"

"I don't know. It just came to me. But I know that's what happened."

"From the universe."

"Hoke has no real grave because he hung himself. Of course he's buried somewhere, but I bet it's unmarked." He jumped up again. "Can we go now?" He helped Mary to her feet.

In the truck he handed her the stick. "That's cool."

"You can have them. I don't use them anymore."

After a brief protest, he accepted the gift. He didn't think he'd ever use it. Even so, he wished he had something to give her in return.

She drove comfortably, more slowly now, with one hand out the window, and one on the wheel. She glanced over at him. "Do you know what matters?"

"What?"

"No, I mean, what do you think matters? Why were you so excited?"

"Well, because. Because they're in love. Because . . . I know why Hoke is upset. They moved the barn, away from Thomas, or Thomas's grave. It's the, you know, the loyalty, the . . . they love each other. These two guys."

Mary regarded him curiously. Her gaze made him falter. Why didn't she watch the road?

"Hey! Watch—"

She pulled the car out of a swerve.

"I think I made a mistake," she said, shaking her head in disbelief. And then again, "Shit! I made a mistake!"

David waited. The woman's shift in mood was unnerving. Had he done something wrong? The car slowed to a crawl.

"Goddamn shit fuck." She turned to him, her face a picture of dismay. "I made a mistake."

56

He went away today. Time stops. He has only been with me for, how long has it been? I cannot keep track of time anymore. It never seems to matter, it slips away and nothing happens. There are no letters.

I miss his questions, his patient listening. His soft laugh. The heart of a child in the body of a man. He is looking for something. So are we all. Looking and waiting. Only I have never been patient.

57

The next morning, David rushed his aunt to get to work early so he could return to the round barn. He'd spend the afternoon with Lucy, so it was his last chance. He brought his pad of paper. He saw the barn differently today: he would draw the inside of it this morning, as if he lived within it. He had a sense now for its inner dynamic. He couldn't explain it beyond that it had to do with holding, embracing, providing sanctuary, but he would trust his eye and his hand to express it. Eventually he would create a miniature round barn for Thomas Fletcher and Hoke, or maybe for Dean Allen. He didn't know why he hadn't thought of it before. In this way, too, he would communicate what he had learned—if there were anyone there to hear it. He found an unadorned section of wall to lean against, with a view he liked. He worked for an hour uninterrupted. Then he looked for a beam from which a man might hang himself, in order to draw that.

This was more difficult. The only beams over which one could throw a rope were in the basement ceiling, and it was too low. David wandered around the barn, with which he was now so familiar. How would he hang himself if he wanted to? And then he thought of the silo. He would extend a pole through the windows of the silo, or hatches as they were called, tie a rope to the pole, and jump from the hatch into the silo.

Suddenly the story no longer seemed romantic but merely sad. And somehow astonishing. To actually end your life, to snap your neck because you had nothing to live for? He had felt sad about Mr. Marcus, but never—. Were his own passions young and foolish? He was looking forward to so much—being on his own, finding new friends, getting laid—and all of it was so prosaic. Was he simply shallow? He hadn't yet lived!

David drew the silo as carefully as he had ever drawn. As he sketched, he called upon Hoke and told him what he knew. He tried to reassure the gruff, angry Hoke; he reasoned with him, argued with him, spoke sternly as if to a recalcitrant child. He didn't care if Hoke were real or not. Perhaps he was talking with himself; it didn't matter.

Dean Allen appeared out of nowhere in his eerie fashion.

"Where did you go? I came back looking for you and found the chicken had flown the coop. The rooster had gone to rest."

"I'm sorry. I'm leaving tomorrow, and there was something I needed to do." David observed Dean Allen with interest. Something was different. Something was about to happen. He set aside his drawing. He had done what he could for the dead, and he gave himself up to the living.

"I trust you were successful," said Dean Allen. "Well. I have been thinking of you and have come to an important conclusion. Come walk with me. I will tell you about the Greeks, about their system of mentorship. I will tell you about Athena. I myself had a mentor once. It was my sister, the fair Cynthia."

58

Because he had Friday off, Tuesday Bailey thought he would take Mary up on her invitation. *Come see me,* she'd said. All right, he would. Why had he ever imposed on himself such a restricted schedule of visits anyway? He drove to the store first, though he didn't expect to see her there. Indeed, her truck was not parked along the side in its usual place.

Take care of Jimmy. He went in.

Jimmy stood behind the register as always, filling out a form.

"Tuesday. You left your change and your milk last time you were in."

Tuesday accepted the bills without comment. "Mary at home? How's she doing?"

Jimmy turned away. "She had a good day yesterday and overdid it. A bad night last night. She's in pain."

"Think I'll go by and pay her a visit."

"Tell her I'm almost done with the ordering and I'll be there soon."

"Anything I can do for you, Jimmy?"

Jimmy shook his head. "Pray, maybe."

Tuesday ignored the front steps where he and Mary had sat and talked as teenagers and knocked on the mudroom door. When there was no answer, he let himself in, as he used to do as a child.

"Mary? You home?"

Mary called from upstairs, not very loudly.

"It's me, Tuesday. You up?" he called from the bottom of the stairs. "Everything all right?"

"Come on up, Tuesday. I'm decent."

Mary lay in bed, in her parents' old room, the big room at the back of the house, the same room in which he had played Pirates, and Monsters, and so many other games. The wallpaper was faded, but the windows were wide open, and a light breeze blew in. With the blue and green striped bathrobe bunched loosely around her, Mary struggled to sit up, as if she had been sleeping.

"Sorry to greet you this way. I'm playing hooky from the store."

Her face was even thinner; she seemed positively little. She had always been short, but round and . . . and full. A card table set up next to the bed was crowded with plastic bottles of medicine, a pitcher of water, a glass. A plastic potty chair sat under one of the windows. Mary reached for the glass.

"The visiting nurse just left. She helps keep me together."

"I saw Jimmy at the store."

"Yep. He's working hard. You can't keep a good man down, Tuesday Bailey. But his heart's breaking and I can't do a thing about it. Come on in, have a seat. Where've you been?"

There weren't any extra chairs in the room. It wasn't set up for visitors. Tuesday sat on the edge of the bed, where she indicated he should.

"You're feeling pretty bad?"

"Oh sure. But I'm not dead yet. Just tired." Smoothing out the cotton blanket. "And you? Are you still lost?"

"I worry about you."

"Well, that's a waste. I appreciate it, though. You always were a kind boy. I've been thinking about kindness lately. Remember the time you found me in the apple tree?"

She reached for his hand. Her hand was small and familiar, as though he'd held it yesterday, running around the barn, helping her up or being helped, after one of them dumped the other off the seesaw. Yesterday, not thirty-five years ago. As if he had spent his life holding her hand instead of wishing for her, missing her. He held her hand lightly—it was so dry—stroking the back of it with his thumb now and then as if reassuring a baby bird.

"I always thought you were magic," Mary said. "For a long time, anyway. It was almost like you could read my mind. It scared me, actually. I never told you that, did I? Somehow the other day I was thinking about that time when you came along and I was stuck in the apple tree. Did I ever tell you how I got there? My brothers put me there. As a joke. They thought it would be funny to see me get down. I did, too, at the time, of course. And then I didn't know how to get down. Then you came along and showed me. I don't remember what you said, or how I did it, only that you came and helped me. And from then on I thought you were magic. But you weren't magic, were you? You were just kind. Why didn't you tell me? I never knew." He wanted to hold her and rock her, she seemed so little.

"I've been thinking about that boy, too, why he was sent to me when he was. He believes in ghosts. He was looking for a ghost, and he found something. But what was he looking for really?"

She seemed to drift off into her own thoughts, rolling away from him as she always had. "What boy was that, Mary?"

"I've been so silly, not to know what an eighteen-year-old kid knows in his bones. A gay kid at that, chasing after a pair of old ghosts—and why? Because they love each other! It's so simple. Is that it, Tuesday? Is that the great question?"

He waited.

"I'm a silly woman," she said again. "I'm going to see the doctor on Monday about starting chemo." She closed her eyes.

He was silent. What was there to say?

"It's never too late to learn from your mistakes, don't you think, Tuesday?" She squeezed his hand. "Remember those bluebirds of happiness." The teasing sparkle returned to her eyes and she smiled at him. "They're yours now. I give them to you."

Tuesday kissed her on the cheek before he left, as if he'd done it a million times instead of never. *Flow gently sweet Afton.*

At home that evening, he worked on his chairs. He spent an hour on one elaborate bluebird, with wings outspread, the tips of the feathers outlined in tiny dashes of red and purple—because bluebirds of happiness are not just blue. This bluebird had a purple underbelly and splashes of yellow on its head and tail, and on the underside of its wings all the colors of the rainbow. This bluebird was the soul of grief, shedding tiny raindrops as it flew ever upward toward the heavens.

59

Mary took a turn for the worse. She was deteriorating fast. On Saturday afternoon, Jimmy and Anne Marie Desautels moved her into the bed that the hospice people had set up in the living room. She joked about being the center of attention.

The day before, Jimmy had arranged with his new manager to take care of business for the indefinite future. He would relieve her when he could, but he did not plan to return for some time.

The visiting nurse would come now every day for a few hours. Mary would probably slip in and out of consciousness. They would do what they could to keep her comfortable, and Jimmy would stay with her.

60

I've never wanted to travel but I would like to go to the sea. I think it is a place where seeing and hearing become one, like lovers. When you hear the sea in a conch shell, the big kind you find at gift shops, you can close your eyes and see the ocean and even smell it. It's not true we become dust when we die; we become liquid. I read about it once. We are mostly water. And the sea goes on forever.

I was a good dowser. When that little boy was lost on Spruce Mountain, the sheriff came to me with a topological map. It was about eleven o'clock at night; Jimmy and I had gone to bed and we woke up to a pounding on the side door. Ira spread the map out on the kitchen table. He doesn't believe in dowsing and only comes to me when he's desperate. His wife is in Fishwives.

"Tell me something about him," I said.

He looked at his little note pad. "Ten years old. He's wearing jeans and a yellow T-shirt and a Phillies baseball cap. His two older sisters were with him. They were on their way down and the kid wanted to go back up; he thought he dropped something."

He went on; I didn't listen. I don't need the information, but I don't like folks watching me while I'm concentrating, so I get them talking. Besides, it makes them feel helpful. Meanwhile I studied the map, but inside myself I closed everything out and just listened. Closed out everything on the outside and opened up on the inside. It's hard to explain, but you know it when you get it right. And then I knew where the kid was. I felt it. I touched the map. Ira circled the spot with a black marker, folded up the map and left. Jimmy and I went back to sleep. They found the kid within a hundred feet of my mark.

I believe that because the continents float upon the water, we can hear the sea beneath us if we listen hard enough. Not the literal sea, not the crashing of the waves that you can hear in a conch shell. I mean a different kind of hearing, the kind you do with your whole body, like sex. Jimmy took me to a play in St. Johnsbury, about Eve—you know, the story from her point of view, how she loved the snake and all. The snake told her that if she ate the apple, she could hear the voice of God in her bones. That kind of listening. I can't talk about it, but this is what I wanted to know more than anything, no matter what it took. I thought I'd get it on my deathbed. And maybe I will. I got a feeling. God forgive my foolishness.

I said to Jimmy while he was sleeping, "When I'm gone, whenever you feel the wind on your neck, that's me." I wanted him to absorb it in his sleep so he'd really know it, without words. And I blew on his neck.

We'd never been to a play together. I went to a play in Burlington once on a high school trip—it was Shakespeare even—and we put on skits sometimes in grade school. I couldn't imagine what possessed him. We left the girl who helps him now in the store and drove an hour away to see a woman act out her version of Adam and Eve. Adam was a bossy jerk, but when Eve came on the first thing she said to us was "I—love—you." Spread her arms wide, took us all in, and said it like she really meant it. My god, how could she do that?

Jimmy gets angry at me in a way he never used to. The other day I was lying in bed and he was hugging me so tentatively, I fussed at him to hold me tight. I told him it hurt me more for him to treat me so gingerly, and so he did, not trying to hurt me, just tightening a little, and I winced, I didn't mean to, but it seems like everything hurts more than I expect, and he jumped away. "Goddammit, Mary!" he yelled. He never used to raise his voice; he's really a mild-mannered man. He was furious, panting and glaring at me. When I finally got him to come back to bed—just to sit on the edge—he started to cry.

I told him I wanted him to get married again. "Not likely," he said. I sat up and held onto him, breathing into the pain like the nurse said.

61

Didi took David to the airport on Sunday morning. He was more subdued than usual. Was he sad to leave? Fearful about the wide world opening up to him in the fall? Or maybe he'd had sex after all—but not with Lucy, surely. But who knew? Here Didi was, older and more sure of herself than David, with a committed, wonderful lover, and she was having dinner tonight with Adrian, in another town an hour away.

But there was no time to ask him about it. They hugged and kissed with much love and thanks, and he was gone.

Maude, Maude. Maude would come home in a week, and who knew what would happen with Adrian after that. Who knew whether she'd ever see him again, socially.

That evening, she waited for him in a bookstore. It was a place she loved, but she did not pull a single title from the shelves. She was not here to buy, or even to browse. She was here to meet someone. A man. A friend. Someone she thought about a great deal. Someone who teased her, who desired her. If men were predatory, as some said, maybe she wanted to be prey. Or maybe this time she was the predator. In any case, this was the first time they'd ever had dinner. A late dinner at that.

She saw him out of the corner of her eye. All of her strained toward him, which made her shy. He kissed her lightly, easily, as if they were old friends. Which was what they were. Not.

"Shall we walk a little?" he asked. He told her she looked well; he'd never seen her in jeans and a T-shirt, but only in work clothes. He looked excited to see her. Where could they go to be alone?

Didi took his arm, as if he were merely a girlfriend, an old pal. A lover. She must touch him. He placed his free hand upon hers. They chatted easily. Then Didi said, "Let's play a game. Let's pretend we're going to take a trip together. Where would we go?"

He laughed. "No, no. I don't want to play that game."

"Oh come on. Would we go to New York? Beijing? Where would you like to go?"

He wouldn't look at her. He ran his hand across his face, through his hair, a gesture she knew well. They turned up a side street, with narrower sidewalks and fewer people. She persisted.

"July in New York is too hot. Maybe we should go to the southern hemisphere. Lima. Or Machu Picchu. Or maybe Alaska. I've never been to Alaska."

He glanced at her briefly, took her hand. "Once you let the cats out of the barn, you can't put them back in."

She was silent, aware of his fingers interlocked with hers. How naturally their hands fitted together. His hands were larger than hers. She said, "I'd like to go to Kyoto and visit temples and walk in Japanese gardens."

He stopped, turned to her, looked at her hard as if he were suddenly unafraid of her or himself. He held her hand between his, pressed against his chest, inches from her breasts. She could smell him, sweet and bold.

He kissed her, not softly, not lightly. Hungrily, as if he had been released, as if he would remove her clothes. She kissed him back. It was downtown in the middle of a city where each of them could know a dozen people, but it was dusk and it didn't matter.

They walked a few steps, kissed again. They embraced like young lovers, or would-be lovers. Or the lovers they were. Didi wondered whether there were an alley nearby, a side road, a darkened doorway, anywhere to have privacy.

He pulled away from her.

"Maybe we could just go up into the woods." She said it jokingly but she was not joking.

"I was thinking more about a warm beach." He smiled at her. "Shall we go have something to eat?" But Didi could not take her eyes from his, could not signal she was ready to stop, and he could not resist her, he leaned toward her and they kissed for a long time.

In silence they walked to the restaurant where they had met before, below the hotel.

It was four in the morning when Didi arrived home, but she was wide awake, knew she couldn't sleep. She dug out her journal, which she had neglected for several weeks, in fact since Maude left. Taped to the front was Maude's last poem.

every girl was once a boy / ask my woman

Didi wanted to scream. Suddenly she hated Maude. She hated poetry. She hated Adrian.

From her pocket she pulled a folded paper napkin she'd brought home from the restaurant. The words on it were blurred, with tiny blobs of ink at the ends of letters. He had laughed at his effort, slid the napkin across the table to her like a child passing a note in school.

It was only a four-inch square, but she had to use three matches to burn it because the flame kept going out. She dropped it finally into the kitchen sink. The fire calmed her a bit. She was glad David had left; she had the house to herself and wouldn't wake him.

She untaped Maude's last poem and retaped it to the top of her desk. She drew a thick red line through it and then another the opposite way. A giant X. She covered the small square of paper with more lines. She drew S-curves between the lines, and tiny circles and arrows, filled the diamonds with more shapes. It looked like hundreds of doodles she had drawn before, in the margins of the telephone book, or on the newspaper left lying around—only she drew now with concentration and the lines were thick and purposeful. She was very thorough, and the letters of the poem peered out from behind her angry design as though hiding from enemy fire. She kept herself from falling into the tiny square. It was too small.

Now she was sorry she had obliterated the words. Where were the other poems? She retrieved them from her desk drawer.

At the side of the drawer she was surprised to see the small box of oil paints she'd bought for David on a whim, and a note. *For you, Auntie.* They hadn't been used. She unscrewed a tube of paint, held it to her nose. Ah, the smell. She closed her eyes. Yes. Hurry.

She took the stairs two by two. In Maude's studio were several prepared canvases covered with green gesso, waiting. They were eighteen by twenty-four, too small for Maude to take because she wanted to focus on larger work. Since Maude had left, Didi had avoided this room, though she ordinarily spent hours here every week reading, while Maude painted.

Didi moved quickly, but with calm. She knew what she was going to do. It would be a portrait of a man; she would use only shades of brown, darkened by black. He was looking off, a moment of nothingness, he was in despair, he hated the world, he looked out a window but saw nothing. The background was a collage made up of the poems, worked into the dark, barely discernible, he couldn't see them, didn't know they were there. It was a portrait of Giacometti, her father's favorite artist because Giacometti cared most of all about the experience of seeing which he tried to re-create obsessively in his own work. But Didi's subject could not see. She saw perfectly how the portrait would turn out. Yes, she would title it *Giacometti,* but it was a portrait of her father.

62

On Monday evening, Tuesday Bailey arrived at his cousin's house to see Anne Marie Desautels leaving in tears.

"We were going to have one last gathering of the Fishwives here, but she's not up to it. We're making her a shroud all in white like she always said she wanted."

Tuesday saw her to her car.

"Jimmy's gone out. Said he'd be back in a half hour. The hospice nurse is supposed to come by at eight. But Mary told me to go on." It was seven now.

Tuesday let himself in quietly, not wanting to wake her if she was sleeping.

It was the first time he'd seen the bed in the living room. One of the two easy chairs had been moved out to make more space. The other was piled with cushions and blankets. Maybe Jimmy slept here.

It smelled strange, too.

Mary looked like hell.

There was no place to sit. *I should've brought the goddamn chair.*

Then, *Mary's dying, where the fuck is Jimmy.*

Tuesday brought in a chair from the kitchen, a plain wooden chair like the ones he was painting. He sat close to the bed. Mary was indeed asleep—or unconscious. A table lamp was on next to the bed, though it was still plenty light out; the living room always was the darkest room in this house. She looked worn out, tired. Like she hurt. His little round Mary was not round at all anymore. Her cheeks showed little lines at the sides of her mouth, tiny wrinkles she didn't have when her cheeks were rounder. She looked older, and strained. Parched.

He held her hand. He sat with her a long time. The nurse came and went, but Jimmy didn't return. Tuesday thought she might have squeezed his hand once. Somewhere in the middle of the night, he started talking to her. Maybe to keep himself awake, maybe to tell her his heart, which he thought she already knew, maybe just to pass time. He talked about everything he could remember. Finding her in the tree, the white blossoms full of bees, her little feet dangling, her sweet voice singing, singing. Playing with her outside, hiding from her brothers, eavesdropping under the porch, running around the barn singing that Harry Houdini song, remember, Mary? *Harry Houdini, marry Houdini, marry Harry Houdini.* Getting the puppy, naming her together: Henrietta, Henrietty, Harrietty. Playing with the puppy like it was theirs.

"Remember when you got the truck, that old red thing nearly falling apart, riding all over kingdom come? Stopping at Joe's Pond—remember how it wouldn't go into reverse? Remember how mad you were? Cussing up a storm. Not too keen on my laughing. But I wasn't laughing at you—just thinking, *Funny girl, there's no one like her in the whole world.* It's still true.

"Remember when we were little how you used to tell me about things? About water under the earth, and the universe in motion? You always wanted to learn new stuff. Remember that funny woman who did yoga on her head? And then when you made the Fishwives try yoga ten years ago. You laughed so hard. You always liked that weird stuff—like meditating. For a while. I remember when you found dowsing.

"You were always looking for answers. What answers, I said. Answers to what's important, you said, so you know what matters . . .

"You know what matters, Mary. Not things you can talk about. Just things you know.

"Remember? Funny girl." He wiped his face with the back of his hand.

Mary opened her eyes. They were full of pain, but clear.

He held her hand in both his own, couldn't speak.

She whispered, "I remember." Or was it just, "Remember"? She nodded at him, kept her eyes on his face. Then mouthed, "Where's Jimmy?"

"Here. Just gone upstairs to get a pillow. He's here with you."

She closed her eyes.

Remember, Mary. Always remember I love you.

He sat with her, rocking, sometimes murmuring softly, sometimes silent, for hours. Some hours later, in the early morning, Mary slipped into a coma. He had never seen anyone in a coma before, but he knew. Had she squeezed his hand again? He wasn't sure.

He sat with her a while longer, until it started to get light.

Jake's was the only all-night bar, forty minutes away. There he found Jimmy, slumped over the bar, all alone. The young bartender was waiting for relief.

Tuesday stuffed Jimmy into the cab of his truck and drove home. In the kitchen, which he reflected Jimmy had never seen before, he propped Jimmy over the sink and ran the tap. He flipped the drain-stop so the sink filled with water. Jimmy was smaller than he, and Tuesday held him down easily. He held Jimmy's head underwater.

There was cold in the hollow of Tuesday's back. He should have killed Jimmy years ago. Jimmy'd had a hold on him ever since. Jimmy struggled. Tuesday let him go.

"What're you, crazy? You nearly drowned me! Fucking asshole!" He sputtered and cursed.

Tuesday threw him a dish towel.

"I saw your truck outside Jake's on my way home. Had an all-nighter at the museum. Figured you needed some help."

"Shit. Life sucks, you know that, Bailey?"

"Yeah."

Jimmy dried his head.

"What time is it? Where's my truck? I gotta get home before the nurse leaves."

"At Jake's."

"Oh great." He was sober enough, but helpless.

"Look, man, go home, all right? Come by later and I'll take you to Jake's. Here. Have my truck for the day. Get out of here."

"Yeah."

Tuesday watched the truck churn up dust on the driveway, turn onto the dirt road, and disappear. The dust settled slowly. The wind had stopped, for the first time all summer.

63

July 21
Dearest Cynthia,

It is getting very bad. But fire is good. It takes away what is rotten and evil. That boy is not sweet. I made him come to me. I made him. The big friendly giant. I am charming and good. He said so.

I am sorry. I do not love anyone

Well Cynthia

You will understand that perhaps. You are

He came to me in the round barn. Now I will have to make amends, for Cynthia. Are you sorry? Poor Cynthia. Where are you? Cynthia loved me, you know. I will never

Behind the carriages. David and Saul. David and Goliath. The carriage was made by Goliath Carriage Company, 1847.

64

July 22
My dear,

I would have you understand something. The nature of evil is that it is invisible. It hides behind old jails and in barns, inside circus cages and antique carriages. You must be ever vigilant. It wears the face of charm. This I know. It attaches to your face like a shadow and you cannot shake it off. Once you are brushed with evil there is no hope. That is the truth. There is nowhere you can go, no one you can be. No devil, no giant, no Ulysses, no Gilgamesh, no Odin, nobody. You must tease and seduce and eat the young soldiers and spit out the bones until someone comes and mercifully puts out your eye and then you can try to escape with the sheep but there is no escape, for Cordelia is dead, and you are left rotting in an old cave full of carcasses. Only fire purifies. I would be the one chosen by God to lead. I would be the maid.

65

Perhaps the great wind of July twenty-third arose in the vacuum created when Mary Bailey Daly's soul was sucked from the earth at 2:27 that morning. Or perhaps it came from the fluctuation of tides and planets that causes all earthly winds. Perhaps it was not the tides at all but the power of human desire.

After an unnaturally still few days, the wind began on Thursday in earnest and blew with increasing force all day. No hurricane or tornado was predicted, only clean, gale-force winds. But the museum was secure; there was no cause for alarm. Tuesday had gone home on Thursday evening exhausted as he had been all week, waiting to hear of his cousin's death. He was deeply asleep at 2:27 in the morning, and just as deeply asleep when the phone rang two hours later.

The round barn was on fire.

What? How—?

It was Sam. "It's bad. The power's out down here, the alarms didn't go off."

"The alarms?" Tuesday repeated, struggling to dress. "The sprinklers?"

"Somebody turned off the water supply. The alarms didn't go off. We have a power outage. We heard the fire engines before we even knew there was a fire. A neighbor saw it."

What was this ungodly wind? Tuesday had sped too fast over the back roads twice this summer already—but tonight he had a hard time keeping the car on the road. He hunched in his seat and gripped the wheel with both hands. Trees and brush bent and swayed madly along the side of the road, visible in the low tunnel of light ahead of the truck.

He didn't get it. The smoke alarm didn't go off. The fire alarm didn't go off. The smoke and fire alarms were wired into the security system, but the power had been knocked out. The sprinkler system, which reacted mechanically to heat, had been disabled because the water supply had been turned off. It was impossible.

Someone purposefully set out to burn down the round barn?

Tuesday cursed the distance, cursed himself for holding onto the house in Eustis so long. He should have moved to town years ago. He'd only stayed—it was true, he could say it now—for Mary. Mary! He hadn't thought of her since he woke up.

The tightness that suddenly gripped Tuesday went straight to his bowels. He stopped the car on the road, left the motor running and the lights on, and relieved himself in the woods, which thrashed and wailed around him.

For an hour, he imagined flames licking the upper two wood-framed floors, flames reaching into the sky, roaring and popping, throwing sparks so people had to move further and further away. The heavy streams of water from the hoses arcing fiercely into the roof, the firefighters high in their cherry-pickers, the powerful water pressure breaking windows. Firefighters unable to find the seat of the fire in this wind. The side walls of the barn were so thin, they would burn like paper. He saw a charred outline of the structure. It made him feel sick.

By the time he got to the museum, the sky had begun to lighten. The fire was out. The air smelled of smoke. Around the barn were three fire trucks and the ambulance that came with them, and a small group of onlookers.

It wasn't as he'd imagined. The barn looked like a cut-away model. Half of it had no exterior walls; supporting timbers had collapsed, the floor planking of both second and third levels had simply disappeared. For the ground it looked as though a bomb had exploded and ripped away half the barn. The other half stood nearly intact, singed and charred at the edges but not destroyed.

Charles Hopper, the police chief, Sam Desautels, and a few others were talking as Tuesday approached, unhurried now, slowed by dread. The fire chief turned to him.

"Tuesday. They're just going in now. I was just telling Charles that it's the wind that saved the barn. The fire started on the north side of the building; a north wind would have taken down the whole thing. Because it was a south wind, it blew away from the core. Of course any wind at all makes it a bitch."

The wind had already lessened. By the time the sun rose, it would die completely.

"How'd it start? Do you know yet?"

The chief, in radio contact with firefighters inside, held up his hand. He was being asked to come take a look.

"They found something," he said without surprise. The standby team of three additional firefighters followed the chief.

Tuesday, Charles, Sam, the few others, including a small group of neighbors, waited. The pumper operator rested against one of the trucks. A local AP reporter—not Adrian—arrived to ask questions and take pictures.

What followed then was something of a jumble. The firefighters inside had discovered two five-gallon cans of gasoline. The fire chief called the state police. Then they discovered a body, unrecognizably charred, not far from one of the cans. The ambulance crew chief was summoned to verify the death. Nothing was touched. They called the police again; it was out of their hands now.

The primary team of four firefighters began the two- to three-hour inspection of the barn, checking for fire extension in the walls and for hot spots.

Outside, the fire chief explained all this to Charles and Tuesday and Sam, who had waited in silence, and to the reporter, who drew him off to the side with more questions. Tuesday, Charles, and Sam avoided each other's eyes. They knew who it was, who it had to be.

The sky lightened from pink to blue. The wind had blown off the haze that sometimes hung over the Adirondacks in the summer. In the clear morning air, the mountains across the lake loomed so sharp and close you could almost see leaves.

Tuesday Bailey wanted nothing more than to sleep for a week. He returned to his office and made himself a cup of cold instant coffee; there was still no electricity.

Mary had died in the night, he suddenly knew. He knew it the way Mary had always seemed to know things about him, when he was sad, or happy—when he walked up the road to her house in his youth to find her sitting on the front steps, waiting for him. Jimmy would have been with her, he was sure. That was right.

He had a lot to do. He'd given instructions about blocking off the barn, and agreed with Charles they needed to close for the day—and in a few minutes he'd meet with Charles and Didi and the other senior staff and the president of the board, and they would talk about what to do. But now he walked wearily along the gravel path, sipping his cold coffee, observing the buildings around him, seeing them with the eyes of a stranger, a new visitor, as he sometimes tried to do. The schoolhouse, the general store, the horseshoe barn, the circus building, the jail, the steamboat, the many old houses in various stages of disrepair known only to his crew, but nonetheless intact.

Mary had wanted to release him, but he had been stuck, like a ghost trapped in a barn until it burns down and he is set free—to return to wherever he came from, or to roam.

He came to the bench where Dean Allen had sat, the last time they had spoken. He ran his hand along the top of the bench automatically and noticed it needed painting.

He'd never given Mary the chairs. Never mind. He still had to finish them anyway. In wild colors, swirling and exploding, all but covering the red. Next to the bluebirds of happiness—which he would fix to look less like feathered blue monsters with great multicolored wings—next to the bluebirds, wild whistling blackbirds and cicadas singing. It would be a noisy chair, lots of noise. He would paint, yes, the mouse, and the seesaw, and the apple tree not just sturdy but bursting into bloom, flinging its blossoms left and right. And singing. Beneath the apple tree, wild rivers rolling to the sea, and rivers under the earth pushing up rocks, rocks flying everywhere, and mountains and trees marching to meet lakes. All of it singing.

Always remember.

I remember, Mary.

Tuesday Bailey set out purposefully for the emergency meeting at the other end of the museum's grounds. He felt the slightest breath on his neck, as if he had been grazed by the wing of a small bird, and he looked up.

Epilogue

Tuesday Bailey had a heart attack in November but survived it. Under strict orders from Dr. Smith to express his feelings and get more exercise, he took up hunting. He crashed through the woods, singing and yelling, and shot occasionally into the sides of hills. It did him good.

After making dozens of dark portraits of her father, Didi began painting female torsos that when turned on their sides looked like landscapes. She titled them Secrets #1, Secrets #2, etc. She had a small local show and sold several. Maude and she were happy.

David constructed a miniature round barn during his first semester of college. He kept it all his life, and many years later, he donated it to the museum in honor of his adopted son's graduation from medical school, which he attended with his long-time companion, John Barenholz.

Jimmy Daly ran the store alone for ten years and expected to die alone. But then Sam Desautels was killed in a car accident involving a moose, and a year later Jimmy married Sam's widow, Anne Marie. Since they both believed they'd had the best the first time around, neither expected to hear bells, but they did all right.

Frieda Maxwell visited Lucy at college the next fall for the first time. She was pleased to see Lucy's new painting on the wall. Lucy and Frieda never became close friends, but many years later, when Frieda was dying, and Lucy asked her what she had loved, she was able to say truthfully, *I loved you.* "I love you too, Mother," Lucy said.

And Hoke Smith? Somewhere over Eustis, in that floating universe in which evil is vanquished and good things come to those who wait, Hoke and Thomas float hand in hand through the ether, dropping starry blessings on everyone who looks upward into the dark night.

Reading Group Guide

Questions for Discussion

1. The author has chosen to braid together a number of story lines in this novel. What elements unite these various story lines? In what ways are they distinct from one another?

2. Each story line centers around a different character—Tuesday, Didi, David, and others. How does the author make each character distinct? What different techniques does the author use to signal shifts in stories and point of view?

3. These characters exhibit various forms of desire—romantic, sexual, artistic, spiritual. In what ways do these desires shape their behavior and attitudes? What are some of the specific forms that desire takes for these characters? How are they united or differentiated by their responses?

4. How do the characters respond when their desires are frustrated or thwarted? What are the different ways in which this happens? What accommodations do they make with their desires?

5. For many of the characters, one result of the frustration of their desires is a sense of isolation from other people. To what extent are they truly isolated, and to what extent is this just a subjective response? How do questions of isolation and connection play out throughout the novel?

6. Many of these characters practice various forms of creative self-expression—everything from painting to birdhouses and sandwiches. How do the characters differ in their attitudes towards issues of creativity, self-expression, and art?

7. To what extent are these creative activities private and to what extent are they social? (David builds his birdhouses for himself, e.g., but collecting the materials puts him into contact with other characters.) How do the characters themselves differ in their attitudes towards questions of privacy and community?

8. To what extent do the characters suffer from erroneous or incomplete understandings of one another? How does your own attitude toward Dean Allen, for example, differ from the opinions that the other characters hold of him? To what extent do the characters suffer from imperfect self-understanding?

9. What do you make of the museum in the novel? What kind of a museum is it? What sorts of preconceptions do we tend to have about museums and what they might or might not legitimately hold and collect?

Author's Note

I began this novel with Tuesday Bailey, a man filled with a quiet, lifelong longing for someone he couldn't have. I wanted to better understand his story and his choices. When I realized he was head of buildings and grounds at the museum, the other characters there began to emerge. The fictional museum is of course based on the Shelburne Museum in Shelburne, Vermont, which is a place I love—a magical place so rich in history and so naturally exciting to the imagination that characters like Tuesday Bailey and Dean Allen and Frieda Maxwell easily spring to mind. Of course I see these characters and others so clearly, blessed and doomed as they are, because they are all aspects of me.

About ten years ago, when I worked with the Vermont Council on the Humanities, I often traveled and led programs in the Northeast Kingdom. Paradoxically, I think it was my encounter with the poverty and the low literacy there that sparked the creation of Mary Bailey Daly, with her spunk and her ardor and her good humor. Maybe Mary thrives in the Northeast Kingdom—captures its spirit—because up there, in that vast landscape, there is enough room for her.

Finally, this is a book about people who love each other and at the same time are searching for what's important. I had a sense throughout its writing that their stories existed somewhere out there, if I could only hear them. Not that this was easy. But every day when I walked my dog in the woods, I tried to listen, the way Mary dowses, and that helped.

An Interview with Suzi Wizowaty

> *Though this is your first novel, you have worked as a freelance writer and editor, and as an advocate of reading and literacy. What brought you to fiction? How have your previous experiences contributed to your fiction?*

This is my first adult novel, but I've written three (unpublished) children's or young adult novels. The real truth is I've been writing fiction all my life. All the other related work I've done—including teaching, editing, freelancing—has grown out of my fiction writing, as a way for me to work with words and stories and still make a living. I suspect that editing and teaching have made me a more careful writer, but not a better one. I'd love to write a big, sprawling, spectacularly messy book someday.

> *Can you say a bit about the importance of reading and literacy issues in your life? What have been some of your experiences working in these areas?*

I began my professional life working in bookstores. Then I spent nine years working in libraries, doing outreach to low-income and elderly citizens, and later organizing programs for kids and adults. For several of those years I freelanced for Vermont's humanities council, leading book-discussion series both for highly educated readers and for adults newly learning to read. Later, as the council's program director I oversaw these programs and created similar programs for child care providers and other groups. (The teaching, editing, freelancing mentioned above I've done mostly around the edges.) Thus in some sense all my working life has focused on promoting books and reading. Why? Because for me literature is not a luxury. It's an absolute necessity. It can save your life. Those of us who take this for granted don't always know how lucky we are.

You say in your Author's Note that the book began with Tuesday Bailey. Was there anything that surprised you about him?

With Tuesday Bailey I wanted to explore what it felt like to long for someone you couldn't have. He loves Mary so much and gives up on loving anyone else. I was indeed surprised to discover that ultimately he felt trapped without perhaps realizing it. I had no idea that when Mary died, he would feel, underneath all the terrible grief—I can admit this even if he can't—some relief.

The Round Barn *features a number of interwoven stories. What were the challenges of braiding the different story lines together and keeping the characters distinct? Did the novel always have this form?*

For me of course the characters are entirely real and I know them better than I know any breathing humans. But how to tell their stories was another matter. I tried several approaches that didn't work. Finally, after several years, when I knew all their stories quite well (and had rewritten them many times), I made a complicated chart in which I listed day by day what each person was doing between early May and late August. Amazingly, it turned out that telling the story chronologically—all the stories together—resulted in a narrative line that not only made sense but had an internal rhythm. Events of significance to each character tended to clump together so that I didn't have to bounce around among different stores too much. In a subsequent rewrite I used dates as chapter headings rather than numbers, for clarity. But I myself ignore dates when I read, so I took them out and let the narrative make clear how much time had passed between chapters.

Do you have personal favorites among the characters? Any you disliked? If so, why?

Does it sound too conventional to say I love them all? I know that Mary is more appealing than, say, Dean Allen or Charles Hopper (and maybe everyone else). But I know everyone's struggles. I may have started out thinking that Charles Hopper, for example, was a sleazeball, but when I let him tell his story in his own voice (which is not in the book), I learned about his divorce and his troubled son and his uncomprehending sadness about his life, and I had to love him, too. The way I work, I have to let each character tell his story in his own voice. That's how I get to know them; it doesn't mean I'll necessarily keep any of the material. It is not an efficient process by any means, but I have not yet found a better one.

Why did you choose to have Didi, a lesbian, tempted by an affair with a man rather than a woman? Is there a point to be made here about the limitations of categories and the fluidity of human desire?

Probably, although I think that's the happy task of the reader and not the writer. I don't write about ideas, but about people. For me the question is not why does Didi get involved with a man—we know she had love affairs with men before she met Maude—but why does she stray at all, when she so obviously loves Maude?

You compare your writing process to Mary's dowsing. What appeals to you about the idea of dowsing? Which of the other characters would you say possess a dowsing-like ability?

I think of dowsing as another way of being what a Buddhist might call "awake." Maybe all artists, all creative people, share with Mary that ability, which I'd describe as the ability or the drive to pay attention. In the novel, David most overtly demonstrates a "dowsing-like ability," in that he hears or imagines the ghost, but others—Lucy, Didi, Jimmy, even Dean Allen in his twisted, misguided way—have it to a lesser extent. They pay attention, they listen, they notice.

Frieda Maxwell comes from a very different background than the other characters. Did her story give you perspective on the other characters? Frieda seems to have a rather astringent view of life. Were you concerned that readers might find her too unsympathetic as a character?

I do fear that readers won't like Frieda. One friend called her a monster, which made me sad. Yes, she's chilly and judgmental, but I've seen many, far worse mothers in the grocery store. Besides, isn't she thawing out nicely? I love her passion for art; it doesn't matter where you start, as long as you have passion for something. And I have enormous sympathy for her mid-life effort to reach out to her daughter after all these years. Granted, I don't think

I'd like her in person, but isn't that part of why we write? And read? To understand, and even love, people we'd ordinarily turn away from?

Was the Vermont setting important to your understanding of the novel and its characters? How did the setting shape your writing and your experience of the characters, if at all?

This is a bit like trying to figure out how the air you breathe affects you. The story and all the characters in it emerged from and center around particular Vermont places. Everywhere the characters go—the parks, the woods, the museum, the general store—are all real Vermont sites, albeit with different names. Some characters come from "away," as is the case in the actual state, but what happens to them here could not happen to them anywhere else. Or maybe it could, but it didn't. Of course my Vermont is not everyone's, it's only mine, but this book absolutely represents the Vermont I know and love.

You are also a teacher of writing. How does your teaching inform your writing? What is your own writing practice? Do you write every day? Do you expect to continue with fiction?

I love teaching. I love working with adults trying to find their own voices; their desire and their effort inspire me. Though it takes so much time, I suppose I keep doing it because these open-hearted conversations about the process of writing and about craft remind me continually of how important it is to take risks.

I write in the morning before going to work. When I'm working on a novel, I try to write five days a week, though my job and life often interfere. Like almost everyone, I struggle for time.

Most recently I've been working on something that can't decide whether it wants to be a play or a novel. As soon as I finish it, whatever it is, I will gratefully return to fiction. Of course I'll keep at it. I'm one of those "toiling away in obscurity" writers. If I haven't quit by now, as I'm approaching fifty, why would I ever?

Date Due

NOV 11 2011			
DEC 27 2011			
FEB 24 2012			
AUG 5 2012			